John S. Bolin
1994

Sarah Dunant

FATLANDS

OTTO PENZLER BOOKS

New York London Toronto Sydney Tokyo Singapore

Otto Penzler Books
129 West 56th Street
New York, NY 10019
(Editorial Offices only)

Simon & Schuster Inc.
Rockefeller Center
1230 Avenue of the Americas
New York, NY 10020

First United States edition 1994

Manufactured in the United States of America

10 9 8 7 6 5 4 3 2 1

Library of Congress Cataloging-in-Publication Data
   Dunant, Sarah.
      Fatlands/Sarah Dunant.
         p.   cm.
      I. Title.
   PS3554.U4626F38   1994   94–8933   CIP
   813'.54—dc20

ISBN 1-883402-82-4

Contents

CHAPTER ONE

Route 66?

It was so early even the central heating was quiet. I checked the luminous hands of the clock, and cancelled the alarm before it detonated. 5.24 a.m. I lay staring up into the darkness listening to the night. Outside, London was as quiet as it ever gets; just the odd bird confusing the sodium street glow for dawn and the hum of an occasional car, someone home too late or up too early. Like me. In a small town halfway across the Wiltshire Plain a young girl was sleeping, dreaming, no doubt, of her day in the big city. I thought of the miles between us. Then I thought of the money and hauled myself out of bed.

The place was like an icebox. I considered a hot shower, but with no hot water consideration was all it got. I pulled on jeans and a cute little thermal vest, followed by a sweater and a pair of woolly socks. Designer Oxfam, that's me. Passing the telephone, I fantasized about dialling Frank's number and letting it ring a couple of dozen times, just to give him a head start on the weekend. But he's sharper than he seems and he'd know it was me. Well, who else would it be?

En route to the kitchen I stepped over the curtain rail and the lump of plaster on the floor next to it. But this was a new day and I refused to be humiliated by past failures. I had a vision of myself twelve hours earlier, one foot hooked over the top of the radiator, the other balanced on the edge of the chair back – a dangerous job, but someone had to do it. I had got the screw perfectly lined up and was set to prove that since the invention of the automatic screwdriver men and women are equal in all things, when the telephone rang. No problem, I thought, ten seconds and it'll be over. I switched on. The screwdriver buzzed like a demented bee and the screw pirouetted into the wall, its head coming to rest at a slight but jaunty angle to the wood. Nice one, Hannah. Another simple but conclusive victory in the nature/nurture debate.

I was halfway down the ladder when patriarchy re-established itself, the screw flinging itself out of the wall, taking the curtain rail and a large fist of plaster with it. I was lucky to make it to the phone uninjured. In retrospect I shouldn't have bothered. Frank on a Friday night: what could it possibly be but bad news for the weekend?

'You took your time. What were you doing?'

'Defoliating my armpits with a pair of tweezers.'

'Congratulations. You finally got a date.'

Since it was his phone bill I was tempted to prolong the banter, but I'd recently read this article in a women's magazine, about life being shorter than you think and the importance of making every encounter mean something. 'Excuse me, Frank, is this vital or can I leave you with the answering machine?'

'I thought you already had. Something's just come in. Do you want to work tomorrow?'

'Depends what it is.'

'Chaperone-companion. Usual stuff. Shopping, sightseeing and not losing them on the way to the little girls' room.'

The posh firms call it bodyguarding, it sounds less menial that way. The clients come in all shapes and sizes, but the best ones are usually foreign. Or to be more precise, Arab. I don't have the right style for the men. But the women can be great. I've had some of my most unexpected pleasure getting to know what goes on under the chador. Mind you, it had been a while now. The aftermath of the Gulf War had kept all but the richest at home; and the richest didn't go to Frank. Funny sensation having poor Arab clients. Although in this case poverty is relative. 'Saudi or Arab Emirates?'

2

'No, no, er . . . this one's English.'

'Why the hesitation?' For an ex-policeman Frank finds it admirably hard not telling the whole truth.

'No reason. She's a great kid. I know you're going to love her.'

That's Frank for you. 'What do you mean "kid"?' Always a catch.

'Kid. You know, as in young person. But very mature. At least fifteen.'

Which meant thirteen and a half if I was lucky. 'Oh, come on, Frank, I'm not qualified to handle children.'

'Hannah, believe me, at this fee you'd be qualified to handle anything.'

'How much?' I said looking at the curtain rail and thinking about redecorating the room. He told me. I whistled. It always begins thus. Me with better things to do, him waving pound signs in the air to tempt me.

'I don't get it. Why so generous?'

'You're working for a firm with a reputation, remember? The kind of outfit that can cope with the threat of a custody snatch.'

'Custody snatch?'

'Well, it's only a threat.'

'At fifteen years old?'

'Yeah, well, fourteen actually.'

'Same difference. What's he going to do? Try to lure her away with the promise of a CD player?'

'Not he. *Her*. And she's tried before.'

'The mother? Tell me more.'

'I've written you notes. I'll get a bike to drop them round. So – do you want the address now or shall I ring someone else?'

It's one of our little games, pretending that Frank has a large workforce. It makes us both feel better about our jobs. I already had the pen in my hand. First he gave me the time, then told me where I was going. That way it took me a while to realize I'd been had. 'Oh, thanks, thanks a million. Why didn't you tell me earlier?'

'Because you wouldn't have taken it if I had. And Hannah? Don't be late, eh?'

5.55. In the kitchen there was orange juice, but not enough milk to cover the muesli. I added milk to the already long list on the noticeboard. Now if I were a really original PI, my kitchen would be an Elizabeth David sanctuary, overflowing with fresh bread, runny cheese and a large shiny cappuccino machine. Which just goes to illustrate the misery of conformity. I decided to cut my losses and hit a motorway cafe later.

Outside it was still dark. It had been another frustrating night for the Tufnell Park Neighbourhood Watch scheme. I passed a Ford estate and a Peugeot 205 with their side windows smashed, a straggle of intestinal wires gaping out from the holes where the radios had been. I clutched my fancy car stereo to my chest. Down the road my beat-up Y-reg Polo sat proudly intact under a street lamp. It wouldn't be long before the stereo was worth more than the car. I see it as a public service, really. Beat crime. Make sure none of your possessions are worth stealing.

I slid the radio in and turned it on. Radio 4 was telling farmers what to do with chicken feed, which is not something you need to hear before breakfast, while Radio 3 was broadcasting classical static. There was a smattering of DJs ranging around the rest of the dial, but they all sounded as if they already knew no one was listening. I went for a tape instead. This early in the morning you need old friends. Eric Clapton's fingers danced their way into his voice. It was almost as good as a cup of coffee.

The ride out of London made you see life from the night cabbies' point of view. No cars, no queues, just open road round the park, then amber to green right through on to Westway. Someone had once told me that when the lights

4

were with you, you could drive from the ocean to Beverly Hills without stopping once. Sunset Boulevard. Even the names were right for the American Dream. Here in England we just have the Marylebone Road. If you ever planned to motor west ... I swapped Clapton for Chuck Berry and together we blasted out a litany of Midwest cities while I sped up and over the flyover, flashing past signs for Shepherd's Bush, Uxbridge and Acton.

Still, on the right morning, with four hundred quid at the end of a day's work, even Britain has a frisson of myth about it. Take the M25 – which I did at some speed. At this hour it was touched by stardust, empty and proud, for all the world like a real motorway rather than a gigantic circle of urban stress. It was almost a shame to get off it. I took the long, sleek curve into the M3 like the final corner at Le Mans and hit the motorway without dipping below fifty. I moved into the middle lane and put my foot down. Night driving. Nothing like it, especially on the edge of the day. I was thinking fast track, when a Safeway truck pulled up level with me. The driver shot me a wide grin before pumping his accelerator and leaving me behind. In a disappointment born more of horsepower than gender I watched him go. A mile later he was halfway to the horizon when a sleepy police car on a bridge above yawned, stretched and moved out, lights glinting with the prospect of a kill. I slowed down to make the pleasure last longer. When I passed them a couple of miles down the road, summary justice was being executed on the hard shoulder. I saluted a fallen hero, but he was too busy manufacturing an excuse to notice. Frank tells me that's one of the problems with women. Their hearts get in the way of revenge. In fact it's part of a longer theory he has about wife battering and domestic violence. Like many of Frank's theories it's not quite as crass as it first sounds, but I won't bore you with it now.

I kept my foot at an even 70 m.p.h. Around Andover the dawn arrived, sneaking up from behind, pink-wash streaks

5

giving way, against March odds, to a porcelain-blue sky. The sunrise was still singing as I sped down the long, open hill bottoming out into a wide-angle view of Stonehenge half a mile to the right. At this distance the stones looked like something out of a kid's building box. You could almost imagine reaching out and picking them up one by one, rearranging them at will. I thought of the alternative version: the Druids and the slow pull from the coastal quarries to the silence of the Wiltshire Plain. I thought of Tess, with much thanks to Hardy and little to Polanski, and saw how – in a clear, deserted morning on the edge of spring – there would have been worse places to complete a tragedy. Then I thought about all the other things I could be doing with my life at this moment, like waking to the same alarm at the same time in order to do the same job at the end of the same tube stop. And I felt OK in a quiet sort of way.

On the seat next to me lay a brown envelope. I had read Frank's brief already. Simple and stylish. The Met must have missed him when he went. Her name was Mattie Shepherd, fourteen yesterday, father's name Tom. Her birthday present was supposed to have been a weekend in London with all the trimmings, but his work had intervened. I was the substitute parent. It was my job to pick her up, show her the sights, and deliver her to her dad's house in time for him to take her to the theatre. My contact at the school was one Patricia Parkin, the assistant head. She would meet me in the front reception with Mattie at 8.00 a.m. sharp. As for trouble, well, all I had was a name, Christine, and a brief description which made her sound like every woman in the street. She was, according to Tom Shepherd, 'disturbed', definitely not to be trusted with her daughter. And that was about it. Maybe Mattie would tell me more.

If, that is, I had the stamina to get that far. My stomach, always an alert companion, had joined the conversation. Half a mile on, a Happy Eater appeared in the distance. I pulled in behind the large red dinosaur and went to the main desk. I ordered bacon, toast and coffee to go. The bacon, toast and coffee they could do, the 'to go' was a little harder. We discussed it for a while. I toyed with the idea of recreating the 'hold the mayonnaise' scene in *Five Easy Pieces*, but one of the problems with growing older is that waitresses get younger, and homage only works when you both know what you're worshipping. So I went for pragmatism over poetry – stuck the bacon between the toast, poured the coffee into a plastic water cup and exited, leaving what I computed to be a subtly derisory tip on the table behind me.

The bacon smelt wonderful, which was more than could be said for the way it tasted. Or didn't. Ah well, another day, another hit of cholesterol. Who wants to grow old, anyway, particularly if you're the only one you know who doesn't have a pension plan. I rifled through the glove compartment and found a badly recorded dub of the Who's greatest hits. Hope I die before I advertise American Express.

I left the A303 and reached Debringham with twenty minutes to spare. It looked familiar. Either I had been there before or it was exactly the same as a number of other well-scrubbed country towns, all civic pride and real estate with no sign of mud or cattle markets. The kind of place that makes you wonder if the country really exists any more, or if it's all just a marketing construct of Habitat. Theme-park Britain. Something in it for everyone. If you've got the entrance fee.

The school was on the outskirts and well signposted. The people of Debringham were obviously proud of it. Huge stone pillars beckoned you on to a wide tarmac drive and up towards a suitably stately pile, very nineteenth-century Gothic. According to the recently repainted sign, this was Debringham College for Girls, established 1912; no doubt once the instant ancestral home of some Victorian industrialist who had hit bad times and had to sacrifice the dynasty.

The façade of the house, like the town, looked familiar magazine territory. Maybe in the holidays they made money by renting out the exterior for horror movies – the kind where unspeakable evil afflicts young virgins until Peter Cushing manages to coax them out of it.

It would be an exaggeration to say I hated it on sight. On the other hand, as a child of aspiring but struggling middle-class parents, I have always had a healthy class dislike for the hothouses of the rich. It's a prejudice reinforced by three years at a university where most of the men's entrance credentials had been earned on the river, and where they were happier playing with a rugby ball than a woman. And a good deal more adroit. It's one of the many topics that can still wreck a dinner-table conversation between my brother-in-law and me: the misnomer of public school educa-tion. Except Colin is not even to the manner born, just an eighties upstart with more money than his father and deter-mined to show it. Sister Kate says we never give each other a chance and that we'd like each other a lot if we could get past the politics. But then, as we all know, the political is personal.

OK, Hannah. Enough. I wiped the froth from the corners of my mouth, parked the car in the front drive and went in to pick up the child. Inside, a wide entrance hall lifted my footsteps and flung their echo up a grand stone staircase towards a vaulted ceiling. Very *Mädchen in Uniform*. I looked at my watch. 8.00 a.m. sharp. Frank would have approved. I was looking for someone to talk to, when she appeared. She'd been around too long to be the one you'd have a crush on, but she looked OK, if a little tweedy around the edges.

'Miss Wolfe?'

'Miss Parkin?'

'Mrs,' she corrected gently and not without a certain humour. 'You're very prompt.'

'I left early,' I said, with a touch more belligerence than I intended.

'I'm sure you did. Mattie will be down in a minute.' She paused. 'She's looking forward to it.'

'Good.' I wished I could say the same.

'You haven't met her before?'

'No.'

She smiled. 'She's an interesting girl. Although you may find her a little upset that her father's not here. We only told her this morning.' The inference was that she might have wrecked the joint if she'd found out any earlier. Great. Humiliating enough to be baby-sitting without the tantrums thrown in. Surprising her mother wanted her back, really.

'Mr Shepherd mentioned his wife, Christine . . . Mattie's mother. I wondered if you'd had any dealings with her?'

She looked at me, as if sizing me up. When it came, her answer was non-committal enough for me to realize I had failed the test. 'She visited the school once, yes.'

The tension was killing me. 'What happened?'

'Mattie felt she didn't want to see her, so the matter was taken out of our hands.' Her eyes flicked slightly to one side of my head. Behind me I heard the tap-tap of some seriously heeled shoes. Work calls. I turned to greet the day.

You know what they say about the past being another country. Well, for this one you'd need a visa. She was fourteen going on twenty-four. Tall, maybe five-five or five-six already, with a mane of dark hair caught up in one of those frou-frou elastic velveteen bands that were all the rage. Her clothes – skirt and sweater – were smart, veering towards well groomed, the kind of garments where the label told you more than the washing instructions. Mattie Shepherd – self-possession on legs, and a nice line in Lycra tights. Just what I wanted most for my weekend – a day in the company of a budding Harvey Nichols buyer. But while the clothes gave off one message, the scowl gave off another.

I put out my hand – the better to keep her at arm's length. 'Hello,' I said cheerfully. 'You must be Mattie.' Nice one, Hannah. Narrative and smarm all in one.

She regarded me as one might regard a lump of bird shit. Hard to know what had disgusted her most, my face or my personality. Then, murmuring what was obviously an obligatory 'good morning' in the general direction of Miss – sorry, Mrs – Parkin, she sailed straight past me and out the door into the morning sunshine.

I watched her go, that neat little butt shimmying across the tiled floor. I thought of the money. And suddenly it didn't seem so generous. Mrs Parkin took pity on my outstretched hand. Her face had just the ghost of a smile as she pumped my fingers and said briskly, 'Well, have a wonderful day. Please give my regards to Mattie's father. Tell him she's doing fine and we'll look forward to seeing him next time.' Then she stood and watched as I followed my charge out to the car.

At least she had the grace to wait by the passenger door. I looked at her snarling little face over the roof of the car, and I have to say it played into all my worst prejudices. 'The name is Hannah,' I said with an accent plucked from the playground of a South London comprehensive. 'And I just want you to know I'm looking forward to this every bit as much as you are.'

The scowl got bigger. I unlocked the car and we both got in. I strapped on my seatbelt and put the key in the ignition. She didn't move. 'I think you'd better put on your belt, sweetheart. It's going to be a long drive.'

She was staring out through the windscreen, as if she hadn't heard me. I waited, counting to ten silently. Out through the corner of my eye I saw Mrs Parkin come out on to the front steps, getting ready to wave. Five thousand pounds a year and they can't even get them to put on their seatbelts. Somebody should tell their parents. I started the engine, moved into first, then hit the accelerator at the same time as I released the clutch. The car shot forward, flinging us both back against the seats. Then I hit the brake. The seatbelt bit into my chest. She stuck out her hands against the dashboard, but she was still winded enough to let out a cry.

'Sorry,' I said with genuine gaiety.

She shot me a glance of pure malice, then pulled the belt off its hook. This time, at normal speed, I executed a swift three-point turn and headed for the front gates. In the back mirror I saw Mrs Parkin standing, a trifle anxiously, on the gravel. I gave her a cheery wave. Eight o'clock to five-thirty. Nine and a half sodding hours. Just you wait, Frank Comfort. I'll get you for this.

CHAPTER TWO

Sweet Little Fourteen

The first hour was pure murder. But then, as a private detective, it's my job to get a perverted pleasure out of that kind of thing.

Beside me the Harvey Nichols trainee was fast turning into a bit of a slob. She had arranged herself extravagantly on the front seat, one leg tucked up underneath the other, skirt halfway to her crotch, head back against the headrest as if the world outside was just too boring to warrant her attention. Mind you, she had a point. As we passed, Debringham High Street was tarting itself up ready for business. A classy collection of retail outlets they were, too: a couple of antique shops, an auction house, and a book shop with a display of Dorothy Dunnett and Kingsley Amis in the window (now there's one for *Blind Date*, Cilla). Just the kind of place to drive teenagers into solvent abuse. If, that was, they were allowed to use their tuck money outside school grounds. I wondered if it was worth letting off a small salvo in the hope of attracting a conversation.

'Picturesque little place,' I said with what I felt to be well-judged irony. 'Do they let you out?'

She humphed a bit, then said, 'Saturday mornings and Sunday afternoons.'

'What d'you do?'

'Shoplift.'

The remark came out gin-dry. I found it genuinely funny but thought it wiser to suppress my admiration. I stopped to let an old lady with an old dog cross the road. The dog was moving slower than she was. It was not a life-enhancing sight. 'Do I gather you don't like it here?'

'It's a dung heap.'

I thought of Mrs Parkin's sensible shoes and the bill that must come flying through her father's letter box every term. 'But an expensive one.'

She snorted. 'He can afford it.'

'You're sure about that, are you?'

We were on the outskirts of the town now, the smart thatched cottages giving way to open land, rich rolling fields with early sunlight playing across them. Big farms. I wondered what they grew. But then in my experience the country is always a mystery to girls born in Hammersmith. There didn't seem much point in asking Mattie, since whatever she was looking at it wasn't the countryside. Instead she had her head halfway inside her voluminous shoulder bag, rummaging frantically. She came up triumphant, an unopened packet of Dunhill cigarettes in one hand and a cute little Bic lighter in the other. Bedside me the cellophane crinkled and a flame licked up. I cleared my throat loudly.

It's a difficult one, smoking. I mean all the best PIs hurtle towards death in a wreath of cigarette smoke, and I'd certainly paid my dues to that myth for long enough. But then I met a man who couldn't stand the smell and I surrendered to lust. It would make a better story if it had taken six months of nicotine patches and Mars bars. As it turned out I wasn't quite the addictive personality I had thought. For him or the cigarettes. So I let them both go together. And, yes, my teeth do shine more in the dark, which just means I have to keep my mouth closed on night jobs. It also means that now, of course, I have all the tolerance of the converted. I coughed again. She held out the packet.

'Filthy habit, isn't it?' she said tartly. 'D'you want one?'

I thought of the litany of horrors one should recite to an adolescent about smoking. 'No.' Worth a try? 'And neither do you.'

'It's *my* body,' she growled, still at the stage when death is preferable to reaching thirty.

'But it's my car,' I said sweetly. 'And I'm asthmatic. Cigarette smoke brings on fits.'

She stared at me, and you could see she didn't believe me but wasn't sure how to call my bluff. With bad grace she stubbed the cigarette out in the ashtray, then carefully pushed it back into the packet. And suddenly I was fourteen all over again. 'However,' I said 'there's some dope in the glove compartment if you want to roll a joint. I haven't had one all morning.'

I watched while her eyes widened. With the creases temporarily gone, her face was almost pretty: skin like a fat peach, mercifully untroubled by acne, and what looked like good bones lurking underneath the puppy flesh. She was going to turn some heads soon. If she hadn't done so already. She hesitated, then leant forward and snapped open the little flag. An A–Z exploded out into her lap. In the mess that remained we both saw a mound of tapes, the odd McDonald's wrapping and a couple of packets of gum. I put out a hand and rummaged a little deeper, then said softly, 'Damn, I must have left it at home. Want some gum?'

She shook her head and scowled again. We were getting nowhere fast. I opted for confrontation.

'You know, Mattie, we're going to be in each other's company for the next eight hours at least. Either you can be more polite or I can be less. It makes no difference to me. I want to be here about as much as you do.'

The face stayed thunder, but the eyes sparked a little interest. 'So why did you take the job?'

'Because of the money.'

'He's paying you a lot, is he?'

'More than it's worth,' I said bluntly. 'Except now I'm not so sure.'

'Yeah,' she smiled bitterly. 'That's my father, all right.'

I let a beat of a pause go by. 'Like him a lot, do you?'

'I don't know. I can't remember what he looks like.'

'How about your mum?'

She shot me a dark look. 'What did he tell you?'

'Nothing. Except that she's out to get you back.'

She snorted. 'If she wanted me back, then she wouldn't have left me in the first place, would she?'

And there was genuine pain in her voice this time. That's the trouble with being fourteen. You want people to treat you like an adult, then when they do it hurts too much. I let it be. She sat with her face away from me, looking out. We drove on in silence. Then she put her hand out and angrily took a piece of gum. After she had unwrapped it, she thought long and hard about throwing the paper on to the floor, but in the end stuffed it in the overflowing ashtray. I was more pleased than I allowed myself to show. Or maybe I showed it more than I thought.

Ahead of us the A303 announced its intention to turn into the M3 with no service stations for twenty-three miles. We both watched the sign and the last service station whip past. It was ninety seconds later she said she needed to stop for a pee. Great. Always guard against complacency, Hannah, Frank said smugly in my ear, it's not in the bag till it's in the bag.

'Tough,' I said, to both of them. 'You'll have to wait.' My turn to sulk.

By the time we reached the service station we were in zero temperature again. She got out of the car before I'd properly stopped, pulling her bag with her, and flounced across the forecourt towards the entrance. I watched her go. It would, I decided, be an act of overt aggression to follow her into the Ladies and stand guard at the loo door. There are some places where even a chaperone doesn't go. On the other hand I was being paid way too much money to be just a chaperone. I waited till she'd disappeared through the main entrance then got out of the car.

By the time I got there she wasn't in the loo, or at least none of the ones that were open. I called her name. No answer. She wasn't buying more cigarettes and she wasn't making a phone call. Neither was she having an overpriced cup of coffee. That left the bridge to the other side of the motorway.

I didn't run, but I didn't exactly walk, either. I love those bridges, concrete corridors going nowhere. I've always wanted to have a last-reel shoot-out in one of them, bullets ricocheting while innocent passersby dive for cover. Either that or me flinging myself through the plate-glass windows on to the back of a passing truck underneath. Alas, today was yet another day when I didn't get to fulfil my ambitions.

Neither did I get to find my client. Either she wasn't there or she'd already left. I hoofed it back to the east side. From the entrance to the forecourt I saw a figure standing next to the car. She didn't look anything like Mattie, but what the hell . . .

At least she had the grace to be shifty about it. Though, to be honest, it wasn't her face I was concentrating on. I have to say it suited her better: the tattered leggings with the money belt around the waist, the T-shirt under the sharp little leather jacket and the hair piled high like a black fountain frozen in mid-flow. I had a vision of that nicely pressed Jaeger skirt all scrunched up in the bottom of her bag, but I couldn't summon up any pity for it. She looked – well, she looked more herself.

She stood waiting for my disapproval. I stared at her and saw myself aged fourteen, hair like a sheepdog, miniskirt barely covering my knickers and a long string of beads undulating over lumpy teenage breasts: just another suburban rebel desperate to catch up with the sixties when the decade was already over. In retrospect it had been less about fashion than identity. And I had thought I was so wonderful. It still comes as a shock when I look back at the pictures and see myself as overweight jailbait. Now those would be a set of negatives to kill for.

She was still waiting. I tried to take it seriously. The generation gap demanded it. But I just couldn't do it. I looked her up and down and shook my head. 'You look great. Let's hope your temper improves with your appearance. Shall we go?' And she gave me just the smallest of smiles.

Back in the car we were Thelma and Louise. She strapped on her seatbelt and hit the glove compartment. For a second I thought we might be back to the dope, but instead she had her hands full of tapes, making an instant inventory of the music. I'd seen people more impressed by my taste. She took her time. We were already in the fast lane when she said,

'Who's Bob Seger?'

'He used to play back-up to Frank Sinatra,' I said solemnly. 'Go on, give it a try.'

She slid the tape in and I turned on the stereo, loud. The opening chords of 'Blow Me Away' lifted the car about an inch and a half off the ground. And this time the grin reached her ears. Rock 'n' roll. Bringing the world together.

We hit the rest of the gum and moved towards family matters via education, on which we had similar views, albeit for different reasons.

'They're just stupid most of them. They're so *young*, even the older ones. Half of them are still slobbering over Jason Donovan.'

'Jason doesn't do much for you, then?'

'God, do me a favour.'

'How long have you been there?'

'One hundred and ninety-six days,' she said immediately. 'Not including holidays.'

'If you hate it so much, why don't you ask your father to take you away?'

'Because he wouldn't listen.'

'Have you tried?' She scowled, which was her way of telling me the question wasn't worth answering. 'So where did you go before?'

'A place in Suffolk. Then when we came to London, a day school in Acton. That was OK. At least you could get away from it.'

'But then your mum left and he felt he couldn't cope, was that it?' She chewed on her cheek. 'Maybe he thought it was best for you.'

'Well, then he was wrong, wasn't he?' she snapped back. 'But he doesn't care. As long as he's got his rats to play with.'

'What does he do?' Because she obviously wanted to tell me.

'He's a scientist. Trying to cure the world of cancer.' And although she spat it out, you could feel how it had been a thing of pride not so long ago.

'But not so good with his own family, eh?' I let it sit there for a while but she didn't pick it up. I tried again. 'Is that why your mum left? Because he worked all the time.'

She shrugged her shoulders. 'She just didn't like the idea of being at home any more. Can't say I blame her.'

It was the second time she had refused the jump. Whatever or, more to the point, whoever had made her go, Mattie didn't want to talk about it. Between the lines it was all pretty classic stuff: an only child who'd got all the attention for so long that when the parents started to think about themselves, they discovered they didn't really like each other any more. So Dad compensates through work, and Mum . . . well, maybe she started to talk to the milkman.

'But he does work too hard?'

'Why not? There's no one at home to make him stop, is there?'

'Maybe they'll get together again,' I said, only because I thought she might want to hear it. 'And you could come home.'

'You must be joking. They don't give a toss about each other, any more than they give a toss about me.' She slammed her finger on to the stereo button. 'This music sucks. I'm going to put something else on.'

Watching her face in profile, I had a clear memory of that kind of anger, the one that overtook you from behind and burnt up everything in its path. Mine had been about . . . well, what had it been about? Having parents that loved me too much and wouldn't let me out into adulthood as fast as I was determined to go. At least there was a real reason for her anger. All dressed up for life and nowhere to go, except the school playground or the no man's land of a marital war zone. God, if there's one thing worse than growing older, it would be a slow return to adolescence.

The blue motorway sign told me London was less than an hour away. I thought of other things we could talk about. But she beat me to it.

'How old are you?'

I wondered how to put it. 'Over thirty.' I shot her a glance. You could see she was shocked. 'But it's all right. I work out mentally.'

If she found it funny, she didn't let me know. 'You're not married?'

'No. No, I'm not married.'

'So how many men have you slept with?'

Served me right, really. I mean you can't make the conversation personal and then cry foul. I pretended to give it some consideration. As it happens, I already knew the answer. Men in my bed: just another of those lists one resorts to late at night when counting sheep doesn't work. That and the names of the girls in my last year at school. A bit harder that one, but then we're talking larger numbers.

'Eighteen.'

'Eighteen.' Despite herself she was impressed. You could hear it in the voice.

'Yeah, but a lot of those were SLBA.'

'SLBA?'

'Sexual Liberation Before Aids. I'm much choosier now.' Or *they* are, I thought, but decided not to say. She was silent for a while. My God, I thought, I really have shocked her this time. Then she said, 'My friend Helen's having an affair.'

'Is he better than Jason Donovan?'

She snorted her disgust. Then said, rather eagerly, 'He's the school gardener.'

'Very Lady Chatterley.' I had a thought. 'You know Lady Chatterley?'

'Of course,' she sighed. 'I read it when I was ten.'

'Fine. So, do they meet in the potting shed?'

'He's got a room. In town. She goes there on Saturdays.'

'Ah yes, the morning off.'

'She has multiple orgasms.'

'Lucky her. How about him?'

'He does, too.'

'Well, that's all right, then.'

There was a slight pause. 'You don't disapprove?'

'No, I don't think so.'

'Her father would.'

'No doubt.'

'But then he still thinks of her as a child.'

'Yes, well, he would, wouldn't he?'

She looked at me sharply to check whether or not I was laughing at her. I must have passed the test. 'So you don't think she's too young, then?'

'I don't know. How old is she?'

'Thirteen.'

I glanced over at her. 'You want a serious answer?'

She hesitated, then nodded.

I smiled. 'For me it would have been. In fact I know it would have scared the hell out of me. But maybe for her it's all right. Sort of depends on how he treats her, really.'

'Oh, he's nice to her. Well, most of the time.'

'Then it's probably good preparation for the rest of her life.'

She fell silent. I wondered what I'd just been told. Another sign whizzed past me on the left. London, twenty miles. I looked at my watch. 9.55. The day stretched ahead of us.

'You'd better take the M25,' she said suddenly. 'It'll get us into town quicker.'

I shot her a glance. 'You want to drive or can I stay at the wheel?' She grinned. 'Fine. You got somewhere in particular in mind?'

'Yeah, Knightsbridge.'

I shrugged. 'I've got the time if you've got the money.'

In answer she unzipped her money belt and flashed me a thick wad of notes. There must have been four, five hundred pounds there. I wondered, not for the first time, just how much money someone was paying her father to find a cure for cancer. Maybe the story about the wife and the custody snatch was just a front. Maybe the real reason he needed a private eye was to make sure his daughter didn't get mugged with the family fortune.

'It's a lot of money, Mattie,' I said softly.

'Yeah, well, it's my birthday, remember.' And not for the first time she sounded older then her years.

CHAPTER THREE

S.H.O.P.P.I.N.G.

Somehow we ended up in Harrods. Not what I expected. Given the service station transformation I had her down more as a Joseph kind of girl. But the little black and grey numbers left her cold — she didn't even get as far as looking at the price tags — while around the corner the castle of fairy lights beckoned. One of the seven wonders of the consumerist world.

I had a spiel about Harrods. It went down well with paranoid Americans — a potent story of Western capitalism now owned by the Middle East. A history of our time. Except I didn't think Mattie would be interested. We started in the food hall. Her suggestion. We bought chocolate and almond croissants from the pastry bar and ate them out of the bag with our fingers. Mattie had two. I was impressed. For a fourteen-year-old she seemed enviably oblivious to the evils of carbohydrates. Then we took the lift up to Way In, Harrods' boutique answer to youth culture.

It was so dark in there it took me a while to realize there was nothing worth buying. Mattie flicked idly through the rails. She seemed ill at ease, but when I asked her if she was looking for anything in particular she treated me like a salesgirl, a distinct touch of the get-your-hands-off-me Mattie back again. I left her to it.

Across the shop floor a woman in a chador was fingering her way through some garish costume jewllery. She appeared to be alone, but then he or she would hardly stand right next to her, would they? I spotted him lurking by a make-up counter opposite, and he didn't look happy. Could be he just didn't like having to be so obvious. Or maybe he thought the job was beneath him. Either way you can see now why Frank passes certain assignments on to me. I looked away. He left it a second, then glanced in my direction, just to check I wasn't someone he should be worrying about. I gave him a wink. He looked right through me. I thought about going over and telling him what a good job he was doing, how no one would know he was there, but it seemed unduly cruel, even for me. After all, we both have a job to do.

When I looked round, Mattie was gone. I went in among the rails, but there was no sign. I checked the changing rooms and the rest of the boutique. After the service station incident I was more pissed off than anxious. Or maybe just disappointed. So when I finally tracked her down at the lifts, doors open, about to step in, I'm afraid I lost it a little.

I grabbed her by the arm and yanked her back. Not the most private place for a public showdown, but there you go. 'Where do you think you're going?'

She didn't look at me, just tossed her head: Scarlett O'Hara caught trying to wreck another marriage. And pretending she felt OK about it. 'Downstairs.'

'Come on, Mattie, you know the deal. You want to go somewhere, I go with you.'

She shook her head angrily. 'You're not my father. I don't have to ask your permission.' She still hadn't had the grace to look me straight in the eye.

'Oh yes you do. I'm being paid to look after you, remember?'

She pulled open the zip of her money belt, grabbing a handful of notes and waving them in front of my face. 'How much? I'll give you the same again to leave me alone.'

I sighed. We were evidently providing entertainment for the little crowd waiting at the lift. I wondered what they thought. Not mother and daughter, surely. God save me from that. I pushed down her hand. 'Put it away.' Then louder: 'Put it away, Mattie.'

I could feel all my good work slipping away. I lowered

my voice, keeping it steady. 'Listen, I know you don't like this. I don't like it, either. But look at it from my point of view. If something happened to you, it would be my fault.'

She closed her eyes tight, more petulance than anger now. 'I told you. My mother doesn't want me. She's too busy with her lover. It's an excuse. My father's not paying you to protect me. He's paying you to make himself feel better about preferring work to his daughter. You're his guilt money. Just like me.'

Over the top of her head I spotted the bodyguard from the make-up counter, smirking from behind his client's flowing robes. I looked back at Mattie. And my heart went out to her: to be so alone that she was forced to row with someone who was almost a stranger. I put my hand on her shoulder and this time she didn't shrug it off.

'OK,' I said quietly, 'OK. Your father's a shit. So let's go spend some of his money, all right?'

She pursed her lips, then nodded. I took her by the arm and we stepped together into the lift. The crowd watched us go. I stood by the lift buttons and turned to her.

'One,' she said quietly. I raised an eyebrow. She gave a little shrug. 'Underwear,' she said defiantly.

It struck me later that she hadn't so much wanted her independence as her privacy. Certainly I was impressed by her sophistication. When I was her age it was Marks & Spencer cotton all the way. Maybe things had changed. I had this vision of Debringham College for Girls as a Cynthia Payne training school with Mrs Parkin as the madam. I even made a joke about it.

She gave me the cockroach look, but not without a certain affection. 'You don't think this stuff's for me, do you?' she said disparagingly, looking through an unexpected but clearly deliberate hole in a designer piece of satin. 'It's a present. For Helen . . .'

Of course. Helen and her gardener. 'Don't tell me. He's into topiary.'

24

'What?'

'Nothing. It's just in my day the whole appeal of school-girls was their grey serge knickers.'

She gave a grin, but you could see that for her it was really a serious business. A costly one, too. The smaller the garment the bigger the price tag. My mind kept slipping back to D. H. Lawrence, too busy with the life force to check out the lingerie prices. Did men really care that much what it was, so long as it came off? Maybe that was my problem: not enough spent on underwear. The last time I had been lingerie shopping it had been a clever device to check I wasn't being followed. Frank's idea, I should add, not mine. I hadn't bought anything that time, either.

Mattie, however, was making out like a bandit. She finally settled for six little numbers. And then, rather charmingly, bottled out at the last minute when it came to paying for them. So I got landed with it, along with a bundle of notes to cover the damage. The woman at the till lifted up each garment to fold it properly. Her face was impassive. On balance it must have been easier than selling condoms. 'Will it be Fetherlite, or Rough Rider, Madam?' I stuffed the Harrods carrier into my shopping bag and headed back to Mattie. She stood waiting with an expression caught midway between mischief and pleasure. I was surprised how happy it made me feel to see her so relaxed. 'Well, let's hope they do the trick,' I said, smiling. She hooked her arm over mine and propelled me towards the exit.

The afternoon was easier. The erotic purchases behind her, she seemed happy to be her age again. It was she who picked the Science and the Natural History museums and there proceeded to dazzle me with her knowledge. Of course, being on first-name terms with the dinosaurs is a prerequisite of childhood, but Mattie was something else again. It was biology mostly, but with enough hard science to have me outmanoeuvred within the first half-hour. Either Debring-ham College was doing a better job than she was willing to let on or she was a very bright cookie indeed. I wondered if it was her natural bent, or if she had tailored her intelligence to what would impress her father. I just couldn't believe that he wouldn't be interested in finding out.

On the security front I decided to keep an open mind and, more important, open eyes. But no one showed any undue interest in either of us. In the end I think I probably got careless. Although I don't believe that would have made any difference to what happened later. But then that's for you to judge.

We headed off at around 5.00. Her father's place (she insisted on calling it that, rather than home) was in Sutherland Avenue, in one of those gracious, generous houses overlooking communal gardens at the back. In my student days someone I'd known had had a bedsit in one of them. It was the time of the Notting Hill rapist. All I remember were the bars on her windows and the fear of leaving too late at night. Now it looked different, plush and with less sense of threat. But then now it's my job not to be so scared of everything.

When we arrived she didn't want to get out of the car. I sat for a while trying not to notice, but her aggression made the silence too noisy to stand for long. I put my hand lightly on her sleeve. 'Come on,' I said gently.

She shrugged me off and opened the door. I let her lead the way. At the top of the stairs an impressive array of locks presented themselves. I looked at her questioningly.

'He's paranoid,' she said. 'He got burgled last year.' She rang the doorbell. The housekeeper answered. The hall behind her swung up into a wonderful spiralling staircase, shiny dark mahogany banisters against bright white paint. The whole place looked as if she had recently finished licking it with her tongue, not a hint of dust anywhere, no sign that anyone actually lived there at all. Except maybe the houskeeper. She was a nice enough woman, elderly and a little stout, with a strong face and steel-grey hair styled

26

in one of those pensioners-get-it-cheap-type perms. She welcomed Mattie with a hug, which the girl did her best to squirm her way out of, but it was clear they had once been sort of pals.

Mattie stalked off into the living room, a huge double room with windows looking out on to the gardens, and flung her coat and bag on to the sofa in what looked like a blatant attempt to untidy the place. Then she flung herself on top of them. Home sweet home. Even her body language had closed up again. We both watched her from the door, then Mrs Dayley (I kid you not) set off for the kitchen. I trailed after her.

On a spotless table a tray was already laid, tea with cakes on a boldly designed china service. Classy stuff. Shame about the family.

'She looks thin,' she said as she clattered about with the kettle.

'I wouldn't know,' I replied. 'I only met her today.'

She gave a bit of a snort, as if it was my fault. 'Has she been all right?'

I assumed she was referring to the eight hours we had spent together. 'Depends what your expectations are,' I said, then regretted my harshness. 'She's been great. Interesting company.'

'Good. Dr Shepherd's going to be late.'

'Ah . . .'

'He rang. Asked me to stay on and let you know.'

'How late?'

'He said he'll be back by seven. In time to go the theatre.'

Wonderful. So much for the end of my day. Then another thought, even worse, struck me. 'Who's going to tell her?' She looked at me as if to imply that I was probably earning more than she was. But I had just spent the day perfecting how not to be bullied. 'I think you know her better than I do.'

She picked up the tray and pursed her lips. As she was on

27

the way out of the kitchen I said quietly, 'Can I ask you a question, Mrs Dayley? Mattie's mother – I mean . . . how did she leave?'

She used it to get back at my cowardice. 'Badly,' she said as she exited.

I waited in the kitchen. From the other room I heard the murmur of voices, then some clumsy bashing of crockery. That's the trouble with tea services, break one cup and the whole set is in trouble. Much better just to go for the mugs that come with petrol coupons. A few moments later the housekeeper came in with her coat on. 'Poor child,' she said, under her breath. Then up at me, 'I think it's a crying shame, I really do,' but she sailed out before I could inquire as to whose shame exactly. I heard the front door slam after her.

In the living room Mattie was now sprawled horizontal on the sofa, the television blaring out in front of her, the remote control on her lap. It was an old film, black and white, Bette Davis with an improbably high forehead and a ruff like a gigantic starched doily – the virgin Elizabeth making up to the Earl of Essex.

'You know it's only an extra hour,' I said. 'He'll still be here in time for the theatre.' She ignored me aggressively. 'What are you going to see?'

'A play,' she replied in a voice not dissimilar to the one that Ms Davis would use later to crush the Spanish ambassador.

'Fine,' I said, mad at her despite myself. I sat down on the chair near by and poured myself a cup of tea. She sighed in exasperation at the noise and flicked the sound up a couple more notches. Errol Flynn's whispered passion boomed out across the room. But even at that volume you could see he didn't stand a chance. Less a question of desire than politics. Reverse the sexes and there'd have been no problem. Elizabeth, like her father, could have had her leg over as many times as she wanted. As it was, gender ruled: the queen kept her crown and slept alone.

On the sofa Mattie was doing a good impersonation of watching, but the room was full of her fury. I dragged my eyes away from the screen (I'm a great Bette Davis fan) to look at her. In the end the problem was less her anger than her pain. The poor kid was so storm-tossed, trying not to care. It made her as vulnerable as she was volatile. Maybe that was why no one – her father in particular – had tried hard enough to break through.

'Mattie,' I said after a while. 'Maybe it doesn't have to be like this. I mean I know it feels as if he doesn't love you. But maybe he's as scared of showing it as you are, scared that if he tries to get close you'll push him away. When families smash up, there's so much pain that everyone gets caught in the fall-out.' I paused, she wasn't looking but I knew she was listening. Ah well, I thought, what have I got to lose? 'I know adults are supposed to cope better than children, but believe me, there are some things that being older doesn't help with at all.'

So it was a little pompous. But that wasn't what blew it. What blew it was the vocabulary. *Children*. I of all people should have known better. Since when had I been a child at fourteen, except to thoughtless adults?

'Thanks,' she said coolly. 'You should work for a women's magazine.'

The more they like you the more they know how to twist the knife. That's what Kate always tells me. So Mattie liked me. Big deal. To my surprise I let my disappointment show. She stared at me for a second, then dropped her eyes, gnawing slightly at the bottom of her lip. You could see she was tussling it out with herself, to trust or not to trust. But I think by then she was too deeply into bad habits. She turned her head back to the screen. I did the same. Out through lattice windows an execution block was being prepared. Of course there is a theory that Elizabeth was less the virgin queen than the black widow spider. Either way, poor old Errol.

A few minutes later she stood up and flung the remote on the sofa. 'I'm going up to my room.'

I thought of stopping her, but decided maybe she'd feel better alone, less exposed. I listened while she climbed the stairs. A door opened and closed. I heard the sound of music, the insistent bass beat thudding through the flat. I looked at my watch. It was 6.15. Outside the daylight was starting to seep away. Something nagged at the back of my brain. Something about the evening that I had forgotten. But sometimes trying to remember only makes you forget more completely. It would come back to me.

She had been up there about fifteen minutes (Errol had been axed and Bette was putting a brave face on it) when the phone rang. Someone picked it up immediately. I grabbed the remote and pressed the mute button. But all I could hear was the bass thud and the odd punctuating shout of black rap. The telephone was on a table near the window. I thought about finding out who it was, but, strictly speaking, it was none of my business and, anyway, I couldn't be sure she wouldn't hear me. I put the volume back on and watched the credits roll by. After a while I got bored with adverts and decided to check, just in case. I went quietly up the stairs. The music was coming from behind a closed door. I stood by it, then knocked. No answer. So I went in.

It was her bedroom, that much was clear, only her bedroom younger than her, caught in childhood. On the bed the duvet cover was pink with frills and there was one of those rag dolls you stuff your jammies in. The wall above had a large poster of Jason Donovan (there's no scorn like the scorn reserved for old sex symbols) and by the side a built-in desk unit with a special pen-holder and blotter. Other than that, it was bare and, of course, spotless. On the stereo the switch was pushed to repeat. Second time around the rap didn't sound quite so provocative.

I should admit to a moment of panic: a sudden vision of open windows and fire escapes, the noise of struggle enveloped by endless replays of Niggers With Attitude. Except, when I looked, the window had no fire escape and its lock was untouched. I went back out on to the landing. From the floor above I heard something, a sound of a voice maybe, but very muffled.

I went up another flight towards another closed door, stripped and polished like all the others, with a poncy little porcelain key cover and doorknob. It was cold to the touch. I waited for a second, but although I could hear the sing-song of her voice in animated conversation through the wood, I couldn't make out a word she was saying. I turned the doorknob silently and went in.

The room was stunning: a serious study, every wall lined with books and files, and a large oak desk looking out over the front of the house. To one side were two tall filing cabinets, both of them pulled open with files sticking out. At first glance the place looked like a fourteen-year-old cyclone had just hit it. Even the carpet was lifted half off the floor. Mattie was standing at the desk, her back to the door, folders strewn around in front of her, the phone in one hand and a bundle of papers in the other. She sounded excited and angry all at the same time.

'Listen, of course I have. You think I don't know what I'm looking for . . .' There was a pause. 'Well, what shall I do?' Then another and someone told her. 'Yes, yes. OK. Yes, I know . . .' But then she registered my presence and whirled round. Still, the sight of me made her jump. She let out a gasp. 'Oh, you scared me,' she said in a bright little voice. Then back into the receiver, 'No, not you. Listen, I have to go. I'll see you . . . I mean, you won't be late, will you? OK? Bye.' She put down the phone.

I didn't say a thing, just stood there, waiting for her to make the first move. 'That was Dad,' she said aggressively.

'Really?'

She gave me an exasperated gesture with her hands. 'Surprise, surprise. He can't find the theatre tickets. He thinks he left them somewhere in his desk.'

31

Put it this way. It wasn't that I disbelieved her, it was just
. . . well, maybe I'm a suspicious soul. 'Or in his filing
cabinets?' I said politely.

She looked at the mess. 'If it was a report, he wouldn't
have lost it.' She shook her head. 'He's very absent-minded.'
And it was said with more affection than I'd heard all day.
'They could be anywhere.'

'But I thought he was coming back in half an hour
anyway?'

She shook her head. 'You don't know him. He won't get
here in time. He never does.' She stuffed the two or three
files back into their folders and closed the cabinets. Then
she turned to me. 'It's all right. I'm allowed in here, you
know. Anyway, it's the only private phone in the place.
When Dad was out working, Christine used to use it all the
time. That way she thought I couldn't hear.'

'And could you?' I said after a beat of a pause.

'Well, wouldn't matter much if I did. I mean *children*
don't really understand, do they?'

I closed my eyes. 'You know I don't think that, Mattie.
And I'm sorry I used the word. If it's any help, I think you're
probably a good deal older than I ever was at your age.'

She stared at me for a minute, then dropped her eyes and
shuffled some papers around the desk. 'Yes, well, I'm sorry
I went for you, too . . . you know, downstairs.' She stopped,
making a little lost gesture with her hand. 'Helen says it's a
great way to lose friends I haven't made yet.'

I sighed. Was this really peace in our time or just her way
of deflecting my curiosity? So Mattie went through her
father's filing cabinets to see what was there. Maybe she
was looking for a reason why he preferred work to family.
Let's just hope she didn't find any porn magazines. Well,
whatever his secrets, they were more her business than
mine. 'OK,' I said. 'Shall we go downstairs?'

'In a minute.' She glanced around the room. 'He's . . .
he's very particular about his study.'

And so, only a fraction against my better judgement, I left her to it. She wasn't far behind. In the living room the tea had grown cold, but she poured another cup anyway. On a ledge underneath the coffee table a copy of the *Independent* sat neatly folded. She pulled it out and started flicking through, as if she was looking for something. After a while she looked up. 'I can't find the right page.'

'What you looking for?'

'The theatre listings. Dad says the play's on at the Garrick, but I don't know where that is.'

'Mattie,' I said softly. 'He'll be here.'

She shook her head. 'You don't understand. He wasn't last time. Last time I had to take a taxi and we missed the first half,' she said bitterly. We sat silently for a minute. Then she got up and went out into the kitchen. I heard a cupboard open and the sound of something clinking. When she came back she had a set of car keys in her hand. 'Listen,' she said. 'I'm just going out to Dad's car to look up the theatre in his entertainment guide. I won't be a minute.'

I thought about it. Then I got up to follow her.

'You don't need to come,' she said quickly. 'I promise no one's going to snatch me. And I'm not going to run away.'

I looked at her for a moment. 'Are you sure about that, Mattie?'

There was a pause. She shook her head. 'Where would I run to? Anyway, I'm fourteen, remember. I don't even know how to drive.' She frowned down at her feet, then up again at me. 'Listen, Hannah, I'm glad it was you and not someone else looking after me. But that's the point, don't you see? Everywhere I go someone is always "keeping an eye" on me. The old bats at school, Mrs Dayley here. My father. And now you. I'll go out to the car, get the book and come straight back in again. You can watch me from the window if you're that worried, all right?'

To be honest I still didn't want her to go. But then I was caught. Because, of course, I also wanted her to feel I was different from all the other adults in her life. Because she needed that as much if not more than she needed a chaperone. Hannah, sweetheart, remember you're a private detective not a social worker. Good old Frank. I do the job, he gives the advice. Maybe Mattie wasn't the only one fed up with people keeping an eye on her.

'OK,' I said. 'I'll wait here.'

And after that she did something quite unexpected. She came up to me, put her arms around my neck and gave me the briefest, tightest little squeeze. Then she grabbed her jacket from the sofa and was gone. I heard the front door open, then bang shut, as if on the catch. I stood for a second without moving, then moved to the window. She was down on the pavement. She looked up, saw me, grinned and wagged a finger in mock reproach. Then she walked down the road about fifteen yards and stopped by a dark blue Rover. She opened the door and slipped into the driver's seat.

What happened next I never really saw. Except I think that as the door closed behind her she was leaning over towards the glove compartment. It must have been that because I don't believe I heard the sound of the ignition. No, I really don't think I heard that. But then there was too much other noise to be sure.

The blast seemed to come in two waves. First there was a small one, as if something at the back of the car had caught fire. Then, almost at the same instant, thunder cracked and sky slashed open in a great wound of red and black as the car, the road, even the street lamp above, exploded upwards in a fountain of flame.

CHAPTER FOUR

After the Deluge

It was so foreign to me. You have to understand that. I had worked with Frank for maybe two and a half years. In that time I must have caught a dozen shoplifters, even jumped on a couple of them as they raced down the street, and I'd once been attacked by an angry husband who caught me outside his mistress's house taking pictures. But it never felt like real violence, not the sort which changes everything. The only job where someone had died had been a missing person and, although I cared, I hadn't known her before it happened. And she hadn't been in my charge when it took place.

So, you see, I wasn't prepared. For any of it. I, like everyone else, thought car explosions were the things you saw in movies or on television, where there is a mass of fire and smoke and then you move on to the next scene. It strikes me now that since it's usually the bad guys who get blown to hell, it doesn't matter what happens after. No one ever kills the heroine. Especially not a child.

Because, of course, I knew she was dead. I knew it long before I saw it for myself. It wasn't even the force of the blast as much as the feeling in my gut, as if someone had taken out a piece of me without anaesthetic. She was dead. And suddenly I was screaming. Suddenly I was out of the house and on the pavement amid a sea of glass bellowing her name while my skin hurt from the heat and my eyes poured tears from the smoke, or from something more painful. And all the time knowing there was nothing I could do, that it wasn't a question of bravery or cowardice, simply the irrevocable force of that wall of flame keeping me back.

There were people around, I know that – a man in a raincoat shouted at me to get back, and windows opened all about, voices raised. And then, after a while, there was the sound of police and fire sirens, first in one ear then in the other, like a stereo drama, growing closer all the time. But by then things were clearer anyway. The plumes of black smoke had washed away and through the flames you could just make out the wreckage of the car, a flash of a curve of window frame, a distorted tangle of a bonnet. Steel and wire, misshapen, but good, tough materials, able to withstand a certain strain. Just like the adverts. Not like human flesh.

The black shape in the seat wasn't human flesh, either. It was just a thing, a stump, no real form at all. But that was the point. Because not all of it was there.

I know you don't want to hear this. But I need to tell it, anyway. Because it happened. And because everything that followed was, in one way or another, a result of it. Mattie Shepherd's body had been ripped apart when the petrol tank blew. That was what they said at the inquest, and that was what I saw. Of course we know about such things from reports of plane crashes: how the rescuers come across bits of people scattered over an area of miles in the snow, or the woodland or the desert, or wherever it happens to be. Well, in this case it happened to be Sutherland Avenue, and in this case it wasn't miles. I saw it as the flames died down and I moved closer to the car. And I was still seeing it as the police car screeched to a halt and two men jumped out, hauling me back while I screamed for them to let me be. It – a lump of leather jacket and a part of an arm lying in the middle of the road.

And the only thing I do remember thinking, as they guided me back inside the house, was how terrible it must be for relatives of plane-crash victims: because whatever they find, there is never a body to hold on to, to cry over, or at the very least to believe in, only a collection of bits in a bag, a jigsaw of a person.

And so with that bureaucracy took over. Police procedure. And I was taken over with it. It took them a while to get over their preconception of me as a hysterical female, but then, to be honest, it was a mistake easily made. After I'd stopped shaking – for the record sweet tea was useless, neat Scotch would have been much more effective – I told them who I was. From there they must have called Frank, and they or Frank must have called Tom Shepherd. Later came the third degree. But by then I had become who I was supposed to be: a private detective with a client, a brief, and a brain, not to mention one hell of a story to tell.

I told it a number of times. First to a big curly-headed guy in plain clothes who fancied himself and whose name I instantly forgot, and then, in more detail, to someone who was obviously his assistant. Technically, of course at this point I ought to have been shipped off to the nearest station, in this case the conveniently placed Paddington Green, home of the Anti-Terrorist Squad, and had my whole statement taken down word for word. I would probably have still been there in the morning. But Frank must have put in a good word for me, because for once they let me stay where I was.

I was good as gold. Or at least as near to gold as a girl like me ever gets. I told Detective Winter everything he thought he needed to know. And if I left anything out (which, I might as well tell you now, I did), I swear it wasn't from a conscious desire to deceive. In the event it hardly mattered. None of it made sense, anyway. Which is what gave it away, of course. I mean since we clearly weren't looking at a bungled custody snatch, that didn't leave much else it could be. Admittedly, I'd never seen a car bomb detonate, so had no idea what, if anything, were its distinguishing characteristics. But from the way he looked as I described it, he obviously knew. And now, just as the second explosion ripped its way through my memory, I heard something else, something more immediate. The sound of crying, long sobbing moans more like an animal than a person. At first I panicked, thinking it might be coming from me, but as I listened I realized it was seeping up from downstairs. My interrogator hesitated too, mesmerized for a second, then calmly began to talk over it, reeling me back in to the subject in hand. From there on the sobs ebbed and flowed at intervals, but we both ignored them, pros that we were.

At last they let me go. I refused their offer of a lift home and headed off down towards the front door. In the hall the living room door was ajar. I stopped and stared through the gap. On the sofa, where Mattie had been before, a man sat with his back to me, head deep in his hands. He wasn't crying any more. Opposite him, sitting on the edge of my Bette Davis seat, was the big guy in plain clothes with the dark curly hair, obviously a man with a mission, and, now my brain was working, equally obviously a rank high up in the Anti-Terrorist Squad. This was, after all, bound to be their case. As for Shepherd, well, what can I say? Except it's hard to look at anyone in that much distress and not feel pity. The copper glanced up at the door. He stared for a moment, half looking at me, half through me, then slowly got up and, giving the slightest of nods to the woman PC standing behind, closed the door in my face. Bastard, I thought. And it made me feel better to have some of my old prejudice back.

My car was parked about forty yards down the street on the other side. The fire engines had gone, but the police cars and an ambulance were still there, although the burnt-out shell of the Rover was screened off. There were still policemen everywhere, keeping the onlookers with nothing to look at at bay. Someone said something to somebody and I was let through. I found my car keys in my bag and put them into the lock. Then I slid into the driver's seat and closed the door, like I and a million other people had done a million times before. Except for one. I sat for a moment staring at the dashboard. I reached across to get the stereo out of the glove compartment and as I did so something went very wrong in my stomach. I tried to put the key in the ignition but it was clear I wasn't going anywhere. I got the door open just in time to throw up on the pavement. And so it was that I left a little of myself on the street with Mattie Shepherd.

Eventually, when there was nothing more to leave, I drove home. I was surprised by how empty the roads were, until I realized how late it was. 11.47. Five and half hours since . . . But then I don't suppose she was counting any more. I turned the corner into my street and everything looked the same but different, as if I had been away for a very long time and my memory had played tricks on me. When I got out of the car, I was so tired I could hardly stand.

In my exhaustion I found I'd relocked the front door trying to open it. I knew I just had to get inside and then I could lie down and let it all go till morning. But as the door pushed open I got this sudden hit of tension, almost a physical shock, as I realized that something in the flat wasn't right.

I stood absolutely still, trying to place the fear. And then I heard it, coming from the living room, a soft almost rhythmic clicking sound, once, twice, again, as if someone was trying to make a cigarette lighter catch in the darkness. And instantly I saw Mattie sitting there in her leather jacket, half a stubbed-out Dunhill in one hand and her cute little Bic lighter in the other, flipping down on the switch time after time waiting for the flame to jump. I was trembling so much I had to hold on to the wall. I put my hand on the handle and softly turned it.

The room was dark apart from the street-light glow from the curtainless window and one small, green light dancing in the wall unit. The amplifier was on, and below it the pick-up of the turntable was hiccuping its way round and round an album. Repeating stereos, fast becoming a leitmotif in tonight's drama. I turned and saw the figure laid out on the sofa, shoes off, arms in a pillow behind the head. And then, and only then, did I remember what I had forgotten so completely. That this was Nick's Saturday for not having Josh and that we had agreed to spend the evening together.

I walked farther into the room and looked down at him. He was sleeping noiselessly, his face caught in that slight frown I knew so well. Down by his side an empty bottle of wine sat next to a long-stemmed wine glass, half filled (Nick always picks the best glasses, says it improves the taste). The album on the turntable was Mahler's Requiem, a cover I didn't recognize lying near by, which no doubt made it a particularly special recording, the latest move in his contin- ued, good-humoured campaign to drag me kicking and screaming into adult music appreciation. I put out my hand and turned the switch. The pick-up lifted smoothly off the record and Mattie put away her lighter until the next waking nightmare. I looked at Nick again and was about to wake him when I realized that I didn't know what I would say, or if I would ever stop crying once I had begun to say it, and I couldn't bear the idea of not being in control. So instead I took a blanket from the chest and laid it carefully over his sleeping form. He didn't stir. I went out and closed the door. I brushed my teeth to get rid of the taste of bile in my mouth, but I left the light off so I wouldn't have to look at my face. Then I lay down on my bed and gave myself up to the protection of sleep.

CHAPTER FIVE

I Cain't Say No

When I woke it was another glorious day. It was also half over. I had slept for twelve hours. Lying beside me, in the curve of my body where a lover should have been, was a piece of paper. It read: 'Let me guess. You met a job you liked better than me?' Good old Nick, never one to make a crisis out of a drama. I got up and went into the bathroom. My face looked like my clothes, crumpled and slept in, and my eyes had that closed-up piggy look that comes from too much crying. Which was strange, considering I hadn't done any. I ran a basinful of cold water and dipped my head into it. Electric shock treatment. While I was fumbling for the towel, I knocked over the next instalment, rolled up in my tooth mug alongside the toothpaste. It read: 'Or maybe you've just grown tired of safe sex?'

In the living room the remnants of the night before had been cleared away, and the Mahler was sitting in its new cover on the coffee table, casually ostentatious. I nodded welcome to it, but it just wasn't the morning for a requiem. Instead I put on the radio. The *World this Weekend* was in the Ukraine sizing up the possibility of another nuclear catastrophe from the clapped-out old Soviet reactors. Maybe Mattie had already been news, or maybe the police were keeping it to themselves until they had something to say. I put on the kettle and went in search of breakfast, which, along with the Harrods almond croissant, was the last thing I remembered eating the day before. I wasn't expecting much, so the fridge came up trumps. Sitting on one of my fancy plates on the top shelf with a neat little cover of cling film over it was breast of chicken in a creamy sauce, ringed by a semicircle of new potatoes and some thoughtfully arranged broccoli spears. And on the top, the final and concluding part of the discourse: 'Just so long as it isn't my cooking. Call me on Monday if we're still lovers. Nick.' And this time I smiled.

I peeled the cling film off and stuck my finger in the sauce. It tasted better cold than anything I could make hot. I nuked it in the microwave for ninety seconds (last year's Christmas present from a mother who's finally given up on my domesticity) and then sat down next to Mahler at the table. What are the most important things in life? Food, sex, death and the movies, not necessarily in that order.

I ate slowly, making every mouthful count. The food helped normalize things a little. I suppose I should have given some thought to Nick, about how pissed off he really was. No doubt you've got some questions of your own about him you wouldn't mind answered. But the fact is it wasn't the right time, not with Mattie sitting so close on my shoulder. He'll come up again. And then, I promise, I'll tell you the whole story, or as much as there is. For now let's just say that he's a nice guy with a well-developed sense of humour; that we have a good time in bed (when we manage to get into the same one together) and that I absolutely adore his cooking. Not exactly Abelard and Heloise, but good enough for me right at the moment.

After eating I went into work. I hadn't really planned it that way, but when it came down to it the flat felt too warm and cosy, and I was too off the wall to be comfortable with its comfort. Of the other places I could go – well, Nick, even if I wanted him, had gone south to be a good enough father, and Kate, good sister Kate, was hurtling down the French side of the Alps with Colin in Michelin men suits and bobbly hats and wouldn't be back for another fortnight.

I parked on a meter which during weekdays would have cost me 20p for every ten minutes. It gave me short but sweet pleasure to walk away with the clock reading PENALTY.

Before we get there maybe I should prepare you for the office. I mean the street isn't too bad, as roads around Euston go. A hundred yards farther on and the real estate picks up considerably, but like a high-tide mark you know it's never going to reach us. The whole area has a feeling of the temporary about it, as if being near two of the biggest railway stations in London had infected it with their sense of transience and movement. Frank says he chose it because it was *of* town, but not *in* town (unusually poetic for Frank), but I think it was the only place he could get for the money, and he figured he might pick up some passing trade. The name on the plate reads COMFORT AND SECURITY, the lettering's really quite nice. We buzz you in via the door phone, which sounds good but means the inside comes as even more of a shock. The hall and stairs are communal, so it's not all our fault. When Frank moved in towards the end of the eighties, the television industry was still expanding and a couple of puppy-dog independents took the offices on the floor above and tarted the place up, even put down a new carpet. But then the bottom fell out of the market, not to mention the economy, and failure began to stain the carpet and dirty the walls. What with the name on the door and the state of the staircase, I suspect your average punter could mistake us for a coy version of sex and bondage. But then most of Frank's clients are not average punters. Neither are they glamorous women with skirts slit to the thighs who tell their story through lazy curls of cigarette smoke while the light casts film noir shadows on the wall. In reality most of them are men and most come via insurance firms or Frank's old friends in the Force. (I've often wondered if the boys operate on commission, but even if they do Frank would lie about it, so I've never bothered to ask.)

As for the jobs, well, take away the pizazz of the name, and private detecting is a dull business these days, made duller by the demands of the 'security' industry. I mean you still get the odd juicy assignment: a factory where the books aren't balancing because someone (in my case the son of the owner) is walking away with the goods, or the fire-insurance claim which turns out to be petrol for profit rather than God's little handout to a small business. I've even had some pleasure watching people betray each other through lace curtains and fake hotel reservations, but the line between investigation and voyeurism is painfully thin in those kinds of jobs, and Frank usually off-loads them on to contract labour. Instead I get other run-of-the-mill stuff, like looking after rich ladies in town for the day. Or young girls. Because, according to Frank, I'm good with people and so they feel at ease with me. A talent to aspire to, eh?

Sometimes I think I should have just swallowed my political misgivings and joined the opposition. Who knows, by the time I was ready to begin my ascent up the ranks maybe the police would have learned how to spell equal opportunities. Either way I would have had a much bigger computer to play with. Mind you, as I keep telling Frank, if he hadn't been such a cheapskate and gone for an Amstrad over an IBM, I could probably have hacked my way into their mainframe by now (well, even us girls have our techno-logical wet dreams). As it is, Comfort and Security has to make do with the good will of the boss's ex-colleagues. On the other hand if I had joined the Force, chances are Frank would have already left it. And I'm a great believer that some people are your destiny.

Upstairs the office door wasn't locked. He was standing by the coffee table with his back to me, and from the sound of it he was trying to gouge the last scraps of Coffee Mate out of an empty jar. 'I thought it was your turn to buy this stuff?' he said, grumpily, without turning, as if there was nothing out of the ordinary about us both being in the office in the middle of a Sunday afternoon. I sighed and walked past him to a cupboard at the back, from where I plucked a new jar.

'Thanks,' he said with scant gratitude. I took off my coat

and put it over the back of my chair which sat in a corner and was a little smaller and a little neater than his. 'You want some?'

'Yeah. Please.'

He grunted, and padded off to get another mug from the sink. 'Did you get my message?' he called from the alcove we have graciously called a kitchen.

'No,' I said. But I had known it was him, the little light flashing the number 1 on the answering machine when I woke up. I hadn't really wanted to hear it, whatever it was, but now I was here I was glad he was too.

I stood watching his back through the open door of the kitchen. He's a rumpled kind of man, Frank. I don't really remember his stomach arriving, but it certainly wasn't as much of a feature two and half years ago. There's also been a growth in the amount of chin. If you were cruel you could say he looks just what he is, an ex-policeman gone to seed. But in Frank's case what you get is more than what you see. Because he's most definitely not stupid. Neither is he corrupt, nor greedy. On the other hand he's not exactly Chandler's white knight. He has distinct trouble with some of the isms of life – sex and race in particular. Also I know for a fact he regularly tries to shaft the VAT man. I suspect in his heart of hearts he thinks himself a failure, and it's that which keeps him modest rather than any innate goodness. But he knows more about private detecting than anybody else I know and he's not mean with his knowledge. Also, when things get tough, as they most certainly were that afternoon, he's the one I find it easiest to talk to.

Nevertheless, the etiquette of our intimacy required that I pretend otherwise. He came back and handed me a cup.

'So what you doing here, Frank? I thought Arsenal was playing Manchester United?'

'Saturday, Hannah. They play on Saturday. How often do I have to tell you?' He sat down and put his feet on the desk. 'Ginny had a Spanish class reunion. There are twenty-three people in my sitting room eating *tapas* and talking *Guernica*. I thought I'd get ahead of the accounts.' He took a swig of the coffee. I probably don't need to tell you that Frank has never been ahead of the accounts in his whole life, but it was nice of him to have such a good excuse. 'However, since you're here, maybe we should do a little work instead. What do you think?'

'I think it's better than staying home and crying,' I said lightly, but it still sounded heavy.

He nodded. 'Good girl. So—d'you want to start or shall I?'

I had more to say than he did, but that was only proof of how little he'd been told about the job in the first place. It had come in at the last minute. 6.15 on a Friday afternoon. By phone. The man said he was Tom Shepherd and there had seemed no reason to disbelieve him. He was due to pick up his daughter the next morning from her boarding school in the West Country, but some urgent work had intervened. Frank had offered it to me because—well, take your pick. It sounded like girl's work and he knew I needed the money? Or because a football team he liked had something better to do with his Saturday afternoon?

Then I told him my side. He listened, grunting every now and then. And when the telling got difficult he pushed me through the pain with a few brisk questions. And so we got from the crime to the investigation.

'Big bloke, yeah? Dark curly hair. Not a great bedside manner?'

'Yeah, that's him. I didn't get his name.'

'Don Peters. He's one of the graduate whiz kids that's going to wipe out the IRA and still have time for breakfast.'

'So, it was the Anti-Terrorist Squad?'

'Who else would it be? The way you tell it someone blew up the car.'

'Yes, but not the IRA.'

'Hardly, seeing as the ATS have been made redundant in that area. And even if they hadn't – come on, Hannah, use your brain. You're not that grief-stricken. What's the difference between IRA bombs and the one you saw?'

'Um . . . IRA bombs . . . big, sophisticated, usually made with plastic explosives, imported rather than home grown, Semtex mostly.'

He nodded. 'See. If it had been a bomb like that, you'd switch on the ignition and boom – one big blast to hell, or wherever they think heretics go. But that's not what you saw, right?'

I tried to think about it without really seeing. 'No, no . . . er . . . there were two blasts. A small one, then a bigger one to follow. The second must have been the petrol tank.'

'You got it. And the first was probably petrol too. Fire bombs in the trade. Not the cleverest of devices, but they do the job. They've done it before.'

'Bristol, 1990,' I said quietly. 'The owner of the car was OK, but it took off the fingertips of a passing baby.' I remembered it well. Little niece Amy had been pushchair size then, but Kate had insisted on carrying her everywhere in a sling for the next three weeks on the grounds that if they went, at least they'd go together. It had seemed a bit melodramatic to me, but, of course, I couldn't say it.

Frank, meanwhile, was back in police files. 'Yep, although in that case, interestingly, they used plastic explosives. First time. But the year before, when they went for the university building, it was definitely a fire bomb. Generally works better against property than people. Used in fur shops or department stores, it sets fire to the stock, then wrecks it further when the sprinkler system goes off. Lot of damage to come out of one little cigarette-packet bomb.'

'And meanwhile Tom Shepherd was too busy with his rats to find time to celebrate his daughter's birthday,' I said softly, sitting again in a car looking out over sunlit Wiltshire fields.

'What?'

'Nothing. Just something she said.' It was funny how neither of us had used the words yet. The love that dares not speak its name. The British obsession with animals gone crazy. 'You think it's animal rights?'

He shrugged. 'Animal rights in the shape of the Animal Liberation Front. Who else?'

'But – I mean, they don't kill people.'

'They do now. You start putting bombs under people's cars and it's only a matter of time.'

'But if it was petrol, it would have been connected to the ignition. Wouldn't it?'

'Maybe, maybe not. You'll have to wait for forensics to tell you for sure. If there's anything left for them to go on. Why?'

I shook my head. 'I just don't remember her going for the switch. I mean she couldn't drive.'

'So maybe it was a duff connection. They're amateurs most of these boys. It did the job, anyway.'

'But why Shepherd? I know he was working on cancer research, but so are hundreds of others.'

'Did she tell you that?'

I nodded. I was finding it hard to swallow.

'And did she tell you who he works for?' I shook my head. 'Vandamed. With the biggest independent cancer research department in the country. Shepherd's head of it. Lot of money, lot of prestige, and a *lot* of animals. Prime target.'

'My God.'

'Not only that. He's had death threats before.'

'What! Christ, Frank, why didn't –'

'Because I didn't know.' And for the first time I realized how angry he must be too. 'All I knew was what you knew. A guy rings up wanting his daughter chaperoned. Only possible problem is a deranged wife.'

'So how did you find out?'

48

He made a face. 'Well, not from Don Peters, that's for sure. We never got on, even when I was high enough up the ladder to shit on him.'

He grinned. Only I was too busy to congratulate him. Too busy running it all back, seeing how it ought to have been. How that morning it should have been Tom Shepherd who got up in the dark and walked out to his car, just as I did to mine, with the thought of a two-hundred-mile round trip in front of him. Except his would have proved to be a longer journey. And that way Mattie would have lost a father, but she would still have been alive. And I would not be nursing this gnawing pain at the corner of my soul. I shook my head. I had to remember whose fault all this was, and not blame the wrong person. So he didn't love his daughter as much as his work. It wasn't a crime. Jesus, what exactly could he be doing to his rats that would make it worth blowing him off the face of the earth? And if they were out to get him, then why the hell hadn't he told us? That one seemed worth following up.

'You tell me. But I betcha he's been asked the question enough times by now.'

'Yeah, but not by me.'

We both heard it in my voice. He looked at me for a moment. 'And what good do you think that would do?' he asked carefully.

'It would make me feel better, for a start.'

He shook his head. 'Hannah, nothing's going to make you feel better. That's the point. So he tells you? What do you do then?'

'Maybe I'll go look for the guys who did it.'

He smiled. 'Two years catching shoplifters and she thinks she's Inspector Morse.' In other circumstances it's my role to laugh at Frank's Jewish mamma impersonation. In other circumstances it can be quite funny. 'Hannah, she's dead. The boys don't like animal rights in the first place. So now they've got a stiff on their hands, they're going to be breaking their balls to bust the guys who did it. There'll be a hundred coppers out there, all of them better trained and better informed than you are.'

'So? I've got you. What they know you can find out too. It was a Comfort job first. They'll understand. You're always telling me about their private codes of justice. If I were animal rights I'd probably prefer to be arrested by me than by them.'

From the way he was looking at me it was clear he thought I was reverting to type. In Frank's book even the best women let it happen to them. Emotion versus reason. Or for that you could read passion versus indifference. He shook his head slowly. 'Uh-uh.'

'Frank –'

'Hannah, I know what you're feeling, but it's too big for you.' He paused. 'And, believe me, even if it wasn't, it'd hurt too much doing it.'

I stared at him. 'And how much will it hurt not doing it?' I said quietly.

He sighed and pulled open a drawer. Then he held out an envelope. It was big, brown and fat with soft stuffing. I knew what it was but I asked anyway.

'It's the money he owes you.'

I took it and flicked it open. A cushion of notes, and they weren't fivers. I'm not as fast as Frank, but even I knew there was a good deal more than there should have been. I looked up.

'It's a bonus,' he said evenly. 'From him, not me. It arrived by courier. I think it means the job's over, Hannah.'

And I thought of Mattie's money belt, bulging with crisp little guilt notes. 'Yeah,' I said quietly. 'Well in that case it's not enough.'

CHAPTER SIX

Working in a Coal Mine

As detecting goes, the first bit was easy. Vandamed's London research centre was in the book and Tom Shepherd's home phone number had been on Frank's notes for the job. When I got through to the flat it was a policeman, but then I expected that. Tom Shepherd wasn't there. He had gone into work. Drowning his sorrows, no doubt. I asked the PC if anyone had claimed responsibility yet, but he clammed up and said I have to talk to DI Peters about that. Good old Frank. Never misses a description.

The research centre was on the other side of London, but the traffic was easy. I even parked in the employees' car park. I didn't expect Reception to let me in, so I wasn't surprised when they didn't. I called from a phone booth across the street and got through to the research offices. It rang a long time. When he answered, the voice sounded anxious, as if he was expecting bad news. Maybe I was it. He didn't want to see me, that was clear enough, but when I told him I was standing outside his window and I'd still be there when he got out, he didn't have a whole load of option.

This time Reception let me in and even gave me my own personal security officer to take me to the research building. Shepherd met us at the lift door.

All I had seen the night before had been a head buried in hands, a stubble of grey-black hair and a halo of grief. Now I found myself standing in front of a solidly built man in his late thirties, with well-cut features and a day's growth of beard. OK as looks go, but not the stunner his daughter would have turned out to be. Mind you, it was hard to tell with his eyes in that much trouble. He looked like a man who'd been given sedatives and then decided not to sleep. God knows what his waking dreams had been made of.

He led me into a small office and closed the door. He stayed standing. You could see the last thing he wanted was to talk to me. And now it came to it, face to face with his grief I found myself unsure of what I wanted to say.

'I got the money.' It came out rather abruptly. 'Thanks, but you overpaid me.' He frowned as if he didn't understand what I was saying. And I could see that he was going to have a hard time stopping himself from breaking down, which was exactly what I didn't need. 'I came because I thought it might help to meet me. I mean, I thought there might be things you wanted to ask . . . seeing as I was the last one . . .'

He shook his head. 'There's nothing I want to know from you. Thanks.' He added it almost as an afterthought. It was a good voice, dark and precise. I needed to hear it again, to see if I might recognize any of her intonations, her mannerisms of speech. But I couldn't think of anything to say. Except the one thing he wouldn't want to hear. I said it anyway.

'Well, there's something I want to know from you.'

'Which is?'

'Why didn't you tell us about the threats?' He looked at me evenly. 'The police said you'd received death threats from the Animal Liberation Front. You should have told us. I should have known.'

He stared at me for a moment, and it struck me he might be fed up with emotional women. Certainly I could feel that somewhere the grief had given way to anger – only when he spoke, none of it showed in the dead voice. 'And what difference would it have made if I had?'

Oh, not much, only that I would have checked under the car, that's all. Say that diplomatically. I gave it a go. 'It meant I wasn't looking for the right things.'

'Are you telling me you would have saved her?' And this time the anger came shining through. Mine as well as his.

'I'm telling you I should have known.'

He made a fierce little gesture with his hand, as if batting away my stupidity. 'Do you have any idea how many scientists get threats from the ALF? In this building, for example? Do you know how many people have been leafleted or insulted at one time or another? Most of them. Multiply that by every research establishment in the country and you've got one hell of a number.'

'But the police said yours was a campaign.'

'It was more than one threat, yes, but that hardly registers as a campaign. And there'd been no violence. No bricks through the car window, no razor blades in my personal mail. Nothing special. If you work with animals the ALF is a fact of life. If you let them undermine you, then they've made their point. The reason I didn't tell you was the same reason *I* don't go out every morning and check underneath the bonnet of my car. Because I refuse to give them the satisfaction of my fear.'

It sounded good. Except . . . 'Except this time they were serious.'

'Yes. So it would seem,' he said quietly.

'So why you? I mean what made you different from all the rest?'

'I don't know,' he said for what was obviously the one hundred and fourth time. He was getting angry again. 'Why don't you ask them?'

'Because I'm asking you.'

OK. So I should have been more compassionate. The guy was in pain. But he was also still alive, and all the way down the line he had disappointed her. What's more, he knew that I knew it. 'Look around you,' he said with barely concealed exasperation. 'We're the biggest research unit in the country. And I'm the head of it.'

'Yeah, but cancer. It doesn't make sense. If the ALF are going to blow up people, surely they'd pick their targets with a little more public relations in mind.'

He snorted. 'You don't know much about animal rights, do you, Miss Wolfe? That's the whole point. In the eyes of the ALF all scientists are monsters; it doesn't matter what they do. It's means, not ends, they're concerned with. I believe it's what's called a gulf of understanding. For medical science progress is impossible without testing. For animal rights any test which involves what they see as suffering to animals is no progress at all. There's no middle ground.'

Nice little speech. Word perfect. Still, he was right. Despite all the publicity, I didn't know much about their philosophy. I also didn't know that much about his job. But maybe he wasn't allowed to talk about it.

'So how do they justify the suffering they cause?'

He stared at me. 'I have no idea. Perhaps when you catch them, they'll tell you.'

It was clear the interview was drawing to a close. He rubbed a hand over his eyes. I watched him. His whole face was rigid, the jawbone set against any further feeling. He seemed like a man caught between exhaustion and fury. But what I didn't get now I couldn't see myself getting later. 'I wonder, do you have any of these threats that I can see, Dr Shepherd?'

The answer came slow and precise, as if he was talking to a child. 'No. I have given them all to the police.'

Time to start leaving. I put my bag over my shoulder and held out my hand. Play them right and you can get some of the best stuff from exits. 'Well, thanks for seeing me, anyway.'

He hesitated, then took my hand. His touch was clammy. I tried to imagine being fourteen with him as the centre of my universe, but I just couldn't get there; somehow he didn't seem old enough to be a father. But then he must have been young when she was born, mid twenties or even less. Maybe he had never quite finished with his youth and went looking for it amid the test tubes and lab assistants. It was an uncharitable thought, but then there was definitely something about him I didn't like. Or maybe 'like' was the wrong word – 'didn't feel comfortable with' was probably more accurate. Still, grief turns people inside out I have been told. Parents especially. Fathers and mothers. I wondered how they were going to conduct the funeral. Have separate services and bury the corpse twice? What corpse? I tried not to think about it.

Oh, yes indeed, I still had a whole slew of unanswered questions. I went for a first parting shot. 'About Mattie's mother –'

But he didn't let me finish. 'There's nothing to say about her. My wife is a disturbed, unstable woman. We haven't seen each other for a year.'

'Disturbed and unstable,' I repeated. 'But not violent?'

His eyes narrowed. 'And what does that mean?'

I waved a hand. 'Nothing. Only that I'm trying to find out who killed your daughter. And since it was pretty obvious the device was intended for you, I –'

'My God, you think it was Christine?' This time he laughed. It was not exactly an infectious sound. 'No. She gets too much pleasure from having me alive. Anyway, it's not her style. Christine would have trouble changing a plug, let alone constructing a bomb.'

Well, that sorted out that one. On the other hand it sometimes takes two to be electrically incompetent. Maybe he was the kind of man who needed to do it all himself. In which case I certainly wasn't looking at an absent-minded professor, the sort who regularly misplaced theatre tickets. I saw Mattie whirling round in her father's study, phone to her ear. One last question. I was careful how I phrased it. Right at that moment, apart from the person on the other end of the line, I was the only one in the world who knew about that phone call. And just for the present I wanted to keep it that way. So I asked him when he had last talked to his daughter. He treated it as an odd question, one implying neglect rather than affection. Maybe it did.

'I don't see that it's any of your business. Now, if you don't mind I have a lot to do.'

You betcha. Like finding a cure for cancer before the suppressed guilt makes you ill yourself. Don't reckon your chances. 'Of course. You're right. I'm sorry.'

I got to the door before I turned. 'Oh – stupid thing, really. Mattie was under the impression that you'd given me the theatre tickets for last night. I wasn't supposed to have them, was I?'

He looked at me as if I was slightly deranged. How irrelevant could something be. He'd never know. 'No. They were at the theatre. Why do you ask?'

I shrugged. 'Just wanted to check I didn't owe you some money.'

I went back to the office. Not because I had anything to do there, but because it felt better than going home. Frank had gone back to the leftovers of the *tapas* and the echoes of Spanish cedillas in his ear. One of these days I'll get to meet his family, the indestructible Ginny. As marriages go it didn't sound too bad. At least they weren't out to kill each other.

Of course I didn't believe it was Mattie's mother. I had just wanted to rattle Shepherd into some unguarded remark. In retrospect it didn't rate as one of my greatest interrogations. My technique or his personality? Let's call it a draw. My only consolation was that I couldn't believe the police had done much better.

The phone took the top of my head off, but then the office doesn't get too many calls on a Sunday evening. Frank had put the machine on so I just let it go. After the beep a man's voice said in a chatty kind of way: 'Well, off spending Sunday with the family, eh, Frank? I thought that was one part of this job you used to like. Listen, I thought you might want to know we brought in Ben Maringo, had a few words with him. He says it's no one he knows, but then he claims nobody's talking much to anyone these days. Gave us a few leads, though. I'll let you know when we do. Cheers. Oh, and by the way. Don thinks your girl's a cutie.'

Well, wasn't I the lucky one? In all kinds of ways. A present from the police. How nice. Nice of Ben Maringo to have such a distinctive name, too. Even nicer to find that his name was in the phone book. Granted, it didn't make the rest of Sunday night any easier, but at least for once Monday offered something to look forward to.

CHAPTER SEVEN

God Gave Names to All the Animals

I would have got there earlier if my car hadn't given up the ghost and I hadn't had to sit around waiting for the AA. It was mid-afternoon when I finally arrived at the small Victorian terrace on the outskirts of the Hackney Marshes, its façade badly in need of a coat of paint. Any worry that I might not have found the right Maringo was dispelled by the poster in the front window. SAY NO TO ANIMAL TEST-ING. And the picture of a dog cowering in terror as a hand with a scalpel approached it. For the boys to have him on file he probably had a record. And for them to think him worth a visit, it must have been for something pretty meaty, if you'll forgive the word. Clearly, whatever the consequences, it hadn't done much to change his views.

The doorbell didn't work, but then that's not something to hold against anyone. I rapped the knocker loudly. The door was opened hurriedly by a youngish woman, fair, wispy hair cut short but in no particular style. From under her feet a cat whipped out and into the road. She frowned at me and put a hand up. 'The baby's asleep.'

'Oh, sorry.' I smiled. 'Is Ben in?'

'Yes.'

'Great. Can I see him?'

She opened the door without really giving it much thought. Ben clearly had a lot of visitors. Either that or she didn't know him that well. Two rooms led off the narrow hallway on the right. Friends of Ben would have known which one to find him in. But then that's the nice thing about Victorian terraces – there's not exactly a rich choice of functions. I opened the door to what once would have been called the front parlour. The room was sparsely decorated with a sofa and a couple of chairs, a big dark rug on unpolished floorboards.

And a rabbit. Once you'd seen it, it was hard to take your eyes off it. It was large and white and sitting in a corner. At first glance it was so still you might even think it was stuffed, but look a little longer and the nervous twitching of the nose gave it away. It was sort of implicit in the twitch that this was a bunny who'd been to hell and back. I dragged my eyes away in search of its saviour.

But Ben Maringo had another love as well as animals. In a dark blue carry-cot next to him lay a small, sleeping baby. I don't know what made me think it, but it seemed clear this was his first child. It made him a late father. From his fair, thinning hair and lined face he was at least in his mid forties. He looked up. He was tired. But then the baby was very young.

'Hello, Ben.'

'Who are you?'

There were a number of answers I could have given him, but after a visit from the ATS I thought he'd appreciate it if I told him the truth. He didn't say anything for a while, just looked at the baby, tucking the covers in around the sleeping form. 'So, how did you find me?'

That was a little more tricky. 'I . . . I can't say,' I said apologetically.

'So much for anonymity under the law,' he said, but with more resignation than bitterness. The door opened and the young woman stuck her head round. She nodded rather nervously at me. 'Ben, if you're all right, I'll slip out and get the stuff from the chemist. I think he'll sleep till I get back.' Now I noticed a small, dark spot on her T-shirt front. A nursing mother is always on the run. So says Sister Kate and she should know.

'Yeah, OK. Oh, and Martha. You better get some more baby scissors. I can't find that pair anywhere.'

She nodded and was gone.

'How old is he?' I said in the silence that followed.

'Five months.'

'Does he sleep?'

'Off and on. Hasn't quite got the difference between night and day yet.'

'My sister says you have to train them young.'

'Yeah, well he and I have only just been introduced.' He paused. 'I was elsewhere when he was born. Detained at Her Majesty's pleasure.'

'What did you do?'

'I took some animals for a walk. They hadn't been well and they needed the fresh air. Unfortunately I had some trouble getting their cages open.'

I shot a glance at the rabbit. Police exhibit no. 234, or a trophy from an earlier raid? Neither Ben nor the rabbit saw fit to tell me. To have only just met the child he'd presumably fathered, Maringo must have done, say, a year out of a possible three-year sentence. Which means it wasn't just the cages he wrecked. So he was the real McCoy. No wonder the boys picked him up so fast. On the other hand if they'd really had their suspicions, he wouldn't be back here in the bosom of the family.

'I'm surprised they didn't tell you.'

'I didn't get to you through them,' I said, which was not entirely a lie.

'Hmm. But no doubt you want the same thing?' I didn't say anything. 'You know, I suppose, that the ALF have denied responsibility.'

'No. No, I didn't know that.'

'Of course nobody believes them.'

'Do you find that surprising?'

He sighed angrily. 'Every time the same superiority, the same stupid ignorance.' And for the first time his voice forgot the sleeping child in the room. 'You don't understand at all, do you? I don't suppose you've even thought about it?'

First Shepherd, now him. I was getting tired of being harangued. I wanted to shout back at him, tell him that what I understood was what I had seen on the road that night. Maybe that would shock him out of his pathetic righteousness. Trouble was he was right. I didn't understand. And if I was going to find Mattie's killer, it would be better if I did. Or at least learnt how to pretend.

'So why don't you tell me?'

'Because you'd still think we were nutters.' He shook his head. 'That's the pity of it. We tell ourselves we're doing all this to make people think – about the suffering, the immorality, the cruelty. But because nobody wants to listen, we end up doing exactly what we condemn, using violence to get our message across. And all that does is to make people deafer.' He looked up at me just to prove he was right.

'I'm listening,' I said quietly.

'Are you?' He smiled. 'I doubt that. You wouldn't want to change what you believe. It would turn your life around too much. And you've got too much to lose. Like everyone else. That's how it works, you see. Even when we do make the headlines, nobody's interested in putting our side of the case. When did anyone ever ask you to seriously consider what it's like for animals to be under our power? Or what it does to us to exercise that power?

'*Dumb* animals.' He said it with a sudden impatience. On the edge of my left field of vision the rabbit moved, a small but significant advance towards the centre of the action. Maybe it was reacting against the description. Come on, Hannah, no excuses now. Listen to what the man has to say. 'They're not like humans at all. I mean we've got souls, intelligence, sensibilities. All they've got is instinct: the will to survive, the desire to mate, a need to care for their children. No, not like us at all, eh? And then there's the feelings. Contentment, hunger, stress, fear, panic. Oh, and pain. They're particularly good at feeling pain. So in a way it's lucky they're not like us, isn't it?

61

Because if someone "experimented" with us the way we do with them it would be considered obscene. A crime against nature . . .'

The pause was slight, more to regain his breath than to let me speak, but I got in, anyway. 'Even when their suffering means saving people's lives?'

He smiled. 'You mean the "hundred of them is worth one of us" argument? Sounds good, doesn't it? Except in the end it's got nothing to do with it. We don't torture animals to save lives. Or to get a new kind of bath cleanser. Or even because we liked the taste of meat. You know the real reason we do it? Because it just doesn't occur to us that their suffering matters. Any more than a hundred years ago it "occurred" to white people that black people's suffering mattered.' He paused. 'Because, of course, they weren't "like" us either, were they?'

It was a powerful way to end. But then he knew that. I wondered if he also knew how dangerously thin was the line between philosophic logic and racism. I thought about bringing it up but something in his face made me decide against it. In his own way he was a good preacher, and like all good preachers he convinced himself anew each time around. Painful business. He shook his head. 'And yet it's you lot who call us uncivilized.'

In the carry-cot the baby started to stir. He leant over and touched it lightly on the cheek. It snuffled back into sleep. I thought about what he'd said. It reminded me of a hundred other speeches I had heard about a hundred other instances of oppression and cruelty. The kind of thing you knew would destroy you if you really took it on board. So where do animals come in the list of man's inhumanities? He was right. For most people not very high up. I wondered what I would have done if I'd come across the rabbit wired up to a dozen electrodes writhing in pain. How his words might affect my next bacon sandwich. But I didn't really want to think about it. Which, of course, was exactly his point. He recognized my silence. No doubt he'd witnessed it enough times before. 'On the other hand you could just forget all about it. You wouldn't be the only one.'

'I have to ask you this. Do you know anything about who killed her?' I said carefully.

He smiled. 'It's the wrong question. The question is, would I tell you even if I did?' He paused, then shook his head. 'It was never my scene. Even before Dominic came along I never set out to hurt anyone, except maybe the hunt man I threw off his horse. And now – well, now, I've joined the ranks of the "too much to lose" brigade. I've spent the best part of six years of my life in prison, and apart from maybe a hundred animals that I've saved from dying I haven't achieved anything. I don't think in that time I've converted one single ordinary person to the cause. No, maybe Martha, but that's different. And now I want something for myself. I want to watch my son grow up. And to do that I have to make a pact with this lousy society. I'll take no part in the cruelty. I won't eat or drink or wear anything that has come about as a result of killing or maiming or hurting any animal. But I won't break the law to stop others doing it.'

'But you still know those who will?'

We looked at each other.

Eventually he said, 'You don't feel like the police, so I'll tell you this. The Animal Liberation Front that I know didn't put any bomb underneath Shepherd's car. Three years ago, just before that baby got caught in the Bristol blast, there was a crisis in the movement. And the extremists won out. The side that wanted to shock the world into listening to what we were saying. So they booby-trapped the cars. But a kid got caught in the crossfire and we became indistinguishable from the IRA. Once again nobody listened. And we learnt our lesson. Most of us. As far as I know, all of us. But the movement operates without hierarchy and without leaders. That's the point about it.

There are small independent cells all around the country, and they're largely autonomous in what they do and how they do it. None of them that I know would have put a fire bomb under Tom Shepherd's car. And if there was someone who did, then they're not animal rights in my book. Not any more.'

I wondered how far Dominic was responsible for changing his mind on that one. Those that know tell me babies alter your emotional landscape entirely, blotting out some of the features you liked, as well as those you didn't. But how far could they change someone's loyalties?

'Did you give the police any names?'

He smiled. 'I told them about a few people they already knew who had absolutely firm alibis.'

'You led them up the garden path?'

'I wasted a bit of their time, just as they wasted a lot of mine.'

I smiled back. 'One other thing. Do you know anything about Tom Shepherd's work that would mark him out from all the others?'

It was clear he had already given it some thought. 'All research units have to find new drugs to justify their exist- ence. And he's head of one of the biggest. Any drug he comes up with would have to be tested within an inch of its life, which means a good deal less than an inch of a thousand animals' lives. More than that – well, from what I hear, Shepherd's an ambitious man. He's got one of the plum jobs in the business, and he got there very fast. Who's to tell what he did on the way up?'

And there was something in the way he said it that made it all fit into place. 'Should I ask the same question of you?'

He looked at me for a moment, then said, 'You know it's a big ego boost, thinking that you're saving mankind. He wouldn't be the first to confuse vanity with scientific altru- ism. Just as I said – everyone's got a lot to lose.'

I had to admit it, he was more convincing than Tom

Shepherd, but then he had a child that was still alive. Frank says it's my blind spot, giving so much time to the subversives; that in the end it makes me as prejudiced as the people I despise for doing the opposite. Sometimes, when I'm feeling unsure of myself, I think he's probably right. Now was one of those times. 'And that's all you know?'

The front door opened and closed. The baby juddered awake and started to cry, as if he could smell her presence.

'That's all I know.' Maringo bent over and picked him up, cradling him over his shoulder. I caught sight of a squashed little face, snuffling and rooting in search of something he couldn't give. Martha came into the room and held out her hands. The mark on the front of her T-shirt had spread. I got up and left them to it. On the hall table there were some leaflets. Visitors' material. I picked up a few and took them with me.

I'd been in there a long time. Too long to think of doing much else with the day. Remembering there was nothing in the house to eat, I drove home via the supermarket. In retrospect not a wise move. I spent ten minutes by the meat counter trying to work out exactly what I felt about chickens. I already knew how I felt about rabbits and dogs: the photos and descriptions on the leaflets had been pretty graphic. But then I wasn't about to eat a dog. I picked up two chicken breasts. In terms of comparative cruelty it still seemed to me that Mattie had got the worse deal. But then that was hardly the chicken's fault. I put the portions back again and moved on to the lentils. But the thought of living in close culinary proximity with pulses for the rest of my life made the future seem even bleaker. So I compromised and bought fish. Poor little buggers. Between the Japanese and confused vegetarians they have a hard (and short) life.

By the time I pulled up outside my flat it was already evening. I looked up at the darkened windows. But it all felt too lonely, too much space for me and my thoughts.

Anyway, I wasn't at all sure what one should do with cod to make it worth eating.

His street was fancier than mine. I parked next to his Volvo and called up through the intercom. And waited. Maybe he wasn't home.

'Yep?' a voice crackled.

'Hi,' I said. 'It's me.'

'About time,' he said and buzzed the door open. I took the stairs slowly. It occurred to me I was going to have a lot of explaining to do. Stuff I didn't really want to have to say all over again. He was standing in the doorway, waiting for me. I stopped a few yards away.

'I'm sorry,' I said. 'I meant to call . . .'

And to my horror I realized I was going to cry. He put out a hand. 'It's OK, Hannah. I talked to Frank. It's going to be all right.'

And as I fell into his arms, I remember thinking how relieved I was to see him, and what a vicious joke of fate it was that I didn't really love him.

CHAPTER EIGHT

You Need a Friend

'You want some more?'

I shook my head. He filled his glass and put the bottle down on the bedside table, then put out his arm for me to crawl inside. At the foot of the bed the TV was droning on quietly, yet another detective drama, the lone hero putting the world to rights while his own internal landscape fell apart. I knew how he felt.

It was only 10.30 and I was ready for sleep. Nick had done some inspired things with the cod, and then we had done some rather more predictable things to each other. But against the odds the sex had helped – at least it makes you know you're alive. If you can really let yourself go, that is. In the past that had been a problem for me. I suppose I was scared just where I might end up. But with Nick I've always known where I am. That's the strength of us, but also finally the weakness. I think – in fact, I know – that he feels worse about it than I do.

Not only is he a good lover, he's also a good listener. Part of his job, counselling disturbed kids. Well, you didn't really expect him to be a commodities broker, did you? We talked about Mattie. About the awesome sense of waste when it happens to someone so young, and how if *I* was feeling destroyed, then it would be so much worse for the parents. And once again I was sorry to have been so tough with Shepherd.

'I wouldn't worry. He probably appreciated the chance to get angry. Just as you did.'

'And how about you?' I said. 'How angry were you?'

He made a 'what's a guy to do' sort of gesture. 'I didn't feel a thing after the first bottle. It may surprise you,

Hannah, but I already knew I was having an affair with a woman obsessed by work.'

'You want I should change my job?' I said, although not as well as Frank would have done it.

He pretended to give it some thought. 'Yeah. How about a lawyer? I've always had this thing for lawyers.'

'Is this sexual, or did your mother want you to marry into a profession?'

He laughed. 'Well, she certainly didn't believe in therapy. Thought people should solve their own problems.'

On the telly our man was looking craggy and interesting over a lonely glass of Scotch. In about thirty seconds' time a long-legged blonde would walk into his life and up the ratings. Give me a break. 'Do you think you could have helped her?'

'Who, my mother?'

'No.'

He shrugged. 'Hard to say. Depends how long she'd been feeling neglected. But from what you tell me she had enough spirit to come through it. Everyone gets disillusioned with their parents sooner or later. Sometimes it hurts more the longer it takes.'

I saw again her closed little face, fists up ready for aggro. 'She'd have given you a run for your money.'

'All part of the job.'

His. Not mine. Mine was making sure I brought the client home alive. Not exactly a difficult task, you might think.

'It wasn't your fault,' he said quietly.

'Yeah? So whose was it?'

He looked at me for a moment. 'What happened, Hannah? Did you see yourself in her?'

So I'm the only one obsessed by work in this relationship, am I? I put out my hands in mock defence. 'Do I get reduced rates?'

I thought for a minute he was going to pursue it. But

68

luckily lust got the better of him. 'Only if I get to sleep with the patient,' he said as he slid his hand under the covers.

It might have been a nice idea if the bed hadn't been littered with the remains of the cheesecake dessert. Rule 33 in our relationship: whoever's house it is does the clearing away.

'Don't fall asleep by the time I get back, all right?'

I yawned, just to keep him on his toes, then lay against the pillows and watched him go. I have a special fondness for the back of men's bodies – the way they're so unbalanced; those thick, fleshy shoulders tapering down to neat little hips and buttocks. I find it rather poignant. Others might call it symbolic – getting pleasure from watching them walk away.

Six months. Shorter than some, longer than most. I kicked and stretched my legs to the bottom of the bed, and as I did so my great suitcase of a handbag toppled off the edge, spewing its contents over the floor. I got up to retrieve them and so it was that I noticed the Harrods bag peeking out from the depths of the garbage. I picked it up, and with it came a whole fistful of memory: Mattie's mischievous grin as I stood at the counter waving pieces of silk erotica in my hand. I took them out, one by one.

I was still holding them when Nick came back from the kitchen. He looked at them and then at me, and the delight was mixed with just a little confusion. 'What's this? Post-feminism in action?' Then he looked again. 'Hannah? What is it?'

I shook my head. So Helen never got her underwear. I had been so caught up in my own grief I hadn't given a thought to anyone's else's. Death is death, whether you're thirteen or thirty-three. And a best friend must be a worse loss than a client. I put the silk back in the bag. 'Sorry,' I said distractedly. 'I'm just a Marks & Spencer girl who got led astray. Where's the alarm?'

'Why? How long are we going to fuck for?'

I smiled. 'I've got to get up early.'

'You want to tell me where you're going?' he said just a touch less lovingly.

'Yeah. Back to school.'

I won't tell you about the journey because you've been there already. It wasn't the same, anyway—not the sunshine, nor the landscape, nor the feeling of anticipation. I got there just after ten, and found Patricia Parkin. But when I asked if I could see Helen, she said it wasn't her decision and I had better talk to the head.

The head had the best room in the house, dappled with light and full of wood and history, an obvious exhortation to students to go forward into successful adulthood. She was younger than I expected. She was also tougher.

'I'm sorry. It's out of the question. She's very upset. They all are. I don't think it would help her at all to meet you.'

'It's only for a few minutes. Mattie bought her something. I'd like to give it to her.'

'You can give it to me. I'll see she gets it.'

It would have been almost worth it just to see her face. 'No,' I said. 'That's not possible.'

She paused for a second. Then stood up. 'I'm very sorry, but that's all I can offer. I know how far you've come, and I can understand your concern, but, well, I have to think of their well-being.' And how much their parents are paying not to have them disturbed, I thought uncharitably, but it helped.

We shook hands and she showed me to the front door. She stood at the steps to see me off. Just like the time before.

I got into my car and turned to Mattie, to make sure she had put on her seatbelt. The empty air grinned back at me. Once again it seemed intolerable that she wasn't there. When no one close to you has ever died it takes a while to penetrate the layers and meanings of loss. Maybe I should ring my parents, I thought, and tell them how much I loved them. Just in case.

I drove out and parked in the high street. Then walked the half-mile back into the school grounds. I stationed myself round the side, between the main house and one of the dormitories. There was, of course, more than one way to skin a cat. I saw Ben Maringo's face crease up in distaste. Sorry, Ben.

I waited till I saw a girl that looked around the same age as Mattie, then approached her and told her I was looking for Helen. She told me she was in Recreation and if I wanted she'd go and get her. All in all it didn't seem a big deal. I stood waiting, and I could feel my heartbeat getting louder.

When she came, she wasn't at all what I had expected. She was mousy, covered in freckles and bigger than Mattie, considerably bigger. It struck me she might have trouble squeezing into the cute little garments sitting at the bottom of my bag.

I told her who I was, and that I was here unofficially. Her face clouded over as I talked and she look kept looking down at her feet. I began to see things from the headmistress's point of view. But it was too late to stop now.

'I could have sent it, but I think she'd have preferred it this way.'

I handed her the Harrods bag. She took it gingerly.

'You don't have to open it now,' I said. And as I did so, suddenly, wham, it hit me like a freight train. The whole damn thing. God, sometimes I wonder why Frank bothers with me. Good old Mattie Shepherd. She had style right up until the end.

The girl had opened the bag and was staring down at the contents.

'It's all right,' I said. 'You see, she told me you were having an affair with the school gardener. But you're not, are you?' She shook her head, and her cheeks were pink under the freckles. I nodded. 'How long had she been seeing him, Helen?'

At first she wasn't going to say. But I'm afraid I pushed her a bit. After all, that was her role in life, or obviously had been with Mattie. It came out in a great whoosh. But then some secrets are better in the open.

'They'd all been after him, the older girls especially. Well, he was really good-looking. But as soon as he saw Mattie that was it. I told her she'd better be careful. But she didn't care. She used to go out at night and meet him in the grounds. She said they were really in love and that as soon as she could leave school they were going to start living together.'

'And what did he say?'

She shrugged her shoulders. 'Tony? He kept himself to himself. Apart from Mattie. I suppose he wanted to keep it as secret as she did. I didn't really like him that much, actually. I thought he was . . .'

'Yes?'

'I don't know. Weird. A bit snooty.'

'And you say it had been going on for four months?'

'Since November. She made me take her place at carol rehearsals so she could meet him.' Poor Helen. I only hope it had given her a little vicarious pleasure.

'So where is he now?'

She went into communion with her feet again. 'I haven't seen him. Not since –'

'OK. Listen, thanks for your help. You were a good friend. She talked about you a lot.'

And her face lit up. 'Did she?'

'Yes. In fact I think maybe you should keep them after all. I'm sure that's what she would have wanted and, well, you never know when they might come in handy.'

And she went even pinker as her hand clasped the bag. In the background someone was calling her name. 'You'd better go,' I said.

She nodded and left without looking at me again. I turned my attention to the ground. Of course after what I'd heard I didn't really expect to find him. But I had to try.

Behind the tennis courts and the hockey field the garden became quite dense: an overhang of big trees with shrubbery that had been allowed to go to seed. Creative gardening, maybe. To be honest I didn't feel good about being there. Nothing specific, just a touch of the 'city girl in the country' blues. So when he came up behind me I experienced what I think was a mild version of a cardiac arrest.

He wasn't the one I was looking for. That was plain immediately. On the other hand the man in front of me certainly resembled a gardener. He had a head of hair that looked like bees had made honey in it, and a face worn away by wind and sunshine. Not a trace of the Jason Donovans about him.

I told him I was looking for Tony. He told me so was he. I also got the impression he wasn't surprised it was a woman doing the looking. In fact when I pursued it, grizzle-head admitted that employing Tony had been something of a mistake; that despite impeccable references and a nice line in rose pruning he just hadn't shown the right kind of commitment to the job. In fact, when – or rather, if – he turned up again, it would be to find he didn't have a job any more.

When I asked if he had an address, he told me the boy had been staying in digs in town, but that according to the landlady he hadn't been around since Friday night, and his room looked like he'd left for longer than the weekend. Well, what a surprise. I thanked him for his trouble and left him to his hedge clippers.

As I slipped out of the main gates Helen was waiting for me. She was dawdling by the trees, trying to look as if she wasn't there, which in her case wasn't that easy. I thought of all those photos of myself at fourteen, crammed into little shift dresses for all the world like an overstuffed saveloy, and I wondered if I shouldn't offer her some hope for the future. But if someone had brought it to my attention then, I probably would have died of shame. She didn't say much, just handed me a large brown envelope. I had a sick feeling in the pit of my stomach from the moment I saw it in her hand.

'What is it?'

'Something Mattie kept in my locker. We always swapped private things. Sometimes other girls do raids . . .'

Ah yes, I had forgotten just how nasty young girls could be to one another. I wondered what Helen had swapped. Not a lot, I suspect. As it was, you could see she wasn't at all sure she was doing the right thing by keeping it, let alone by giving it to me.

'Thanks,' I said. 'What would you like me to do with it?'

She frowned. 'I don't know . . .'

Too much responsibility, that was her trouble. To the living and the dead. 'I tell you what. If I think it's important, I'll make sure the right people see it. And I won't involve you. OK?'

'Yes. Thanks.'

She turned. But there was one more question. A case of mopping up, really. 'Oh, Helen, one thing. That night . . . the night she died. Did you by any chance call Mattie at her father's house? It would have been about 6.30.'

She frowned, then shook her head. 'No.'

Girls' secrets? We all have them. Worth checking. 'You're sure about that?'

'Yes . . . I mean, how could I? We're not allowed to use the phone until after seven.'

'Fine. Thanks a lot.'

And she disappeared. I walked back to the car, the envelope stuck to my hand. But I had decided to wait. To open it somewhere where she had been with me, so if necessary she could look over my shoulder. Once back in the driving seat I carefully slit the top and shook out the contents. A set of roughly printed leaflets fell into my lap. I recognized the picture on the front of one: a rabbit with half its fur ripped away and a mark like an acid burn covering the exposed flesh. I didn't need to read the copy to find out how my last suntan had helped to incinerate a thousand animals. The other leaflets told more horror stories, the kind of thing to revolt a young girl's sensibilities and make her think badly of her father. I was looking so hard at them I almost missed the last billet-doux. It was stuck at the bottom of the envelope and I had to tease it out with my fingers. It was worth the work.

I was staring at a blurred black-and-white photograph of a young man in half-profile, hair quiffed back, cigarette in his mouth, a moody look in his eyes. Behind him were what looked like the gardens of Debringham College. It had the feel of a photo taken without his knowing, either that or a fashion editor had spent a number of hours making it seem like that. I looked at the curl of the cigarette smoke and thought briefly of the irony of lung cancer, Tom Shepherd's research and cruelty to animals. But mostly I thought of the boy himself. Twenty? twenty-five? Maybe older, it was hard to tell. But one thing was easy. Even from the semi-profile you could see what all the fuss was about. Yes, indeed. Mattie had got herself quite a catch. Shame about his politics.

CHAPTER NINE

Try a Little Tenderness

'He's trying to look like James Dean.'

'Matt Dillon, more like.'

'Who's Matt Dillon?'

'James Dean forty years on. God, Frank, this is youth culture. You've got to make an effort.'

'I don't see why. My parents never did.' He threw the photo back down on the desk and took a swig of tea. 'Still, whoever he looks like, he's not a man eager to have his picture taken.'

'Well, it is a little incriminating, isn't it?'

'Maybe.' He picked up the leaflets and flicked through them, making faces. Then he looked at me. 'So, what do you think you've got?'

I took a breath. 'I think Mattie Shepherd was having an affair with an animal rights activist, posing as the assistant school gardener. And I think it was through her that the ALF got whatever stuff they had on her father.'

'Woooh! And I think you've got an overactive imagination.'

'Oh, come on, Frank. I know you don't approve of me doing this, but don't treat me like a moron.'

'Hannah, if I thought you were a moron, I would have given you your own personal copy of the telephone answering-machine messages from Sunday night. Ben Maringo, remember? Yes, thank you. I like a girl who has the decency to look embarrassed. Was he a help?'

'He was. Thanks,' I said somewhat belligerently, and repeated what Maringo had told me about the ALF cells, their level of autonomy and secrecy. And their possible extremism.

'And you think this guy's one of them?'

'The timing fits. Shepherd first received threats in early December, a month after Mattie started visiting the potting shed. And if the gardener really had nothing to do with it, then he'd still be at work. Anyway, who else would have given her the leaflets?'

'It could have been a school project.'

'Frank, have you looked at this stuff?'

He humphed in a Frank kind of way. 'You really think she would have shopped her father?'

'Well, she was pretty mad at him. The whole point was his work had become more important than his family. I think she might have wanted to get even with him somehow. Yes?'

'But not to have him killed.'

'Of course not.'

'And that's what you think she was doing that night in his study. Going through his papers looking for stuff.'

'Well, she certainly wasn't looking for theatre tickets.'

'Except if her boyfriend was animal rights then he would have known about the bomb. Which made it a bit late for her to be looking for more evidence.'

'Maybe they didn't tell him.'

'Come on, Hannah, no one plays it that close to their chest.'

I thought again. 'OK. Maybe she wasn't meant to be there in the first place.' Step by step. Like learning to walk: first the basics, then the fancy work. 'I mean the police have no way of knowing when the bomb was put there, right?'

'Right.'

'But since it's not something you'd do in broad daylight, it must have been done the night before. And what was Shepherd meant to be doing next morning? Getting up at the crack of dawn and driving down to Somerset to pick up his daughter. And who would know about that? Mattie and, therefore, loverboy. But then, at the last minute, Shepherd cancels. What time?'

'6.15, 6.25. I was walking out the door.'

'And you're the only one he tells.'

'No, he rang the school.'

'Yes. But the school didn't tell *Mattie* till the next morning because they knew she'd be pissed off. Patricia Parkin said that herself. And by then the boy's long gone. Nobody at Debringham had seen him since Friday afternoon. So as far as he – and presumably, they – are concerned everything's still on course for Shepherd's early-morning appointment in hell.'

'OK. So when did they find out?' And you could see he was enjoying it. Maybe it reminded him of the old days, smoke-filled rooms, men with their ties off bonding over matters of life and death. Truth be told, it was one of my favourite bits too, being a surrogate male colleague.

'I suppose when someone drove down the road to check and found the car still outside the house. But by then there's nothing they can do. I mean they can hardly walk up in broad daylight and take it off again.'

'But they must have realized the next time the car was used it might not be him on his own. In fact it would almost certainly have been the two of them together.'

'Yes.' It was an uncomfortable conclusion. A mad scientist was one thing, his innocent daughter another.

Frank shrugged. 'Well, you're the one who thinks they've got principles. Why didn't loverboy try and warn her?'

And once again I heard the first ring of a telephone call. And I saw Mattie with her back to the door, papers in one hand, phone in the other, arguing with someone. Only a matter of deduction. If it wasn't her father and it wasn't Helen, who else could it have been? In which case why hadn't he warned her? Or maybe he was trying. Maybe he never got around to it because I interrupted the call. '*Listen, I have to go now. I'll see you. I mean, you won't be late will you?*' But see you where? Back at the school? Or sooner? Maybe the visit to the car was just an excuse all along. And once she had got the entertainment guide she would have made a run for it. Whatever it was, she hadn't exactly given him time to answer back.

Frank was watching me. I thought about telling him, but right at that moment I didn't need to feel any worse than I already did. 'I don't know,' I said feebly.

After a while he said, 'I don't suppose you want my version?'

I smiled. 'Would that stop you giving it?'

'The problem with knowing too little is you have to make up too much. You've got a picture of a boy, probably a boyfriend, who may or may not be connected to the ALF. The rest is speculation. Healthy exercise, but not to be trusted.'

Good old Frank, pulling me back from the brink again. 'So, what should I do?'

'Well, I'd say you'd better go looking for Bob Dylan.'

'Matt.'

'Matt.' He grinned. 'I just want you to know I can see through your lies.'

It took me a little while. But then I wasn't expecting it. And I hadn't been there in his heyday. 'That's very good.'

'Yes, well some of us are old enough to remember the Isle of Wight. I never liked him after he went electric. Meanwhile, what are you going to do with this?' He pointed to the envelope.

I shrugged. 'Nothing.'

'Nothing?'

'You said yourself I can't prove anything. It'd be a waste of their time.' I made myself busy not looking at him.

'Hannah?'

'What?'

'Look at me.'

'Yes, boss.'

'You did tell them everything that happened that night, didn't you?'

'Sure. I –'

Telephones. Sometimes I swear they know they're being talked about. He picked up the receiver, but kept his eyes on me. 'Comfort and Security. What d'you want?' He's got a great telephone manner, Frank. If I were in trouble, I'd be round like a shot. 'Yes, it is.' Pause. 'Yes, she does, but I'm not sure she's here at the moment. Can I ask who's calling?' His tone changed. 'If you'd just hold on a minute.' He put his hand over the receiver.' She says her name is Christine Shepherd, and she wants to meet you.' Thank you, Christine.

It wasn't as good an address as her husband's: a purpose-built apartment block off Shepherd's Bush Green, with one of those front gardens that is no one's responsibility except the neighbourhood dogs'. The flat was on the fifth floor. The lift was cleaner than the garden, but not exactly a triumph of design. When I got out on the top landing, all the front doors had different colours and doorbells to them. The whole place had a feel of built-public, gone-private about it.

The door opened on an older version of Mattie: the same great mane of hair, and the same straight little nose and upward tilt of the mouth. But a smile that would never reach the eyes again, like someone else I knew. They might have been at war, but she and Tom Shepherd had more in common than they realized. It made you wish for a happier ending. '*My wife is a disturbed, unstable woman.*' Those had been his words. At first sight they wouldn't have been mine. We shook hands and she stood aside to let me in.

The sitting-room was neat and stylish on a limited budget. From the kitchen beyond I heard someone at work. So Christine's man was new in more ways than one. Maybe she was the one who changed the plugs now. She sat down. I did the same. Except neither of us knew where to start. So you're the woman who watched my daughter go up in

80

flames ... You could see the opening sally wouldn't be easy.

'Thank you for coming.'

'You're welcome.'

'Have you seen Tom?'

I nodded.

Her fingers did imaginary crochet in her lap. 'How is he?'

'Upset. Angry.' Inadequate words, but the only ones I had.

'With me?'

'I think with everything. Maybe with himself if he knew it.'

'If he knew it,' she repeated quietly. 'Yes. Did he talk about me?'

'No. Not a lot.' Well, it was only a small lie.

'I see.'

I sat waiting, staring at the rug. Nice piece, the kind that improves with study. In the end I had to help her. Well, wouldn't you? 'Mrs Shepherd, would you like me to tell you what happened?'

She looked up, but didn't speak. Women, of course, cry more easily than men; it doesn't necessarily mean they feel things more deeply. Still, it was awful to watch. She nodded slightly. I took a breath and told her what she wanted to know.

I don't know if it helped. I mean, what comfort can anyone gain from hearing a story which moves so inexorably towards death? I made it as gentle as I could and I filled it with Mattie's optimism and spirit and humour, as if those things could somehow transcend the tragedy. I said very little about her anger, although I think we both knew I had left it out. She cried silently as I talked, nodding occasionally and wiping her eyes with her fingers, and towards the end when her fingers weren't enough, she put her head in her hands and sat for a while.

I waited, my back to the kitchen door. The clatter of

crockery had stopped midway through the story, and now something made me turn my head.

She was standing in the doorway. It was hard to tell how long she'd been there. She was tall, attractive, with red hair, well cut, and a strong, open face. What really gave it away though, was how she was looking at Christine. She crossed the room and sat on the arm of the sofa, the line of her thigh touching Christine's arm. Then she put a hand gently on her shoulder. And there was, in that gesture, something that transcended any notion of sisterly affection. For her part Christine didn't even look up. She simply lifted her own hand and put it on top of her lover's. And so, gradually, the strength of their physical contact pulled her back into the land of the living.

And, of course, now I knew, far from being strange, it all seemed so obvious. Obvious and almost welcome. Or maybe I am confusing that feeling with relief, because now at last I could understand the ferocity of all the emotions, both in Mattie and her father. So much rage and pain. How else do you cope with a wife who doesn't want a husband, and a mother who appears to prefer another woman to her own daughter?

Over Christine's head her lover offered me the slightest smile of introduction. 'Veronica Marchant,' she said, and it was a voice to match the face, clean and clear. 'Pleased to meet you.' I nodded. She watched me, then frowned slightly. 'You didn't know?'

'No,' I said, because it was pointless to pretend.

Christine glanced up at her lover, then back at me. 'Tom didn't tell you?'

'No.'

'And Mattie . . .?' I shook my head. You could see that it hurt her almost as much as the story I had just told. 'She didn't talk about me?'

'Not much,' I said. 'But she missed you.'

'Yes, I missed her, too.' She caught her breath. 'But I

don't think she ever understood. Maybe it's not understandable.' But then that wasn't mine to comment on.

'I think Miss Wolfe might find it helpful to know what happened, Chris,' said Veronica, watching me over her lover's head. And I wondered if that was the way a man would have put it, or if somehow their womanliness made it all different.

And so it was that I learnt the story of the Shepherd marriage: a modern little morality tale of sex and circumstance, starting with an errant conjunction of sperm and egg cementing a relationship which would otherwise have gone the way of all flesh. But they were young (she at teacher training college, he a post-graduate), unsure about abortion and under fierce parental pressure. The way she told it, it was hard to know whether they gave in or simply gave up.

The early years were a struggle because of money, with Shepherd chasing fewer and fewer government research jobs, and by the time things got easier and he'd become the development officer for the Vandamed livestock division, the emotional fault lines were beginning to reopen between them.

The relationship had never been successful sexually, although she'd done a good job of hiding it, even from herself. But as Mattie grew older and Christine could no longer hide behind the excuses of maternal exhaustion, it became impossible to ignore any longer. Although, as she told it, it wasn't quite that simple. When was it ever?

'There's one thing you should know. Veronica didn't break up my marriage. Tom and I did that for ourselves. And he was as much to blame as I was. Yes, I could have been a more responsive wife. But I never refused him. And if he hadn't left, then I'd probably still be there now.'

'He left you?' Among all the mud Mattie had slung at her father that one hadn't been mentioned.

'I don't mean he packed a bag and walked out. But from the way he behaved he might as well have done.' She was angry now and the emotion sculpted her face in memory of her daughter. 'I suppose I should have seen it coming. From the start he'd always been more interested in his work than in me. I think that's why he was able to block it all out for so long. Maybe that's why I didn't mind. It made things easier in some ways. But after Mattie was born he'd always found time for the family. Until he got the London job.'

'Head of research.' She laughed bitterly. 'Everything he'd ever wanted. Maybe that was the problem. Sometimes I think he was scared he wasn't up to it – there were others better qualified. I don't know. Maybe it wasn't work at all, maybe it was me. Whatever it was, he just closed down completely. Never came home, hardly even saw Mattie or me. He seemed to lose all interest in the idea of having a family. He gave up sex long before I did, spent more nights sleeping in the laboratory than he did with me. And when we did see each other all we did was row. I stayed for as long as I could. But in the end there was nothing to preserve anyway. That's when I met Veronica.'

She broke off. I waited. After a while Veronica touched her hair ever so lightly just to tell her we were still there. Christine moved her head into the caress, like a blind person moving towards sound. Their intimacy was almost painful to watch. I wondered where they had met and how quickly they had both known. And, of course, there were other things I wondered but knew that I would never ask.

'And Mattie?' I asked quietly.

'I would have taken Mattie if I could,' she said angrily, with a voice still steeped in guilt. 'But she was already blaming me for Tom being away all the time, and I didn't know how to tell her. Anyway, by then I was in such trouble she would have been in a worse state coming with me. I was only gone two weeks. No, not two weeks. Thirteen days. Thirteen days compared with thirteen years.' She smiled grimly. 'Nobody seemed to notice that discrepancy. But then they were all men. By the time we got to court Vandamed had had lawyers and private detectives crawling all over us. We didn't stand a chance. But then we didn't have much of a case, anyway, since Mattie said loud and clear that she wanted to stay with her father. I dare say it was her way of punishing me for what I'd done.'

And I think she was probably right. Having your mother leave home for another man is one thing, but – well, put it this way, I couldn't imagine it ever, let alone at thirteen. No wonder Mattie had tumbled so eagerly into the long grass with her sexy gardener. At that age you'd need to do something drastic to convince yourself it wasn't hereditary.

'What about after the court case? Did you make any attempt to get Mattie back?'

She sighed. 'I went to the school once to try and see her. But they refused. I think it was on Tom's instructions.'

No, actually. But why hurt her more by telling her the truth. 'And you never tried to snatch her?'

And for the first time she laughed. 'Can you imagine anyone trying to snatch Mattie? Is that what he told you?' I half nodded. 'Well, he wouldn't be the only one who sees me as some kind of threat to civilization. Poor Tom.'

Poor maybe, but not that stupid, surely? How sexually undermined could a man be? 'Disturbed and unstable.' It was beginning to feel more like a self-portrait than a description of his unfaithful wife. Maybe the death threats had got to him more than he was willing to admit. Poor Tom. Poor Mattie. Poor Christine. It was just another of those stories where everybody gets hurt. Even before one of them climbs into a booby-trapped car. A vicious, stubborn image. Still, at least it reminded me why I was there.

When it came to her husband's work with animals, however, Christine Shepherd knew next to nothing. And when I tried to find out what Mattie's feelings on that subject had been, I drew an even greater blank. Tom Shepherd had stopped talking about such things the best part of two years ago. And as far as she remembered, she and Mattie had stopped asking. That was the problem. She did, though, have a suggestion.

'You could always talk to his bosses? If, that is, they'll talk to you.'

They offered me coffee, but I didn't stay. It seemed to me they needed their own company more than they needed mine.

CHAPTER TEN

Have You Seen the Little Piggies?

For a city-dweller I was spending altogether too much time in the country. But then a girl has to go where the work is, and, according to his London secretary, Vandamed's managing director was spending most of his time at their East Suffolk headquarters. East Suffolk – hardly the most glamorous place for a multinational, but then what did I know? Presumably real estate was cheaper in the country. And presumably if you went that far out nobody could see what you were doing to the animals.

The journey ought to have been a breeze. The instructions I had got from the secretary got me as far as Framlingham, but from there things began to get difficult. After I had passed the pet food factory on the way out of the village for a third time, it struck me maybe she had meant right but said left. I tried it. Right took me out of town, where at least I could no longer smell the pet food so strongly. After a few miles the air was sweeter, the surroundings prettier, the roads smaller. And I was lost.

Above the hedgerow on a slight hill I spotted a sign in the distance. Maybe it would say 'Vandamed – this way.' I speeded up and took the corner. Bad idea, really.

Ahead of me a tilted farm truck blocked the lane, its offside wheels caught fast in mud, the driver's window crushed into the hedgerow. The real problem, however, was not the truck, but what was escaping from it. The bolts holding the tailboard in place had obviously jolted free on impact. Either that or the pigs had picked the locks. The effect was the same. They were everywhere, a great bristling herd of them surging and snorting out of the darkness of the truck down the ramp and on to the lane, filling it instantly with their bulk.

Interesting animals, pigs. You don't usually come across that many of them all in one place. In fact the only time I had ever really seen them before (apart from vintage Pasolini, or in between two slices of bread) was in fields, where distance gives them a particular, reassuring perspective. Move closer and they're altogether more alarming.

I thought about reversing, but with a couple of them already pushing by me and more on their way it seemed wiser to wait for them to pass. They were moving fast and although I was narrower than the truck, it was still a tight squeeze. The car rocked as three tried to get past the driver's side together, taking part of the wing mirror with them. I opened the window to yell at them to stop.

'Turn off your bloody engine.' The voice came from somewhere behind me. I did as I was told. The car was completely surrounded now, juddering to and fro with the force of a couple of hundredweight of meat, and the scrape of tough skin against bodywork. If I could hear them I could also smell them. What do they say about pigs being clean animals really? Bullshit. I rolled up the window, but the smell rolled in with me.

Behind me, in my mirror, I saw a second truck backing its way into the lane, effectively blocking the pigs' exit. The man who had called to me was standing in the ditch guiding it in with hand signals, slapping the side when he wanted it to stop. Then he scurried to the back and let down the hinges. The tailboard fell into the lane, nearly making minced meat out of a particularly large porker careering towards it. The man, who was almost as wide as the pig itself, rapped the animal smartly on the flank with a small stick. Against the odds it seemed to placate rather than enrage the animal, and it scampered up into the dark belly of the truck, squealing loudly. So much for the great escape. The others followed mindlessly, battering against each other (and me) in their stampede. I stopped counting after twenty. I was glad I was inside the car.

When they were safely locked in, the farmer turned his attention to me. I opened the door of the car and glanced down at the bodywork. No obvious scratches, just a hell of a lot of grime and mud. When I looked up at him, he was grinning. 'It needed a wash, anyway. Country life, eh?'

'Excuse me, but I'd call it more of a public nuisance. Those pigs were out of control,' I said, but the indignation sounded tight-arsed in my London accent.

'Well, excuse *me*, but if you hadn't come round that corner like a bat out of hell those pigs would still be sitting in the truck, good as gold. City buggers. Why do you think we've got a country code?'

And when had I last read it? I thought about ranting some more, but decided it wasn't worth the energy. He pulled the sleeve of his jacket down, spat on it, then rubbed the paintwork. 'There you go. Right as rain with a wet cloth.' We sort of knew we were both in the wrong.

'Big animals,' I muttered looking back at the cloud of dust wafting up from the back of the truck.

'Yep,' he said, happy to chat now I had withdrawn all threat of damages. 'Big and beautiful.'

'Bit nervy, though, aren't they?'

'Yeah, well, they know where they's going. Not stupid animals, pigs.'

'No,' I said, thinking otherwise. 'I wonder if you could help me. I'm looking for the headquarters of the drug company, Vandamed. I was told it was around this way.'

And he looked at me in a way which made it clear that he now knew why I had almost run into his pigs. Women drivers. 'Vandamed? You'n just driven straight past it.'

Not that it was that obvious from the road. I'm not an expert on the headquarters of multinationals, so all I can tell you about Vandamed was that it covered a lot of ground and every inch of it was well protected. It was about a hundred yards off the road. Razor wire lined the perimeter wall, and the gates were about as inviting as an entrance to a detention centre, which was probably where they had recruited their security staff from.

The problem, it appeared, was that the appointment I said I had was not registered on the guard's security computer. This was an even bigger problem since it was clear that the computer and the guard had a big thing going between them. I tried suggesting that he circumvent the power of the beast by ringing the managing director's office direct, but he didn't take kindly to being told how to do his job, and made it clear that this was the cue for my exit line.

I went like a lamb. That way he had no reason to check where I was going. Not that I had any kind of plan, certainly not one that took into account a couple of kilometres of razor wire, but as sometimes happens at such times, lady luck indulged me with a little sisterly solidarity.

I had parked my car out of sight near the main road and was walking back to the gates when a BMW passed me and schmoozed up to the main entrance. The security guard, recognizing sovereign power, rushed out to greet it. With regal magnanimity the back window on the driver's side slid down for a word of greeting to the unworthy one. So busy were they preserving the status quo that they never noticed powerless little me slide round the back of the security hut and into the compound.

I covered the first hundred yards doubled up and running, keeping to the edge. Then, when it was safe, I cut across to the tarmac road which ran through the centre of the complex. From there I thought myself into the role of your regular research scientist and hoped the body posture would follow. Not that I met anyone to challenge me. In fact, the place seemed remarkably quiet.

The problem was that I had absolutely no idea what I was looking for. Just another private eye in search of a game plan. If I waited long enough maybe it would find me.

I smelt them before I heard them. The stench of sweet

decay and defecation. It was becoming almost familiar. I stood like the Bisto kid trying to work out the direction of the scent, but it was the noise that gave them away, a cross between squealing and grunting, coming from the edge of the compound in among some trees. As I got closer, I saw two buildings. The first was a vicious concrete construction, with no windows at all. The other, from where the noise came, was joined to the first by a short brick corridor. It looked like an old farm building, low slung with a row of tiny dormer openings, more like portholes, high up in the eaves. I hoisted myself up via some faulty pointing on the outside brickwork, and managed to get my head above a window just long enough to take in a vision of some serious factory farming.

Below me, lit by artificial lights, were lines of open concrete compartments with heavy galvanized iron gates, and crammed together in each of them several huge pigs, snorting and grumbling, their noses buried in long troughs of food. The sight was more surreal than horrific, but then I was on the outside. I tried to invert it, to imagine people rather than animals in similar conditions. But the only images that came to mind were the Nazi trains to the camps, and all the animal rights leaflets in the world couldn't bring those two things together. I wondered what Ben Maringo would have said to convince me, but by that time my left foot was already beginning to slide and I needed all my concentration to get back down the wall without breaking a leg.

'I should be careful. They're very particular about their privacy,' the voice said as I hit the earth with less grace than I would have liked. I whirled round to see a man in a suit standing about fifty yards away from me, just as a shriek of alarm bells went off all around us. 'As *we* are, I'm afraid,' he shouted, making a face at the noise. 'Electronically triggered. There're sensors round the window frames. It's one of the reasons we ask guests to check in at the main gate. It's easier on the security guards that way.'

When they arrived, they were more out of breath than I was, but the uniforms looked good, and they had a numerical advantage over me. The man in the suit waved them away, explaining that the alarm was faulty. They seemed satisfied, though one of them, the computer freak, kept looking back over his shoulder, obviously recognizing me from ten minutes before. One up to Vandamed. Believe me, not all security guards have that long a memory.

The man in the suit offered me his outstretched hand. 'Miss Wolfe, I presume? Alan Grafton, head of Vandamed livestock research division.'

'Pleased to meet you. Is that the livestock you're researching?' I said, gesturing to the building I'd just fallen off.

He nodded. 'AAR. The pigs are part of the final trial.'

'AAR?'

'Our new performance enhancer. It would have been on the guided tour if you'd waited. Would you like to see more now, or would you prefer some coffee?'

It's important to recognize when you've just been outwitted, if only to make sure it doesn't happen again. Alan Grafton and I got on famously as we sauntered back across the compound towards the main office. He even apologized for the behaviour at the gate, but then four days after a bomb . . . well, I would obviously appreciate that security precautions had been stepped up. I said I understood. He shook his head.

'My God, poor Tom. I can't tell you how devastated we all are. She was such a lovely child.'

'You knew her?'

'Not really. But when Tom worked here he used to bring her in occasionally. She was younger then, of course. But very bright.' Yes, indeed. Very bright. 'I gather . . . well, I gather you were there –'

'Yes. I was.'

He nodded, but didn't say anything, which I appreciated. We had reached the main building. We took the lift up to

92

the third floor. The doors opened on to some very nice interior decorating, the kind of thing that pigs just wouldn't appreciate. 'Marion Ellroy,' he said by way of explanation. 'Vandamed's managing director. He and Tom have known each other for a long time. He asked to see you.'

The door to the main office was open. He was sitting at his desk with a commanding view over the compound, but got up immediately we came in. He was a tall man with a broad face and a good head of hair, greying in all the right places. Not unattractive if you liked that sort of thing, and well packaged, in a suit blending eighties flair with Savile Row sobriety. In a word, distinguished; the very model of a modern British plutocrat. So it was a surprise when he turned out to be American.

'Miss Wolfe. Tom should have let us know you were coming.' And he held my eye as well as my hand. All the right training. Except it wasn't that long ago I had met another American businessman. He had been younger with more obvious sex appeal, but that was hardly an excuse. It was still a raw memory, how easily I had fallen for the charm. I didn't intend to be that gullible again.

'Tom didn't know.'

The hint of a raised eyebrow. 'I see. Should I ask why not?'

'I didn't want to bother him,' I said evenly.

'Whereas you don't mind bothering us.' Although I have to say he didn't sound that bothered.

I shrugged. 'Do you mind?'

'That depends on what you want.'

Verbal foreplay – after three years of conversations with Comfort I could take a degree in it. I smiled confidently. 'A little information?'

He looked at me for a moment without answering, then picked up the phone and pressed a button. He was still looking at me as he told his secretary to put his next appointment on hold and bring up some coffee. Then he sat down and put his feet up on the desk.

'You got fifteen minutes, Miss Wolfe. You ask. I'll answer.'

And so, basic power relationships established, the talking began. Starting with Shepherd's present job and its scale on any ALF hit list.

'It's no secret. We're not the only people doing this kind of work. Genetic engineering could, in theory, enable us to counteract the development of cancerous cells; basically stop the cancer before it begins. Of course genetics is an emotive subject: dabbling with God's plan, that kind of thing. But that's not the point. The ALF didn't blow up Tom's car because what he did was any worse then anyone else. That's nonsense. Vandamed scrupulously observes the letter of the law in its use of animals for research. No question of that.'

'So why *did* they pick him rather than anyone else?'

He shrugged.'Tom has a very powerful job. Over the last ten years funding for independent medical research in this country has diminished dramatically. I'm an American, so I don't need to have an opinion about your political system. And in many ways I had an enormous admiration for Mrs Thatcher and what she did here, but in terms of the opportunities for government research, well, take it from me, you've got one hell of a brain drain on your hands. Vandamed's cancer programme is not only one of the biggest in the country but also the most securely funded. Now that gives us a high scientific profile. And Tom is part of that.'

'So it wasn't what he did, but who he was?'

'Exactly.'

'And you've been targeted before, right?'

'Over the past five years we must have had a dozen attacks on our laboratories, here and in London. Animals released, computer research destroyed, in one case even the publication of stolen documents.'

'You surprise me. I wouldn't think you were that easy to penetrate.'

'Apart from you, you mean,' he said, and it wasn't clear with how much humour. I thought about looking guilty but it didn't seem worth the drain on my acting abilities. 'Yeah, well, in the past our security arrangements have left something to be desired.'

I let it go. 'And before Shepherd got the job as head of research, what was he doing?'

'He was in charge of our farming development division.'

'I've already told Miss Wolfe a little about AAR,' said Alan Grafton, who had been so quiet we'd both forgotten he was still there.

Ellroy glanced at him, then back at me. 'Then you'll already know how proud we are of it.'

'Not really.'

He looked at me, as if deciding how much to tell. He took a big breath. 'How much do you know about pig farming?' Pig farming? About as much as I could write on a side panel of a beat up VW. Or less. 'Not a lot, eh? Well, believe me, you will. AAR is going to revolutionize the industry. You British are very fond of your eggs and bacon. You eat a lot of pigs. Fact is, right at this moment you eat more pigs than you've got. At last count you were importing something like nine hundred million pounds of bacon and ham. And you're not the only ones. The Germans are crazy about their sausage and Eastern Europe's getting hungry for everything as long as the price is right. Your pig farming's pretty efficient already. Working without subsidy it's had to be. But it could be better. Everybody's trying. You even got hybrid pigs with more teats for more piglets. But what you really need is to get little pigs to become big pigs quicker. Ideally before puberty sets in, so you don't have to cope with castration or boar-tainted meat. That's where AAR comes in.'

He stopped to take a well-deserved mouthful of coffee. It struck me my fifteen minutes were almost up, but he was cooking now. Nothing like business talk to get them going.

'What is it? Some kind of growth hormone?' I asked, because I never really liked lectures and because Ben Maringo's leaflets had a lot to say about how miserable things could get for animals pumped with growth hormones. Not to mention for the rest of us. The worst had been the story about Italian babies developing oversized genitalia after eating baby mush made from calves stuffed with growth hormones. Talk about the twilight zone . . .

He shook his head. 'Wrong,' he said almost gleefully. 'AAR is not a growth hormone. It's a performance booster. Very different. We're talking entirely synthetic compound here. It was developed out of a drug for asthmatics, a drug which was shown to have side effects in increasing muscle production. Of course the implications for livestock farming were obvious even then, but it took a lot of work to perfect the right – safe – compound.'

'And was that what Tom Shepherd did?'

'Yes, indeed. AAR was his baby. And as a result, when it goes into full production later this year, AAR will produce bigger pigs and leaner meat, which not only makes it more profitable for the farmers, but cheaper and – most important – healthier for the consumer.'

'What about for the pigs?'

He smiled. 'I told you, it's not a growth hormone. Also it doesn't need to be injected or implanted in the animal. AAR was specifically developed to be given through the feed.'

'The research?'

'All totally legit. You have my word. Tom Shepherd was not allowed to torture the pigs.'

And that, as they say, was that. Assuming he was telling the truth (and a little independent research would confirm or deny it), then Tom Shepherd and his bosses were squeaky clean. What was a girl to do? Go home, give loverboy's photo to the police and forget the whole thing? Well, you know me. Why give up when there was the possibility I could work even longer hours for less money? I tell you, being in opposition to eighties culture has it drawbacks. I dug into my bag and pulled out the big brown envelope. Well, why not? After all, they knew more about animal rights activists than I did. Maybe they all combed their hair in a certain way? Or smoked the same brand of cigarettes? A kind of freemasonry of terrorism . . . I held out the photo to Ellroy.

'This is probably a waste of time, but have you ever seen this man before?'

He picked it up and stared at it for a good long time. Then he shook his head. 'No. I can't say I have.'

He handed it back to me. Alan Grafton leaned forward. I passed it to him. He took a look, then another look. And I saw the slightest flicker. If Marion Ellroy hadn't noticed it, he certainly noticed I had.

'Alan? Do you know him?' he asked quickly.

'I – I'm not sure. Maybe. Is it important?'

'It could be, yes.'

'Then I'd better check. I mean, assuming that's all right with you, Marion?'

This time the boss glanced at his watch. But what could he say? The door closed on Grafton and there was a moment of silence. Then Ellroy said quietly, 'Is this guy someone I should know about?'

'Probably not,' I said.

'You know, this conversation is beginning to feel a little unbalanced.'

I smiled gaily. 'I think we're on the same side.'

He made me wait for it. 'Yeah, well, I hope so.'

I smiled. Female charm. Not Marion Ellroy's favourite topic when it came to the Shepherd family, but I got there somehow. His face darkened at the mention of the she-devils, but he kept his cool, until in passing I repeated Christine's comment about how the job had maybe been too much for her husband.

97

'I tell you, Miss Wolfe, this is one hell of a guilty lady you're dealing with, and you should bear that in mind. In terms of the job she doesn't know shit from Shinola. Tom Shepherd is one of best scientists it's ever been my privilege to work with, a man of unassailable talent and dedication. And if he'd maybe got a little more support at home, all their lives would have been different.'

'Is that why you paid for his lawyers?'

'I don't know what all of this has to do with the scum who wiped out his daughter, but yes, we did. And we'd do it again. Vandamed's a company that believes in helping its employees. And at that particular time in his life Tom needed more help than most. I think –'

Except I'd never find out what. He hit the phone almost before it rang, said yep a couple of times, then wrote something down.

When he turned back to me, I knew the story had a future. 'Alan says he can't be sure, but the photo looks a little like a young guy who worked for us sometime last year. A temporary cleaner, went by the name of Malcolm Barringer. Our records say he was a student from Ipswich Polytechnic. So, you want to tell me who he is now?' The hesitation gave me away. 'Listen, Miss Wolfe, we've been more than co-operative with you today. But I didn't become managing director by being a complete Mr Nice Guy. Or a complete idiot. Are you telling me we've been infiltrated?'

I shook my head. 'I'm telling you I don't know.' He waited, watching me closely. After a while I shrugged. 'Sorry.'

'I doubt that,' he said, but with remarkable good humour. He played with his pencil for a while, then chucked it lightly on to the table in front of me. 'OK,' he said on a long sigh. 'How about I put it another way? Since you're clearly not working for Tom Shepherd any more, how would you like to work for us?'

Well, well. You play hard to get and everybody wants

you. 'Looking after your employees' interests, you mean?' I said because I couldn't resist it.

He shook his head. 'How you British hate the corporate ethic, eh? Yeah, I suppose you could call it that. Or you could see it as a way of getting the bastards who blew up a fourteen-year-old kid. His job killed her. Which means I'm partly responsible for her death, too. And that feeling's never going to go away. But then you'd know all about that, I guess.' Clever old Ellroy. Recognizing the strengths and weaknesses of others. All part of the job. I dropped my eyes. 'You see, Hannah, right at this moment you seem to be doing a better job than the police.' He paused. 'I'm presuming whatever it is you haven't told me you haven't told them either.' I don't think I actually shook my head, but I certainly didn't nod it. 'So, how about we do it together?'

It wasn't that I didn't like him. Or even that I didn't trust him. Because in some ways he'd been pretty straight with me. So let's just say I was having too much fun being on my own. He didn't give me long to answer, but then I suppose in his position he's not used to hesitation. He made a little clicking noise with his tongue.

'Well, no need to decide now. Give it some thought, OK? You know where to find me.'

CHAPTER ELEVEN

Leader of the Pack

Give or take a bypass, Ipswich was on my way home, but the minute I got back in my car I realized I had a more pressing need. Another case of too much coffee. Of course feminism has given us girls the confidence to pee anywhere, but it had been a long time since breakfast and if I was going to stop I might as well make it work for me. *En route* to Vandamed I had passed a rural little pub with some beaten-up farm vehicles outside: local people, local gossip, and with luck everything I ever wanted to know about pig farming. Unfortunately it took me a while to find it again. In fact, in the end I had to ask. Twice in one day. I won't tell Frank if you don't.

I pulled off the road into the forecourt of a farm. Two men were in the yard. As I got closer, I saw one of them had the back of an estate car open and was carefully lifting into it something wrapped in a large rug. I caught a glimpse of a dog's head lying heavily at one end. It didn't look well. The vet – at least that's who I assumed it to be, though he didn't look anything like his TV counterparts – made his patient comfortable, then gently closed the back.

'I'll call you as soon as I know, Greg.'

The farmer was shaking his head. He looked pretty upset. If you hadn't seen the dog you might have thought it was his wife they were taking away. 'Aye, but you bring him back, OK?'

'I'll do what I can.' But he didn't sound hopeful.

I felt a little hesitant about interrupting, but they had spotted me, anyway. I gave them my best stranger-in-a-strange-land smile and told them I was looking for a pub where I might get a good beer and a sandwich. The farmer was too preoccupied with his dog to answer, but the vet said that if I followed him he'd point me out somewhere on the way to the surgery.

I tailed the estate down a few narrow lanes till we came to a T-junction, where he rolled down his window and signalled left while he went right.

It was the same pub. Inside it had the feel of a working man's retreat: no horse brasses or gilt-framed prints, just solid old wood tables and simple chairs. There were three men sitting at a table by the fire, and a dour old character propping up the bar, no doubt put there by the local tourist board. They glanced up as I came in, and it was clear from the look they gave me that the establishment did not double as the singles bar for suburban Framlingham. The atmosphere had a distinct touch of *An American Werewolf in London* about it.

I went to the loo, then sat at the bar. I really wanted a large vodka, but a driving licence is important for a girl in my profession, so I settled for half a lager and two antique cheese rolls. The chap on the end bar stool fixed me with an Ancient Mariner stare. I smiled and raised my glass. He kept looking. I found myself thinking of the Government's failed policy to provide adequate community care for mental patients.

The conversation of the men sitting by the fire came across the room in waves: dog trials, silage, a new outbuilding which had stretched somebody's mortgage to the limit. And pigs. A lot about pigs. The size of them, the state of them, and how soon they could be looking to sell the meat of them. Final trials. Outside as well as inside the perimeter fence.

In the end my curiosity got the better of me. I picked up my drink and wandered over, using the excuse of the fire to get closer. They noticed me, but pretended they didn't.

I went in all guns blazing: I was the bright-eyed reporter from a national newspaper who'd just interviewed the managing director of Vandamed about his new wonder drug, and now needed some first-hand evidence. OK, so it's every private eye's worst cliché. The fact is more often than not it works. But then I generally use it in the city. Could be that they like the media better there.

I shifted emphasis to the problems of pig rearing in an age of EEC subsidies. That's the great thing about living in a television culture – everybody knows almost nothing about something. This time I hit raw nerves. Two out of the three of them jumped immediately. Seven minutes later I could have gone on *Mastermind*. How much more money a year does a Welsh hill farmer earn from keeping two thousand sheep in pasture rather than pigs? Pass. Answer: sixty thousand pounds. Yeah, well, I was surprised too. And once their indignation was aroused, it was but a small step to the new world order as heralded by AAR. For the first time in a market economy, it seemed, pigs could fly. And so could the men who farmed them.

'So Vandamed's right. This is going to revolutionize pig farming? I mean the meat yield of these animals will be really that different?'

'Aye, well, according to the trials it certainly seems to be.' The man who spoke was small and wiry, with a shock of black hair peppered with grey, or maybe it was paint.

'Come off it, Duncan. You don't need any trial to tell you that. Just take a look at the buggers,' chipped in his fair-haired companion.

I was sitting at the table now, notebook open, scribbling furiously. The man to my right, Mr Silence, was watching me. I wrote 'big buggers', but in a squiggly handwriting so he couldn't read it. Then I looked up. 'That's amazing. And what about the taste? Vandamed says the drug encourages muscle production and therefore leaner meat. Is that true?'

'Well, that we wouldn't know.' The fair-haired man again, eager to chat. 'Seeing as it's still in the trial stages we're not allowed to eat it. Still, we have it on good authority that it's delicious, don't we, Duncan?' And he grinned at his companion. The nudge-nudge implication was obvious. With so many pigs round for the slaughter-house they obviously didn't notice when the odd one went missing.

I wrote down 'meat delicious'. 'So what about the pigs themselves? How has it changed their lives?' This time farmer number three seemed more interested. I nodded encouragingly at him. He was a ruddy-faced man with a definite touch of the Van Morrisons to his physique. In Oxford Street people would have turned to look at him. But he wasn't the one who was out of place here.

'You a meat eater yourself then, are you, Miss, er . . .?'

'Parkin. Helen Parkin.'

'Miss Parkin?'

'Yes. Course,' I said meeting his gaze. Well, one cod does not a vegetarian make.

'So, you like pork?'

'Yes. And ham and bacon.'

'And you'd buy more if it were cheaper?'

'I suppose so, yes.'

'Then what does it matter to you how it is for the pigs?'

The wiry man shot him a half-glance. He pushed his beer forward on to the table and leaned back in his chair. 'No, Duncan, I think we should talk about it. Our young reporter here is obviously interested, aren't you, Helen?'

He hit the Christian name with just a touch of the inverted commas about it. I nodded. Rumour has it that Van Morrison has a considerable temper. I've always as-sumed it was something to do with talent and the music industry, but maybe it goes with the build.

'I expect you're too young to remember rationing, aren't you? One egg a week, a square of butter, couple of rashers of streaky bacon or Spam and a scrawny chicken every two months if you were lucky. It's all different now, of course.

Now we've milk coming out of our ears and larders overflowing with meat, poultry, fresh vegetables, the lot. And all cheap at the price. You work for the environment section, do you?'

'Er, no. I work for everyone. General features, but I've an interest in country matters.'

'Of course you have. Then you probably know most of this, anyway. I read a piece by one of your colleagues once. It said that the average British family now spends a third less than it used to on food. A third less. Bloody miracle, eh? And thanks to what? Us farmers? Well, we certainly do our bit, subsidies permitting. We're still working all the hours God gave us, still trying to earn an honest living, doing the best for our animals. But it doesn't make for that much more food. At least not in the quantities you lot want to eat it. No, to really increase production, you see, we need help. We need pesticides for the crops, and factory farming for the meat. Factory farming and drugs. And the more intensively we use it all, the more food you get. And the more food you get, the cheaper it is, and the cheaper it is, the more you lot want to eat of it.' He broke off for a last swig of beer. No one said anything. But then it was obvious he hadn't finished. I had stopped scribbling.

'Don't suppose you need to write this down, do you? Intelligent girl like you knows it all already, eh? So, where were we? Oh yes, how is it for the animals? Well, put it this way. They've got a lot less going for them than in the old days when they were suckled until eight weeks and then sat out in the pig pens with their noses in the muck watching the world go by. Now it's a little more . . . well, intensive. Now your average piglet is weaned at twenty-one days and on the butcher's slab five months later. In between, it spends its life stuffed in with hundred of others eating, shitting and generally enjoying the pleasures of life. I doubt it'll notice AAR. It'll just grow a little faster and die a little sooner, with a little more help from the vet on the way.

Either way I wouldn't want to be one of them. And I expect you wouldn't, either. But then until you, and all the folks like you, are willing to give up some of your meat, or pay one hell of a lot more for it, then that's how it's going to be, isn't it?'

The place was silent when he finished. And everyone was looking at me: the Ancient Mariner, the barman, all of them. Town versus country. They produce, we consume and both sides feel exploited. Old animosities, going back a good deal further than BSE. I played with my pencil. 'So what about this new drug AAR? What does it do to the animals?' I asked quietly, staring at him. 'You don't think it could have anything to do with Tom Shepherd's car being blown up?'

It caused a ripple among the other two, but Van the man didn't even blink. 'You're missing the point, young Helen. It's not the drugs that are the problem. It's you lot.'

'So why don't you take a stand? Make us listen.' He shook his head, as if he couldn't be bothered with me. 'I mean it. If you don't approve of drugs, then why use a new one?' It sounded good, but we all knew it was a last-ditch attempt to get back in the ring.

'Because if AAR saves one week in the rearing of two thousand pigs, that adds up to the kind of money that if I don't make, my neighbour will. Which means that me and every pig farmer like me would be out of business before you could say "free market" if we didn't use it. And because in the end it's a matter of degree, and when it comes to the best interests of my animals I still know more than the nutters who want to tear down the farm fences and set them all free. Although you, of course, may have some sympathy with that viewpoint. Now, which newspaper was it you say you were from?'

I swallowed. 'I didn't. But it's the *Daily Telegraph*.'

And he gave me a big smile. 'Well, then Miss Parkin, We'll look forward to reading your article. If, that is, they publish it.'

I closed my notebook and got up with what little dignity I could muster. I put out my hand, but no one took it. They were still looking when I went out the door.

In the car park it took me a while to find my keys. I wouldn't like you to think I was shaken, only a bit stirred. I had ridden into all of this on my white charger consumed with the ideals of justice and truth. Stupid, really. You'd think by now I would have learnt that in most cases the good guys are just less mean than the bad ones. The keys continued to elude me, so I upturned my handbag on the bonnet of the car and started all over again. Which meant that I had my head turned away when he walked out from what must have been the other entrance to the pub. Which also meant I didn't really look at him until he had reached the motorcycle on the other side of the car park and was lifting up the helmet. So I really have no idea at all if it was just a trick of the light, a trick of my eye, or a trick of my desire that made that half-profile look suddenly so familiar. Because by the time I registered it in my stomach and turned to face him, the helmet was on and he was already astride the bike. He stopped for just a second, to take the cigarette out of his mouth and toss it into the hedgerow. Then he kick-started the motor. It sprang into life just as I yelled out. He didn't hear. I scooped the debris off the bonnet, clutching the keys and fumbling with the lock. I was as fast as fast could be, but it wasn't fast enough. By the time I got the engine started he was out of the car park. And by the time I was out of it, he was nowhere to be seen, and the sound of the bike had faded, leaving no possible clue as to which direction or where to go.

I sat still for a moment, my heart thumping like the drum section of a Dave Clark record. I pulled the photo out of its envelope and stared at it. Who knows? I thought of going back into the pub to ask, but I just couldn't see them being that helpful. If it had been him, then what on earth was he doing so near to Vandamed? Unless, that is, his cover was better than I thought: just another young student who used to work at the research centre coming back for a couple of pints with the lads?

Too many questions I couldn't answer. Time to go back to higher education.

CHAPTER TWELVE

My Boyfriend's Back

Ipswich Poly was a wretched, decaying sixties building, concrete streaked with rain and birdshit – the kind of thing to drive Prince Charles into a frenzy of carbuncles.

I waited in the reception office while they tried to track down a grant cheque for a girl who looked altogether too young to be so old. Grants. They were about as distant as childhood now. Maybe when I'm eighty, it'll all come back. Will it be worth the wait?

The registrar couldn't put a face to the name. I would have shown her the photograph, only it might have made her suspicious. As it was, it didn't take her long to track him down. Barringer, Malcolm – third-year computer sciences. Where would he be? Well, why didn't I try the computer labs? I didn't hold out much hope. Somehow, animal rights aside, he just didn't look like the kind of chap to spend his days in communion with a machine.

The labs stretched out over two floors. The students, huddled around terminals in groups, reminded me of the pigs in their concrete compartments, making meat for people who didn't want to know how it was made. Between the philosopher and the farmer I was fast heading for a crisis of conscience. Maybe Malcolm Barringer would be my road to Damascus. I asked a girl at the coffee machine if she knew him. She said she did, and that she had just seen him come in. He was working at the end terminal in the room opposite. Sometimes everything just falls into your lap.

I thanked her and headed on in. He was sitting with his back to me. He wore blue jeans and a white T-shirt, and there was a tatty leather jacket on the back of his chair – the uniform of yoof. I thought I remembered the jacket from the bike. I walked up behind him. He was deep in concentration, head down writing something. The nape of his neck had a splattering of blackheads on it. I took a breath and got ready.

'Malcolm Barringer?'

He turned, and as the profile flashed by I knew immediately it wasn't him. Oh, the resemblance to the photo was there, all right. You could see how Grafton might have made the mistake: the same age, the same colour hair, maybe even something approximating to the same shape of face. But there it ended. The young man I was looking at now was still a boy, podgy and ordinary with a chin that was already giving way to weakness. Not at all like the young James Dean. Or Matt Dillon. I have to admit I was a tad disappointed. Disappointed, but not exactly surprised.

It didn't take long. But then there wasn't much to ask. Yes, he was who he was supposed to be, and no, he had never applied for any vacation jobs with Vandamed, although in his first year he had done some vacation work with a small subsidiary drugs company in London and they would probably have references for him. As for last summer, well, he'd been travelling round Turkey with his girlfriend. Didn't get back until the day after term began.

So whoever it was had simply used Barringer's name, his college details and probably even given his past vacation job as a reference. All easy facts to find out. And equally easy to check without exposing the fraud. Vandamed obviously hadn't thought it worth probing any deeper. So much for their improved security service. Maybe Frank should tender for the contract. He could do better with his eyes closed. As for me I was bored already.

Over the top of his head I spotted the clock. Ten minutes past five. This time it wasn't that I'd forgotten, just that I'd got carried away with the job in hand. I tried calling the institute to warn him, but the trouble with having an affair with a therapist is that they are always talking to someone else.

*

Had it been any road other than the A12 I might have made it. But the long, slow urban sprawl plus heavy-duty road-works meant that by the time I got into the West End, it was gone eight o'clock. Then came the relaxing business of finding a parking place. You really need two cars in London. One to drive and the other to pick up from the pound. I eventually squeezed into a tiny space in Chinatown. By then there wasn't much point in rushing. I got to the theatre at twenty-five past. He had left the ticket at the box office, and had gone in without me. Not a great sign. And when I tried to follow, I discovered it was *verboten* till the interval.

I sat in the bar cradling a Perrier and sorting out my excuses, then moved on to an analysis of the day past. Funny. When I woke up this morning, pigs were just another form of fast food. Now they seemed set to become the meaning of life. Or worse.

In retrospect I should have thought less and spent more time feeling guilty. But then I didn't realize he was going to take it so hard. Well, even therapists have to lose their temper sometimes.

'I'm sorry.'

'You're always sorry, Hannah. It's becoming a theme in our relationship.'

'Nick. I left enough time, I swear. It's just I got caught in traffic.'

'Yes.'

'Listen, come on. This way at least you don't have to queue for your interval drink.' I pushed a Scotch and soda across the table. He looked less than convinced, but shrugged his shoulders and took the drink. 'OK. So now you can tell me what I missed.'

It turned out to be a little more complicated than I had expected: one of those moral thrillers where no one is quite what they seem and where you need to know everyone's versions of the same event to get to the answer, which may or may not be the same as the truth. It was a problem I was not unfamiliar with. But right at that moment I didn't have enough energy to work out my own plot, let alone anyone else's. For a start, who was Malcolm Barringer if he wasn't Malcolm Barringer, and what was squeaky-clean Vandamed not telling me about their precious Dr Shepherd?

'Hannah?'

'What? I mean, yes, it sounds wonderful. Obviously it really is as good as everyone says.' He didn't reply, just looked at me. Sometimes I wish he wasn't so good at hearing what people are trying not to say. I leant over and squeezed his hand. 'I am listening, Nick, honestly. It's just I've had a weird day.'

'Like yesterday and the day before, you mean? And the week before that. It's work, Hannah. Like everybody else you have to make a decision as to where *it* stops and *you* begin. And if I did this to you, you'd be the first to shout foul.'

I took it on the chin. Because sometimes you don't have time to duck. 'I know that. It's not that I don't –' At which point, some might say luckily, I was saved by the bell. 'I'm sorry –'

He closed his eyes and gave me a fake friendly swipe. 'And will you stop saying that.'

Given that I didn't understand what was happening, the second half was really pretty good. I listened hard so I could contribute fully to the conversation afterwards. But as it turned out, we didn't talk much on the way back to the car. At first I thought he still had the sulks. It took me a while to realize it was all a little more serious.

At the driver's door he kissed me goodnight. As kissers go Nick can have quite a way with him, so you really know when it isn't one of his best. He let me go and stood back. I opened the door, but he didn't move. 'You're not coming back with me?'

He shook his head. 'You're humming like a generator. I find it easier to sleep with the power turned off.'

'You could always help me to relax,' I said coyly. But it's never been my strongest suit, flirtation.

'Yeah, but could you do the same for me?'

I smiled. 'OK. Point taken. I'm sorry . . . I mean, I'm not sorry. I'm . . . er . . . Listen, thanks for getting the tickets. I promise to be better behaved next time. When do I see you?'

He gave a little laugh. 'Well, in my diary it says this is the weekend that Josh is with his grandparents so we get to go away together. But . . . you tell me.'

'The weekend. Oh, Yes, I . . .'

He let me flounder for a bit. But it didn't do either of us any good. 'Oh, come on, Hannah,' he said at last, fuelled more by impatience than anger. 'It's not that hard to work out. You seriously think it's going to damage your independence, sharing the same hotel room with me? We've known each other for almost six months. I don't want to marry you, I don't want you to have my children. I'm not even sure if I want to spend next Christmas with you. However, I would like to feel that when we're together you're not always somewhere else. I know work is important. It isn't exactly irrelevant to me, either. And I know how cut up you are about the girl. It's just I'm not interested in someone who doesn't know where she is. I had that for seven years. And I don't need it any more. OK?'

He stared at me. A couple walking down the street looked over at us and then passed on, thanking their lucky stars it wasn't them. It's a good reminder. There's always someone somewhere in the world having a worse time than you are. I looked at the ground. How come when anyone gets mad at me it makes me feel like a child again? Something to do with my father, no doubt. Maybe we could talk about it post coitus sometime. If there was another post coitus, that is.

In the end I said what I felt, although I must admit it sounded feeble. 'You're right, Nick. I'm sorry.'

He shook his head. 'Yeah, well, so am I. I spend my life

talking to too many kids. Mary always said it made me sanctimonious. Let's leave it open, OK? If you want to go away, let me know. Otherwise call me when you want my company.'

I watched him go. Nice body. Back view again, eh? Fact is, when the mood is upon me (which is usually when I have made him somehow more unattainable), I still fancy him rotten. But that's why moods are such dangerous things. You can't guarantee how long they'll last. And what happens if the sex gets interrupted by the image of a herd of overweight pigs stampeding through my libido? I slammed my hand against the window of the car. God damn it. How come what you want to give is never the same thing as what they want to take? Maybe I should talk to a therapist about it.

I drove north with the stereo blasting out something young and carefree. To add insult to injury I was starving. Only two cheese rolls since breakfast. It's always seemed a severe misjudgement of nature to me, people having to eat so often to keep going. I went home via the back streets and stopped at my local take-away, otherwise known as the Golden Cockroach – the only place likely to be serving after 11.30 on a weekday night. Peter was busy over the charcoals, as he has been ever since he arrived from northern Cyprus thirty years ago. Maybe it reminded him of the heat he had left behind. It's still not enough to make him happy, not if the amount of whisky he consumes every night is anything to go by. On the other hand he's one of those people who are only truly happy when they're miserable – or maybe it's the other way around. I had been buying my kebabs from him for two years before he even deigned to notice me. Then one Monday night while I was waiting for a take-away he leant over the counter and poured me out a slug of rot-gut. From there we proceeded to drink each other under the table. I'm not ashamed to say that he won. Everything I know of him comes from that one night. So now I am the daughter that he never had. Greek sentimentality. Pathos with style.

This evening he was darker than usual. Just like fathers can be. I stood and watched the doner kebab going round and round, drops of meat grease falling on to the tray below. The smell made me sick with hunger. If that was a leg of lamb, then it came from a bigger lamb than I had ever seen. Lamb. Funny how the word meant a piece of meat rather than a fluffy bundle of young life.

'Do you ever think about the animals, Peter?'

'What d'you say?' he growled.

'The animals. Do you ever think of them playing in some field rather than turning on your spit?'

But he was way too far gone for such things. 'Listen. You want the kebab or you no want the kebab?'

'I want the kebab.'

I did. Vegetarianism would mean not only no more lamb, but no more Peter. I decided to decide tomorrow. Or the next day. Blessed are the weak, for they make the strong feel even more righteous.

The flat felt cold and unlived in. Tough shit, Hannah, you make your decisions, you pay the price. But there were a few words of welcome. On the answering machine the 'message received' light was winking 2 coquettishly at me. I spooled it back.

Number one. 'Hi, Hannah. Why don't you get out of the bath? It'll be worth the walk.' Frank, like Peter, a little the worse for wear. I saw him, feet on the desk, nursing the bottle of Glenfiddich from the bottom drawer of the filing cabinet. 'OK. I thought you'd like to know that Shepherd has been trying to get in touch with you. Says it's urgent. I gave him your number. Maybe he's worried that now you've met her you'll side with the wife.' So Frank knew the sordid details, too. I bet the boys had enjoyed telling him that one. I was glad I hadn't been in on the conversation.

The machine beeped. Number two. 'Hello. This is Tom Shepherd. We need to talk. I'll be at home from midday.'

You see. It was just as well I'd come home alone. We would have been goosing each other all the way up the stairs, and then I would have lost interest. That's the trouble with my job. There'll always be another man. Tom Shepherd. About bloody time.

CHAPTER THIRTEEN

Love Hurts

I got there on the dot of twelve. For a workaholic he was spending a lot of time at home. I hadn't been back there since that night. I needn't have worried. There was nothing left to remind me. The windows in the houses near by had all been replaced and another car was parked in the spot. Nothing so forgotten as yesterday's news.

But if places don't remember, people do. Shepherd opened the door with the chain still on and he looked awful. The five o'clock shadow had four days' more growth and his skin was like pastry that had been rolled too many times. As grief goes, his now seemed more devastating than his wife's. But then he had no one to love him through it. I had learnt a lot more about Tom Shepherd since our last meeting. On balance it ought to have made me more sympathetic. I had once had a lover who had discovered the other sex halfway through our affair; but it was a long time ago, and I hadn't been married to him for thirteen years. No question. Tom Shepherd certainly deserved sympathy. Problem was, I was still having trouble feeling any.

He led me into the sitting room. I had seen it a million times since that night. Now I saw it again, Mattie crashed out on the sofa, the remote in her hand, angry at everyone because she couldn't be angry at the ones who mattered.

I chose a chair. He sat on the edge of the sofa, elbows on his knees, like someone under starter's orders. He launched straight into it, at first not even looking at me, just staring at the carpet, giving it a hard time.

'I want you to stop talking to people. You have no right to be talking to people. It's not going to help anyone."

'You mean it's not going to help you?'

'I don't know who you think you are. She wasn't your daughter. You only met her for a few hours. It doesn't help – what you're doing. It makes everything worse.' Of course there are scientists who give up words in favour of symbols. But I hadn't figured him for one of those. Maybe it was the pain that had decimated his language, making him sound like a child. Even the voice had a ring of petulance to it. 'I told you this once already. This whole thing is none of your business.'

I could think of a number of replies to that one, but we weren't going to get anywhere if I let him get to me. 'How did you know?' I said after a while.

He closed his eyes. 'Edward Brayton.' I frowned. 'The farmer in the pub yesterday. He rang to tell me some girl had been poking around asking questions. He thought she was animal rights posing as a journalist. I think she was you.'

Well, it didn't take a Nobel prize-winner to work that one out. I was animal rights, was I? Thinking back on it, Farmer Brayton had done a pretty good job of tying me in knots. No wonder. So, had all that stuff about the poor little piggies been for real, or simply a clever way of winding me up?

'He told me some interesting things about AAR,' I said, to see what kind of reaction I would get.

'AAR has got nothing to do with anything. You don't know what you're talking about. If animal rights were worried about performance boosters, they would have blown up a dozen people before they tried me. It's just another farming aid.'

'Fine. So if it wasn't AAR, what was it?'

'I've told you, I don't know. And I don't care. Don't you hear what I'm saying? Finding out why they did it doesn't bring her back. I want you to leave her and me alone. You've already done enough damage.'

I looked at him. I could see where she got her stubbornness. But I also knew about my own. 'And what does that mean?'

'It means I paid you a lot of money to keep my daughter safe.'

'But she's dead and I'm alive, is that it? Well I'm sorry that I didn't get blown to bits too. No doubt that would have made things better for you, wouldn't it?'

I meant it as sarcasm, but maybe it was the truth. Maybe having me on his conscience would have been easier than having me here in the flesh accusing him of something, but not knowing what. It certainly felt that way.

'I'm warning you, Miss Wolfe. If you persist in bothering me or my friends, I'll be forced to bring in the police.'

And tell them what? Of course, he shouldn't have said it. He should have realized it would only make me mad. But then to be honest I don't think he was thinking that clearly. I was, though.

'Tell me, Dr Shepherd, what kind of papers do you keep up in your study?'

'What?'

'I mean do you have stuff there that might be of interest to the ALF?'

'What do you mean?' And I have to tell you, he was very nervous all of a sudden.

'I mean it looks like you do. You've got enough locks on the doors. And I believe you were burgled – sometime last year, wasn't it?'

'I don't know what you're talking about.'

It wasn't that I smelt blood, so much as revenge. I was about to do something that I was pretty sure I wouldn't be proud of later. But that would be then, and now was now. And I had had it with men giving me lectures about my responsibilities. 'I'm talking about the fact that your daughter was having an affair with a boy who once worked undercover at Vandamed. This boy then came to Mattie's school as a gardener, got to know her, and got her interested in animal rights. Her locker was full of pamphlets. Then he persuaded her to start digging up some stuff on her dad –

the dad whose obsession with work had, in her eyes, sent her mother off with another woman and her off to boarding school. All so he could get on with his precious research.'

And you could see from his face that whatever he had feared, this was somehow worse. He swallowed a couple of times, and I watched his neck muscles work overtime as the saliva made a painful journey down his throat. 'You've no idea what you're saying,' he said at last.

'Haven't I? Then I suppose you can explain why I found Mattie in your study before she died going through your filing cabinets. And I have to tell you she certainly looked as though she'd found what she was looking for.'

Only now did his defences really crumble. He looked across at me and his face was ashen. He got up slowly and turned away, moving slowly, like a man who has suffered some kind of stroke. He stood with his hand on the back of a chair to hold himself up. I began to realize just what I had done.

'Did she say anything?' The voice was hoarse.

'No, nothing. Listen, Dr Shepherd, I don't mean to cause you pain, but if you'd just tell me what it is you're trying to hide, I promise you I'll find the men who killed her.'

And I meant it. He turned. And for the first time he looked like someone I might have been able to talk to. Except he still didn't want to talk to me. 'I . . . I need some time on my own right now. If you don't mind.'

I sat for a moment, hoping my stillness might change his mind, but he already seemed to have forgotten I was there. I got up slowly and gathered my things. At the door I turned. 'Dr Shepherd, I don't believe that Mattie set out to hurt you. But whoever put that bomb under your car did. And if you don't tell me what it is you know, then I really think it's possible they might try again.'

Well, it was a good line. It would have made *me* listen. But he was beyond hope. Now, too late, I felt sympathy. Bad timing. Life's full of it. I closed the front door behind me, making sure the locks slipped into place.

I walked slowly towards my car, past the spot where she had become my future as well as my past. I wanted to get as far from it as possible, but once in the car I found myself paralysed in the driving seat. I looked back up to the house. A light went on in the study. Tom Shepherd following in his daughter's footsteps, checking the files for what he might have lost. He had his guilt, I had mine. In that same room I had interrupted the phone call between Mattie and her activist. And so she had put down the receiver too quickly, taken the car keys and walked out to her death. Not all my fault. But how many people can one blame for a single action? Shepherd was standing in the window. He was holding something in his hand. I got out of the car and walked across the street to get a better look. He didn't notice me. He was too busy talking on the telephone.

I went back to the office. After the elegance of Maida Vale, it looked even tattier than usual. It always does after I haven't been there for a couple of days. Neither had Frank from the look of it. It was getting on for one o'clock. Either he was out on a job, or just out. If it was the latter, he wouldn't be hard to find.

He was sitting in a corner with a half-pint in front of him, the mobile on the seat next to him. I wondered if he was depressed. I can usually tell the signs, but then I hadn't been looking recently. I know that sometimes he misses the Force. But the one time I asked him about it he waxed lyrical about the freedom of the self-employed. Even after nearly three years I don't feel I know him well enough to probe any further. But being needed usually makes him feel better. And need him I did. I sauntered back from the bar with a pint, a Scotch and two packets of crisps. Beads and trinkets. I slid them on to the table. He looked at the glass, then up at me.

'What d'you want?' he grunted.

'What makes you think I want anything?'

'It's a pint, isn't it? Costs twice as much as a half.'

That's what I call a fair cop. 'All right. How about five minutes of your time?'

'You know, you disgust me, Hannah. You call yourself a feminist, then shamelessly play up to members of the opposite sex.'

'Frank, it's your brains I want, not your body.'

'I tell you, you should be careful. Not all male egos are as buoyant as mine. Remarks like that in the wrong company will get you a fistful of fives one of these days.'

I smiled and drew up a chair. 'Thanks.'

'You got this much information, with a multinational offering to pay you for it, and you call it a problem?'

I shook my head. 'I don't want to work for them.'

'I know. They were nasty to a gay couple, shocking, isn't it?' I made a face. 'Or is it the amount of profit they make every year? I know how hard you take such things, Hannah. But I've told you before, detective work brings only suffering and disillusion. This may be the case where you have to accept that the good guys are not automatically the bad guys.'

'Oh, come on, Frank. They were way too nice to me.'

'You're a private eye. They're always too nice or too nasty. Like the police, it's a reflex action.'

'And that's it, is it? I mean that's the analysis I paid one pound seventy pence' worth of beer for?'

'Yeah, well, you should know better than trying to bribe an ex-copper. OK. You're sure it was him?'

'No. He was a fair distance across the car park, and the photo wasn't exactly a give-away. But it certainly looked like him.'

'But "him" wasn't Malcolm Barringer?'

'No. That I am certain of.'

'Hmm. Doesn't fit, though, does it? I mean if he was who you say he is, then why should he still be hanging around?'

'Well, if no one knows who he really is, then why not?

Maybe he likes to live dangerously. I'm getting the impression he's that kind of guy.'

He looked at me quickly. 'Getting to know him, eh?'

'A little, yes.'

'Better watch your step. Nick'll get jealous. So? What do you think you've got? A rebel with a cause, or something nastier?'

I thought about it. 'I don't know yet.'

'But you do know Shepherd had something to hide – something worth killing him for?'

I thought about Shepherd's face, so sunken and pursued. Hard to sort out the grief from the guilt. But not impossible. 'Yes.'

'Well, of course, you claim to know more about these nutters than I do. But from where I'm sitting it's hard to see what exactly he could have done that made him worth blowing to smithereens. I mean how bad can a pig feel? I suppose you're sure it is the pigs?'

'Frank, to be honest I'm not sure about anything.'

'Hmm. Course, you could always give it to the police. They'd be delighted to find out how much more you know than them.'

'Thanks.' He looked at me, and waited. I took it more seriously. 'I know you think I'm withholding evidence.'

'Not *think*, Hannah. *Know*.'

'Listen, Frank, if I give it to them it's not mine any more. And I'll always be the one who let her walk out to the car.'

He shook his head. 'In my experience it's only worth blaming yourself for things you get wrong. She was fourteen years old. She asked you to let her go out and get something from the glove compartment. You weren't to know the car was booby-trapped.'

I closed my eyes. When Tom Shepherd had said it, it had made me mad. Now it just made me bereft. I shook my head. 'I still should have been there.'

He smiled. 'Determined little tick, aren't you? You know,

when you first came to me I only took you on because I felt sorry for you. Well, that and the fact that you'd been on that computer course. But you've not done bad. For a girl. Well, I don't have any miracle answers for you. Looks like loverboy's still your only trump card. Why don't you give Maringo a copy of the photo. Maybe some of the moderates will recognize him and sell him for thirty pieces of silver.'

I shook my head. 'I can try, but I don't think Maringo's the kind of man to name names.'

Frank shrugged. 'Even if he took the Fifth Amendment you'd know you'd got something. Other than that, I think it's a question of buying more beer. I mean if it was him coming out of that pub, then someone has got to remember him.' I had got there without him, anyway. But it always helps to have your judgement confirmed. 'But, Hannah. Be careful, all right? If this guy is animal rights, then he's more IRA than Sinn Fein. And by now it sounds like that's what half the farmers around Vandamed think you are, anyway. There'll be a lot of bad feeling after her death. Watch out you don't get your high heels caught in a cattle grid. They might be tempted to leave you there till the cows come home.'

I had thought about that one, too. But in the middle of a London day with the sound of traffic all around it just seemed like paranoia. 'Don't worry.' I grinned. 'I'll wear Doc Martens.'

He nodded and drained his beer. 'If you wait till the weekend, I'll come with you, if you want.'

It was, I think you probably know, far above and beyond the call of duty. That more than anything else made me realize just how worried he was. But it also gave me an idea.

'Thanks, but – well, they'd have you down for a copper the minute you walked into the place. And you'd hold it against me for ever if you missed Arsenal.'

'Chelsea.'

'Chelsea. Anyway, I've already got a man.'

CHAPTER FOURTEEN

Saturday Night's All Right for Fighting

The weather came out to greet us, for once behaving according to the season. It was the last official day of winter. Soon the clocks would move forward an hour and the light would make everything seem possible again, until another summer disappointed. Nick and I had set off on Saturday afternoon and stopped for lunch as soon as concrete turned to country. By the time we hit East Suffolk he was driving and I was navigating. It was a good team. A voyage of discovery, for one of us at least.

'Why Suffolk?' he had asked when I told him.

'I found some lovely country when I was there on Wednesday. And according to the guide book this particular hotel is spectacular.'

'You sure you can find it?'

I had the map upside down on my lap. I find this helpful, having the real roads and the map roads going the same way. Most of the men I know think it is indicative of women's lack of direction. 'They gave me impeccable instructions. OK?' I said primly.

'OK,' he mimicked, glancing my way. 'You look good.'

'Do I?'

'Yes. I don't think I tell you that often enough.'

Well, certainly not recently. Of course it didn't make me feel any better hearing it now. You think I'm a slimebag, right? Using my boyfriend as a cover for work. Well, you may be right. But he would never have come if I'd told him, and who said it was all going to be hard grind? If the hotel was anything like the brochure, then breakfast in bed could last until dinnertime, with the briefest of visits to the local pub in between.

We had just passed it on the left. According to the map the hotel was about half a mile away, up the hill and then off to the right. We were coming to the turn-off when we spotted a funeral cortege ahead of us – two big black limos piled high with flowers and a motley collection of cars behind – creeping its caterpillar way along the country lane. We slowed down and crept too, waiting patiently until it turned off into a tiny churchyard overlooking a long, rolling sweep of country. As final resting places go, it would be more inviting than most. Burying the dead. Such ceremony. If we did as much for every leftover animal carcass, there would be no room for humans. Maybe that would make us think a little more about the nature of slaughter. Although I suspect it would depend on how hungry we were at the time. I was so heavily entrenched in shoddy philosophy that I missed the turn-off.

'Right.'

'What?'

'Right. You should have gone right.'

'You mean the one we just passed?'

'Yes.'

'Great navigating.' He slammed on the brakes and backed into a field. Across the hedgerow I saw the first car after the hearse stop outside the church and a middle-aged woman get out, pulling her black coat around her. Strange how when it's not your grief it all seems so far away. In the field behind the graveyard a couple of cows looked up from their pasture, then down again. Another meat-eater bites the dust. They didn't seem that interested.

When we got there, it looked even better than the brochure: neat, formal, and very Georgian, with an avenue of small trees leading up to it and apple blossom everywhere. Out of all the weekends in the year we'd picked the right one.

Nick drew up outside the front entrance and turned to me. 'Well, the girl done good,' he said softly and leant over to kiss me. Serious stuff. I registered it as a slow burn – the rush of sex, or the adrenalin of betrayal? What is it they say about infidelity? That it's one of the more piquant arts.

Our room overlooked the gardens, a snooker-table lawn fringed by beds of spring flowers sloping down towards a well-stocked pond. It was here the carp, according to the blurb, lived and died for the guests. They were lucky it hadn't been fire-bombed by fish freedom-fighters. I threw open the windows and looked out. It was still and utterly silent. If I wanted, life could be like this always. Take a different kind of job, earn a different kind of money, meet a different kind of person. You can do that. I know people who do. Would it really make me so boring and complacent?

Nick had been snooping round the bathroom, testing out the water power. He came up behind me and linked his arms round my waist. 'You still thinking about work?'

'Uh-uh.' And for once it was true.

'Good. You know, you got a great ass.'

I smiled. 'That's *my* line.'

He ran a finger down from the edge of my chin towards my breasts. 'Do you want to go for a walk?'

'Where to?'

'How about the bed?'

To be honest, the anticipation proved somewhat better than the act. Sex. However far it takes you away from yourself, you still have to come back alone. Makes you wonder if it's worth the journey. Or maybe I was still feeling guilty. We lay for a while, watching the shadows move across the ceiling. By rights, this should have been the quiet place in the story where the private eye recharges the batteries ready for the last big push towards the summit of the plot. Once again the reality fell miserably short of the myth. All I could think of was Mattie, of all the beds she would never lie in, and all the men she would never lie next to. Maybe I should have been grateful that at least there had been one. Let's hope he had a good body underneath those gardening overalls. A good body and great technique. Now, now, Hannah. Remember what Frank said. Getting to know them is one thing, fantasizing about them is another. I climbed off the bed, kissing my lover as I went. Just like the movies.

We ate early, in an oak-panelled dining room. I don't remember the food, except that I compromised with scallops and Nick had a radicchio and bacon salad, which he claimed was so delicious that I wondered what the pig must have been fed on to make it so tasty. He drank more than I did, but then he usually does, even when I'm not committed to keeping my wits about me.

When we finished, we decided it would be nice to go for a walk, seeing as it was such an unexpectedly balmy evening and the perfect time to celebrate the coming of summer. It was a mutual decision. What was less mutual was our route, not that he noticed being guided. Halfway there it struck me I hadn't taken Frank's advice. They weren't exactly high heels, but they weren't Doc Martens, either. But then whoever heard of Doc Martens with a Jean Muir dress? (Thank you, Sister Kate, a woman of wealth, dress sense and family charity.)

We reached the pub just after nine. 'Oh,' I said, with delighted surprise. 'This must be the village local. Do you fancy a nightcap?'

To me it sounded about as convincing as Ruby Wax auditioning for Juliet, but Nick was a happy bunny, filled with good food and even better wine, and I was his for the weekend. Off duty. A bad thing to happen to a therapist, really.

We chose the lounge bar. It was cosy and not too crowded. I looked around. In the far corner Duncan, the wiry little farmer from three days ago, was sitting with a middle-aged woman and a couple of men. But he didn't notice me and, casually, I picked a table where I could sit with my back to him.

The man at the bar had turned into a girl, which was a good deal more promising when it came to remembering the faces of pretty young men. But I could hardly go up and shove the photo under her nose, particularly with Duncan sitting there harbouring memories of animal rights sympathizers.

While Nick was buying the drinks, I checked out the public bar: a lot more fellas, with a lot more beer and what looked like a serious game of darts in progress. A couple of them glanced up at me. I tried to look local and feminine. They looked away. It was hard to tell whether that meant I had failed or succeeded. I stood there for a while. There was something uncomfortable about the atmosphere. Maybe it was just the relentless masculinity of it all. One thing was for sure. Nobody there had ever had their photo taken in the garden of a girls' school.

When I got back, Nick, with his cognac and my Guinness, was already at the table. 'Where've you been?'

'Just looking around.'

We sat and drank in silence for a while, listening to the chatter of other people: TV programmes, spring gossip, village business. It would have been relaxing had it not been for work.

'Another world, country living, isn't it? Did you ever want to try it, Hannah?'

'Uh-uh. Not me. I don't know enough about Agas. And I'm scared of the dark.'

He smiled. 'Ever thought you might be in the wrong job?'

'All the time.'

To the right of us a woman started to laugh, a great, peeling blast of sound, joyful, very unselfconscious. It made me want to laugh with her. I watched her. Maybe she would recognize the photo. Her or the man next to her. There had to be somebody here who knew more than I did. As I turned back, I noticed that Duncan had left his seat. I wondered whether it was worth worrying about.

'You seem preoccupied.'

'No. No, I'm fine. Just a little tired. Must be the country air.'

'Hmm. You know, when I first met you, I used to wonder whether it was the work that made you so self-contained or the other way around.'

'You mean all private eyes are natural misanthropists?'

'Something like that.'

If I hadn't had so much else on my mind, I might have found it an interesting idea. Maybe I should have just referred him to my family. He'd get a clear enough answer from them. I was, apparently, always a secretive child. Kate says it used to drive everyone crazy. The way I remember it, it was just a defence mechanism from being the youngest and needing to carve out a world of my own. Guarding my own secrets. So, now I'm grown up, I just go ferreting for other people's. 'And what did you decide?'

'I decided you just hadn't met the right man yet.' He said it with an impeccably straight face, but then that was his speciality. When I came to think about it later, it struck me that he may have been hiding behind the humour to say more than he intended. But that was then, and this was now.

I dipped my finger into the top of the Guinness froth and flicked it at him. 'I can't believe they let you loose on children.'

He shrugged. 'Well, you know my views on political correctness. Death to the imagination.'

There was a little silence. The door to the lounge bar opened and a bevy of young men, obviously fresh from the triumph of the bull's-eye, muscled their way in. None of them was the one I was looking for.

'Do you think it'll make any difference if you find them?'

I pulled myself back to the table. 'Who?'

'The people who killed her?'

It gave me quite a shock, my thoughts being so transparent. 'I don't know. I'll tell you when I've got there.'

'Well, anyway, I'm glad you're off duty tonight.' And he put his hand over mine. I smiled, then froze. Over the top of his head I saw a couple come through the main door. She was stocky, early to mid fifties. He was a little older, although always hard to tell the exact age with Van Morrison. I bent down to scratch my ankle and kept on scratching. He wouldn't recognize me. I looked too different.

I sat up and ran straight into his stare. Clearly it needed more than a Jean Muir dress and a dab of Clinique mascara to turn this swan into a princess. His wife had spotted some friends and was making her way over to the other side of the bar. He was making for me. I dragged my eyes back and smiled hastily at Nick. If we had world enough and time . . . but I didn't.

'I thought we made it clear we didn't like your sort around here?' he said with the kind of projection that would bring the dog back from a couple of fields away. The hubbub level around us dropped significantly.

I looked up at him. 'I'm sorry,' I said, 'have we met before?'

'I'd get out of here, if I were you. Before somebody puts you out.'

Nick was on his feet before I could stop him. He was taller than Brayton, but nowhere near his girth. 'Excuse me,' he said in a tone that could best be described as firm but fair, 'I think you must be mistaken. This lady is with me.' Oough. Hard to know which was more embarrassing really, the attack or the defence.

Brayton snorted. 'Then you should watch your company, laddie.' You could almost hear the clash of their antlers. Men. It's got to be hormones. No other explanation. I was on my feet trying to get between them. But not quite fast enough. Brayton was already in for the kill. 'Or maybe you don't know that this lady, as you call her, is one of the reasons that Tom Shepherd's daughter was blown to bits.'

The hush was now complete. I closed my eyes. 'Nick,' I

said, 'it's OK. I do know this man.' He stared down at me, uncomprehendingly. 'I've been here before. Mattie's father worked near by. I was hoping someone might be able to help me.'

His face made a rapid emotional journey, leaving confusion and arriving at insult via injury. 'I'm sorry.'

'Oh, Christ, Hannah.'

'I was going to tell you,' I said quietly, trying to keep it private.

'Like hell you were,' he said, blowing a bloody great hole in my intentions.

By now most of the bar was waiting for my reply.

'Listen, could we go outside. I –'

'No. No, I've got a better idea. How about *I* go outside? Then you can just stay here and get on with your "investigating".' Great. Why don't you say it a bit louder, Nick? I don't think quite everybody in the village heard that.

He saw my look. 'Sorry. Was that one of your secrets? I don't know why you bother with other people, Hannah. They just get in the way. I assume you can find yourself another chauffeur back to London.'

Well, it was no more than I deserved. Except how was I to know this was meant to be the weekend when we broke through to a deeper level? I watched him go. We all watched him go. Even Brayton knew when he had been upstaged. The door slammed behind Nick and the audience turned back to me. Free entertainment. Well, at least I had everyone's attention. I took a deep breath. I addressed myself to Brayton, but I was really playing to the gallery.

'I know what you think, but I'm not animal rights, OK? I'm a private investigator, looking into Mattie Shepherd's death. And I'm here because I need to find someone. He goes by the name of Malcolm Barringer or Tony Marriot, or someone else. Young, good-looking chap, fairish hair, used to work at Vandamed. I think he rides a motorbike. I've got a picture of him if anyone wants to see it?'

But nobody did. Trouble was, of course, I didn't have their confidence. You could see that. It was the way they were staring at me. Could be my manner. Or my dress. Or my accent. Take your pick.

Brayton shook his head. 'Whoever you are, lady, we don't like being taken for a ride.'

'Well, for Mattie Shepherd's sake I just hope not everybody feels the same way,' I said loudly, picking up my bag and coat. 'If anyone wants to take it further, I'm staying at the Hortley Hotel, OK?' It was a weak exit line, made even weaker by the fact I had nowhere to exit to. I was afraid of meeting Nick in the car park: unless I knew what I was going to say to him it would be better to leave him there. Which left me no option but the back door.

I found myself in an inner courtyard with a few benches and tables. And opposite, two doors, a stick figure on each, one with a skirt on. And so it was I did what ladies always do when covered with embarrassment. I went to powder my nose.

The place was empty. I slid into one of the cubicles and locked myself in. Once on the loo seat I found to my fury that my legs were shaking. I took a few deep breaths to steady myself. Bloody stupid. All of it. All of them. Me. Me most of all. Maybe Frank was right. I should just have given what I knew to the police and let them get on with it. At least they would have had the proper resources to look for this guy. All I was getting was nowhere fast. A clear case of hubris over justice. What did it matter to Mattie who found her killer? Just so long as someone did. I wondered what Frank would have done. Well, not cower in a toilet, that's for sure. But then faced with Frank's physique Brayton might have thought twice before throwing his weight around. I tell you, sometimes it sucks being a girl. It was time I had more courage.

I was still hauling myself out of the slough of despond when the outside door creaked open. Then someone pulled at the cubicle door. I made with the loo paper, just to give a sense of business as usual when a man's voice said quietly but clearly: 'Down by the stream at the back of the pub after closing time. And don't bring your boyfriend.'

Boyfriend? What boyfriend? So someone had something to tell me. Maybe my Sarah Bernhardt act hadn't been such a bad idea after all. Of course, by the time I got the cubicle unlocked the man had gone. And by the time I had catapulted myself out into the courtyard, the door to the public bar was already closing. I pushed my way in, but it was a rugby scrum in there with sixty, maybe seventy people, at least twenty of whom could just have come through the door. I looked at my watch. Just after ten o'clock. Boy, did I need a drink. But I also needed to make pax with Nick. And I only had an hour to do it in.

CHAPTER FIFTEEN

Dancing in the Dark

I had expected to find him in the car park, kicking up the gravel and trying hard not to cool off. But he wasn't there. I stood about for a bit waiting. Then I made my way back to the hotel. The walk took thirteen minutes, which if I was to make my closing-time appointment left thirty-five minutes for the reconciliation. I could sort of see it wasn't going to be enough.

But maybe it was as well I didn't have to try. He wasn't in the bar and he wasn't in our room. Neither was his suitcase. I changed my shoes, repacked my handbag and headed downstairs. And there was something else missing, I realized as I looked out over the car park on my way to the front desk. The receptionist told me he'd checked out ten minutes before, then tried to soften the blow by saying he'd settled the bill before he went. There was no message. Well, I suppose he'd said everything he wanted to say. Ten minutes, eh? He hadn't given me much time to come crawling back.

Ah well, face the facts: I was a woman without a lover. The hotel bar looked warm and inviting: dark wood, comfy chairs and a fire in the grate. I could sit until the early hours and cry into my handkerchief. Except I never carry one. I went up to the bar and ordered a Scotch on the rocks. I stood and watched as the man poured it, enjoying the cracking of the tiny icebergs and the dark, rich swirl of the liquid. Then I picked up the glass and, in homage to a hundred other private eyes more experienced and charismatic than I, downed it in one. Never mind the vintage, feel the fire in your belly. I gave the easy chair a brief salute, and headed for the front door. I had another mile to walk tonight, there and back. I prevailed upon the girl at the front desk to lend me a torch. You could see she was worried about me. Maybe she had Ophelia fantasies. I gave her a big grin and went out into the night. Shame about Nick. Even more of a shame about his car.

It was just before eleven when I got to the pub. As I walked round the back, I heard the bell for last orders ring twice. The garden was benign enough: a little pond, a rusty climbing frame, a few tables caught in the thin light of a half-moon between clouds. At the bottom my torch picked up a gate leading to a narrow, sloping strip of land, below which I assumed to be the stream. Behind me the noise of closing-time was a comfortable companion — doors slamming, people's footsteps, car engines, laughter, talking. I opened the gate and made my way down to the water's edge. With the torch and the sneakers I felt like a professional.

The stream was wide and gushing. Across on the other side there were trees, where the night was dense and my torch made little impact. That, presumably, was where whoever I was to meet would hide. I thought about crossing over but couldn't without making a fair amount of noise and I didn't want give him a reason not to turn up. I cleared my throat, just in case he was already there.

If I told you I wasn't scared, you would think me a liar. But the truth is I wasn't. My stomach was, and my heartbeat was, but I wasn't. In my brain I was sharp and alert, ready for whatever was to come. Call it the Scotch, call it my impatience, call it the cute little can of mace that I keep tucked away in the bottom of my bag for emergencies. Call it what you will, the fact was I was running on high. Whatever happened here tonight was happening to me. I was still in this plot: it was mine and no one else's.

'Do you always talk to yourself?' said the voice from deep in the trees. It was a harsh, forced sound, like a person pretending to be someone they weren't. It was only scary if you let yourself think about it.

'You're late,' I said loudly, singing it out into the night. 'I've been –'

'Shut up. You came to listen, not to talk. I'm going to say it just once, OK? What is done is done. Nobody can undo it. She's dead because of something her dad did. Our mistake. We're sorry. But we'll live with it. And so will you. As long as you leave it alone.'

The words were designed to make your blood run cold. Except maybe that was the problem – the amount of design about them. I found myself caught between chill and cliché. Heroes and villains. Since we all watch the same movies, it shouldn't be any surprise that we all play from the same script.

I got hold of the chill and chewed on it till all its juice was gone, then I swallowed it down as far as it would go, along with childhood fears of dark woods, country lanes and madness on the edges of the night. 'You're scaring the hell out of me,' I shouted into silence. This time it didn't answer back. I stood for a moment waiting. In the quiet I thought I heard the rustle of undergrowth. 'What's wrong? Don't you like it when the girls answer back? Or am I a bit too old for you?' I yelled in the direction of the sound. The lines were all right, but I didn't seem to have the correct stage directions. I thought about crossing the stream and trying to follow him into the wood, but at the last moment, like a horse refusing a fence, I just couldn't do it.

I stood there for a while longer, just me and the night, until in the end there wasn't anything to do but get up and go home. I climbed my way back up the embankment and through the gate, turning every now and then to check I wasn't being followed. I crossed the garden and through into the pub car park. The lights in the bar were still on, but the road was deserted. I looked at my watch. It was 11.45. I had been communing with the devil for longer than I realized. I thought of going back and throwing myself on the landlord's mercy: one more cup of coffee for the road.

But what would I say? Half a mile away the hotel bar beckoned, anonymity and another glistening Glenfiddich.

Of course there are those who say that the Archbishop of Canterbury's envoy, Terry Waite, went back into Beirut that last time knowing full well he was going to be kidnapped, because that was the only way he could atone for having let himself become the pawn of the CIA. I wouldn't have the chutzpah to put myself in the same league but, looking back on it, I did have a little atoning to do.

On the other hand, the way I saw it I had logic on my side. Whatever the terrors of darkness, it wouldn't make any sense for him to jump me now. Better to let me stew in my own fear and the echo of his threats. He could always clobber me later if I still seemed curious.

I started to walk. The torch picked out a wavering path in the darkness. I followed it, amusing myself with thoughts of childhood. About how when I was seven I would creep to the loo in the middle of the night and then run hell for leather back to bed with the sound of the flush ringing in my ears. Sweet terrors.

The night was colder now. I must have been halfway there when I heard the footsteps in front of me. I stopped and turned off the torch, instinctively sliding my hand into my bag, fingers moving over the smooth metal of the canister. You find it corny, no doubt, that I should resort to such girlie aids, that I shouldn't be able to fell a grown man at ten paces with my flying feet? Myself, I prefer to see it as the triumph of technology over muscle. I did try martial arts once but do you realize how long you have to study to get your foot as effective as a squirt of tear gas? It would leave a girl no time to earn a living.

From the darkness ahead I could now hear voices. They were moving closer. There was a small humpback bridge in front of me. I moved softly to one side of it. A moment later I saw the flash of a torch and heard laughter. They came roving into view, two dark shapes not all that steady on their feet. Saturday night, country and town alike. One of them spotted me and gave me a cheery wave. 'Evening.'

'Good evening,' I said.

'Nice night, eh, love?' said the other loudly, then giggled. His companion gave him a shove and he staggered forward a few steps. They both laughed. I watched them go. Interesting how easily men own the space around them, while women just feel like visitors without a permit. I waited till they disappeared down the road, then headed for home. Somewhere to the left I passed the churchyard and its new soft grave with the worms working overtime at safe-breaking. Which meant the turn-off to the hotel could be only a couple of hundred yards away.

If he had come out of the bushes, I would have been ready for him. Well, I like to think I would. But that wasn't how it happened. The wire was strung across the road. He must have had to take it down, then reset it after the lads had gone by. But he'd done a good job, got the tension just right. One minute I was upright and invincible, the next sprawling head first into the dark.

I knew instantly what was happening. In fact, though I have tried to forget them, those next ninety seconds were clearer than almost any other time in my life. I was back on my feet fast, the fear temporarily numbing the pain of the smashed elbow and bruised ribs. My hand was out of my bag, can in place. I whirled round holding it like a pistol in front of me. But he was quicker, coming out of the dark from the side rather than head on. He used the first blow, hand chop against forearm, to knock it out of my grasp. That left me with the torch. But even in karate left hands aren't as strong as right. He flung himself against me. As the torch spun into the air its crazy beam of light spiralled into the blackness and I caught a flash of a face in front of me: fair hair and skin, soft, almost silky. Then it was gone. I felt rather than saw the next blow coming and put up my hands to protect myself. Instinct. Whoever told you it could

138

save your life had read too many books. The force of his fist connected with my stomach somewhere where the womb meets the centre of the soul. It was a kind of disembowelment. I heard my voice shriek like a banshee as the breath was driven back up my windpipe. At the same time I doubled up and fell sideways on to the ground. Nothing in my whole life had ever hurt so much. I couldn't breathe, I couldn't see, and all I could feel was a great wedge of matter forcing its way up my throat. I lay in the ditch, retching. It seemed to last for a long time. I felt him standing above me, watching. But he made no move towards me. When I got some semblance of my wits back, I used the vomiting as a cover to pull myself nearer to the edge of the road, where the bushes would offer me some protection. But he spotted me and leant down to haul me up. I used my free hand to grab my bag. I've joked enough times about the weight of the crap I keep in it being enough to lay out any mugger. Now as I twisted the strap I understood the limitations of humour. I swung with all my might. And the blow connected. But the strap was too long. It missed his head and smashed against his neck and shoulder. Nevertheless, the force made him reel backwards. I turned and started to run, but my stomach was still in the ditch and I couldn't stand upright. He grabbed me and as he pulled me back towards him, I heard the words, 'Oh no you don't,' before his fist hit my face. I heard the crack and felt the tooth shatter. I swear to you, I actually felt it happen. Strange how you can sort out one particular instance of pain from all the rest. My mouth filled up with liquid. I understood it was blood. I also understood that this wasn't a regular beating-up. That to be inflicting this much damage the guy had to have something on his knuckles. Oh God, please don't take my eye out, I remember thinking over and over, like a terrible litany as I waited for him to hit me again. And if there had been time, I would have thought of Mattie, and the shaft of fury and flame that had blown her away and brought me to this. But there was no time for her. Only for myself. And for him. Now he came closer, emboldened by my helplessness. In the darkness all I could make out was the sour smell of him and the sound of his breath. He put out a hand towards me, as if to touch my cheek in some appalling inversion of tenderness. Or maybe he was going for my throat. As his fingers reached near, I lunged forward, opening my mouth and snapping my jaws closed on them. I still had enough teeth left to do some damage of my own. I felt the blood pour out from my lips, mingling with his. I heard him yell. And I felt this small, fierce whoop of triumph inside. Don't mess with me, it said, in neon letters lighting up the night sky. I'm not your victim. He used his left hand to beat my mouth open. But, I tell you, it didn't knock the adrenalin out of me. And it still didn't make me a victim. Neither did the next blow, although as my eye closed underneath the metal on the fist I realized a more appalling truth: that in the end no one up there was going to protect me, any more than they had protected Mattie.

CHAPTER SIXTEEN

Just the Way You Look Tonight

If my life hadn't flashed before me, it stood to reason I was still alive. The philosophical conjecture was backed up by physical proof: I hurt too much to be dead. Amazingly, I came up smelling of roses. Their scent was everywhere, wild and sweet, almost overwhelming. Smell before sight. At least my nose couldn't be broken. I sent a message to my eyes. But only one of them obeyed. Severe tunnel vision brought back the panic of the night. I wanted to bring up a hand to check but I was too scared about what I would find. I worked on what I had. I was staring at a Dutch still life: roses, maybe two or three dozen, in an elegant vase, a jug of water and glass next to it. Behind, sunshine (early morning or late afternoon) filtered through classy cream blinds. And everywhere more flowers. BUPA, I thought. Either that or a funeral parlour. I moved my head. Near the end of the bed there was a chair, with someone sitting in it: Nick, hunched forward, staring at the floor, in his fingers a scrunched-up handkerchief. Compassion filled the air, rolling in on the sunlight, soft and sticky. The pain returned – in my stomach, in my chest, up through my face. It felt unbearable. I closed the only eye that was working and went back to sleep.

The next time I opened it the roses were less colourful, the still life dimmer, ringed by charcoal air. And the water jug had been filled up. I took this as a good sign, that I had noticed the water level and remembered it. The room seemed smaller, but that could have been the effect of the night. The chair had moved nearer to the bed, and the figure in it was stockier, more rumpled. It was also watching me carefully.

'Hello, Hannah,' it said.

'Hello, Frank,' I replied, and he gave a wincing smile as the words came out mangled and a little slobbery. I tried to smile back, but someone had sewn up the edges of my mouth. 'I hurt,' I said, clearer this time.

'I know, babe. I know.'

Good old Frank. Let him be my mirror. If he lied, I would see it in his eyes. 'What do you see?'

'Well, you're not pretty, but then you always were more of a character girl.' He watched me. And he must have seen the lip tremble. 'You're lucky. It looks worse than it is. You've got a badly bruised face, a split lip, and you lost a tooth.'

'My eye?'

'There's a long cut under the eyebrow. That's why you can't open it. It's going to leave a scar but nothing to stop you pulling the boys. They were more worried about your ribs and stomach. But the consensus is it's just internal bruising. Did they kick you?'

Did they kick me? 'Not that I remember. But he had metal on his knuckles.' And I heard my voice go funny again.

'Yeah, well, that figures.' He swallowed hard. His anger sat like static around him. Not like the usual laid-back Frank at all. I was touched. I was also afraid. He put his hand on the bed near to mine. I couldn't remember him ever touching me before, short of the occasional slap on the back. I could see he didn't know what to do. He wasn't the only one. I tried to make it easier. 'You'd have been ashamed of me, Frank. I wasn't even outnumbered. I forgot everything you ever taught me. Though I did bite him.'

Frank nodded. 'Let's hope it's somewhere we can recognize him.' There was a pause. 'You don't have to tell me, you know.'

Oh, but I did. At least some of it. It was OK while we were on the firm ground of facts: the row in the pub, the voice in the loo, even the hissed warning from the woods and the start of the country lane. But when it came to the ditch and the bile in my mouth, the taste was no longer yesterday's supper but my own humiliation. Even without the sex, violence is a sexual violation, too intimate and painful to be shared.

He looked away and busied himself with the water jug. I took the offered drink and sipped it slowly. My tongue found the gap between my back teeth and probed it carefully. Ah well, it had been a tooth with too many fillings anyway. I tried to climb back on to dry land. 'How much does a bridge cost on the National Health these days?'

'I'll make it your Christmas bonus.'

'Thanks. I'm OK really,' I said. 'Just a bit shaky.'

He looked at me and frowned. 'Take my advice, Hannah. Don't bury it until it's ready to be buried. It won't help.'

He was right. I already knew that. I took another sip of water. Then probed further than my gum. 'I think I still feel frightened, Frank.'

'Yeah, well that'll take longer to heal than your face. You know the worst thing? He's going to forget you a lot quicker than you forget him.'

'Is that how it works?' I said quietly.

He looked away and there was almost an embarrassment about him, as if our intimacy had upset him. Our intimacy but his confession.

He shrugged. 'Different strokes.'

Well, well. All the pints of beer and banter and I had never known. There was a small silence. I felt drowsy, but safe. Safer. 'Who was he?' I said in the sure knowledge that I wouldn't be misunderstood.

Frank made a face. 'Just some little punk I once nicked. A man with a vicious memory and a couple of friends.' He stopped. I wanted to ask, even though I wasn't sure I wanted to know. He looked up at me. 'They were waiting for me in my car in an all-night multistorey. They hit me with a baseball bat. Bust both my arms, nearly bust my head. Then kicked a few ribs in. I don't remember a lot.'

'Were you scared?'

The air between us was charged, like the beginning of a love scene. How extraordinary, I thought. Frank and I are having an affair. 'Yes.' He nodded. 'Yes, I was scared. I thought they were going to kill me.'

Secrets in the night. Such a big admission. 'And afterwards?'

'Afterwards I got angry. But it took a while. For a long time I was just glad to be alive.'

I wanted to ask how long. Add it to the list of questions. 'What did you do?'

'Spent some time in hospital. Took some leave. Went back to work.'

'Did you get them?'

'Oh yes, I got them. He pulled another job. Him and one of his friends. We got a tip-off.'

'And you bust them?'

He nodded. I waited. 'It was just him and me in the interrogation room. I hit him. Once in the stomach, once in the face. I hurt him.'

The earth moved beneath me. I couldn't even hear my heart beat. 'Did it make you feel better?' I said it at last.

And he started to laugh. 'I was shaking so much I had to leave the room so he wouldn't see it. I had to hand the interrogation over to someone else. I . . . well, they finished it for me. I suppose they thought it was a favour. Can't say I feel good about that.' He stopped. 'But that's the point. There is no good to be got out of it.'

I should have the luxury of such a doubt. What would I do? Even the idea of it made me shake.

He looked up at me. 'The best thing you can say about it is, it passes. And you do get over it,' he said, already a man climbing back into his clothes, combing his hair, straightening up his tie. 'I don't wake up at night any more. I can park in a multistorey car park without feeling sick. And his is not the face I expect to see in hell.' All dressed up and ready to go. A little bit of me was sad. This Frank and I might never meet again. But one-night stands can set a lot of the world to rights, as long as you understand that is what they are.

'Thanks,' I said.

'Think nothing of it.' I nodded. To look at us no one would know. 'So, if you're up to it, you've got a couple of visitors.'

I shook my head. 'I don't want to see him. Not yet.'

He shrugged. 'He's in worse shape than you are.'

'I know. That's why I need to wait.'

He nodded. 'OK. Him I can stall. The others are going to be more difficult.'

'I know you think I should tell them. And you're probably right. But not yet. Give me a little time.'

'We don't have any more time, Hannah.'

I thought about it. 'The local police won't know what to make of it, anyway.'

'It's not local we're talking about. The London boys are up. Don Peters and Co. They want to talk to you about Tom Shepherd.'

'Shepherd. Why?'

Frank looked at me. I suppose he thought it would come better from him than from them. 'Because it seems you were the last person to see him before he injected himself full of poison.'

After they had left, I asked the nurse to give me something to make me sleep. And so Sunday became Monday, and brought time for reflection. The question was just how guilty was I going to let myself feel? I mean nobody forces anybody to take their own life. So I had told Tom Shepherd some unpalatable facts about his daughter. It couldn't have made him feel any worse than her death had done. Could it?

It seemed to me he must have been planning it, anyway. Peters said the housekeeper had found him early next morning, and that according to the pathologist's initial report he'd been dead for at least eight hours. That left an afternoon and a bit of an evening. The local chemist's had no record of anyone buying any obvious kind of poison that day. Which meant whatever he used, he must have already had it hidden away in his bathroom closet. It was the method that chilled me most of all. So very scientific. But his choice. His life. Not my fault. No, not my fault. In the end not a question of guilt. Only a question of who exactly he had been phoning just after I left the house, and about what? Maybe when I hurt less, my brain would work better.

Frank's diagnosis of the stomach pains turned out to be a little premature, and they insisted I stay in for more tests. The pursuit of profit or the fear of malpractice suits? Private medicine. It was just what I needed to get my aggro level back up to scratch. Still, if someone else was paying for it . . . The interesting thing was who.

It seems news travels fast in the country. When the girl bartender and her boyfriend found me (we'll gloss over what they were doing out in the dark in the middle of the night), they remembered enough from my public performance in the bar to know what to tell the local police, who then contacted Vandamed. Well, they didn't have much choice. At the hotel I had let Nick register us under his address, and all they got from his home number was an answering machine.

Of course, by rights, even without him they should have been able to get all the info they needed from my handbag. But that was the point. There was no handbag. Well, what would you do if you were a professional thug who wanted to make a beating-up look like a mugging? Except it was worse than that. Bags can be precious things. Driving licences, cheque books, credit cards – all that kind of stuff is replaceable, and anyone who walks the mean streets without a duplicate address book is asking for trouble. But some things you can't replace: in this case a certain brown envelope containing a photograph of the man who had mugged me.

And, of course, once I thought about it that way, it all began to make sense. To say there was no point in beating me to a pulp so soon after the warning may have been logical, but only as far as it went. This way he had killed two birds with one stone. No Hannah, at least for a while, and no incriminating photo of himself. Brain as well as brawn, eh?

Of course, Vandamed would probably have a photograph of the student who had infiltrated them. But security mug shots always make people look like convicts, even the good-looking ones, and anyway, mine had been a more personal memento, not to mention the only real proof of the affair which had so effectively brought down the house of Shepherd.

Anyway, the fact was that as I lay unconscious in Ipswich Hospital the only person who knew anything about me was one Marion Ellroy, managing director of Vandamed, plucked from his, no doubt, expensive bed to the bleak horrors of an NHS casualty ward. And from there the rest was private. Well, I already had ample evidence of how well Vandamed looked after its employees. In this case, even someone who hadn't agreed to go on the payroll. The flowers, the room, the medical care – it was all on them. Impressive, eh? And the kind of offer you couldn't refuse, particularly in my condition. I did the decent thing and wrote Ellroy a note to thank him. He, equally decent, did not try to visit me.

So I sat in my private room with my flowers, my television and my telephone while my face turned from black to blue and my eye opened enough for me to see the extent of the damage.

On Monday afternoon they offered me a hand mirror – I suppose they decided I was ready. But some things you can't share, even with professionals. So a little while later I made my own solitary visit to the bathroom. And there, above the sink, made the acquaintance of the new Hannah Wolfe.

You never really know how vain you are until you lose the looks you've got. Maybe the worst thing about what I saw was that I was still recognizable. I think I'd had this fantasy that the violence had somehow transformed me, turned me into someone else, someone ennobled by suffering, and that this new spirituality would shine through the pulp of my face. Well, it didn't.

The main problem was not so much the smashed lip or the bruises, as the fact that there was just too much flesh. My whole face had blown up like puff pastry, as if to protect the bones from any more damage. Maybe that was why my eye had closed, in preparation for another crack of the fist. In its place there was a long, livid gash held together by a couple of stitches and an expanding purple-black bruise which dragged the side of my cheek down towards my mashed lip. Altogether a stunning sight. Gone were the pleasures of working incognito. From now on the private eye had an all too public face.

I thought of Jack Nicholson in *Chinatown* pulling Faye Dunaway into bed with a slashed nostril and sticking-plaster: injured hero, aroused heroine, a symbolic variation on a common genre theme. I put my hand up to the mirror, running my finger from my split lip up to the line of the eye. 'Why, Miss Wolfe, I do declare I just love that cute little scar.' But some kind of gender equalities are simply impossible. And my Southern accent left a lot to be desired. The more I looked the better it didn't get. I would have cried, only the salt would hurt the stitches too much.

After the second day I stopped looking. There wasn't any point. I wasn't going anywhere. And, after all, someone else was doing the work now.

Considering how little I had told him, DI Peters had been quite civilized about it. Well, you can hardly hit a lady when she's down, and, anyway, I got the impression it was no more than he expected from an employee of Frank Comfort's. Of course he was still not to know whether this new truth was the whole truth. But that was his own fault, really. He should have waited till the painkillers had begun to work and my head was less fuzzy. As it was he just jumped too quickly, got so excited about the gardener and the envelope with the leaflets and photo that he didn't give me time to get back to that 'forgotten' phone call that Mattie had taken that night in her father's study.

I didn't feel too badly about it. After all, at least they had a lead now. They moved fast. When they couldn't trace either student Malcolm Barringer or gardener Tony Marriot to any known animal rights activist groups, they made a public appeal. The day I was due to be released the papers carried a small, blurred photograph of a young man somewhere between the age of eighteen and thirty. Vandamed's mug shot – as I predicted – was a joke, apparently a completely different person from my moody black-and-white love study. To add insult to injury, Peters let the Debringham College schoolgirls loose on an Identikit picture for a television crimewatch programme. Their version – a cross between Christian Slater and Ian Brady – looked like yet someone else entirely. According to Frank, the boys got over six hundred calls from people who were sure they knew him. Police work. The indefatigable in search of the indistinguishable. Sometimes it pays to be a one-man band.

And so I was allowed to go home and pick up the pieces of my life – the largest one of which was Nick. As you know he had waited all through Sunday night to see me. Frank had stalled him, but it was left to the pretty young nurse to do my dirty work for me, assuring him that it was only natural for me not to want to be seen by my lover in my present state. 'Give it a couple of days,' she no doubt said. 'She just needs a little time.' And, of course, as an excuse it was not without its truth. You and the bathroom mirror both know that. But you also know it wasn't the whole truth.

Except it could only get worse the longer I left it. So I rang him on Monday night and agreed that we would meet in London when I got home. He had left his car for me. Maybe he'd hoped I would ask him to drive me back, but he understood when I said I wanted to drive myself. I knew he would.

I liked the drive. It gave me a chance to be alone but in the world again, and, truth be told, I was quite grateful to get out from under the roses. There can be such a thing as too many flowers. If I had been nearer, I might even have gone back to the pub, just to have a look at the lane in daylight, exorcize my demons. But the A12 beckoned and it didn't make me a coward to listen to its call. Apart from odd moments at traffic lights when I would find the driver next to me staring uncontrollably, the journey home was uneventful. It was early evening by the time I arrived. I parked outside my flat. The lights were on and the curtains drawn. But then you have to expect that when you give someone your key. The only people I had seen for three days were policemen, nurses and doctors. What the hell was I going to do with a lover?

I climbed the stairs slowly. He must have heard me, because he was waiting in the doorway. It reminded me of that time at his house a couple of days after her death, when I had been so unexpectedly pleased to see him. We stood for a second looking at each other. He made no move towards me. 'Hi, Hannah, welcome home,' he said quietly, then stood aside to let me in.

The flat felt warm, I went into the living room. It was unbelievably clean and filled with flowers (no roses, thank God) and, wonder of wonders, the curtain rail had flown back up to is rightful place above the window sill and the wall around it had been redecorated. It was a great testament to the power of recovery.

'I stuck to magnolia,' he said. 'It seemed safer that way.'

'Did you use a Rawlplug?'

'That and a tube of Polyfilla.'

'It looks great.' Which was more than could be said for me, eh? Oh, what the hell. Why didn't I say it? It was what we were both thinking, anyway. 'I've been contemplating doing the same to the other eye. Just to give it a sense of symmetry. What do you think?'

OK in theory but a mess in practice. It came out angry with no humour to undercut the pain. The doctor had warned me before I left – something about my emotions taking longer to heal than my face. Smart guys, doctors. When it comes to other people's bodies. Nick took in a small, sharp breath through his teeth.

I shook my head. 'I'm sorry.'

'No. I'm sorry. I should have said something. Except you wouldn't have believed me. It's already so much better, Hannah. I mean compared with Sunday night you look –'

'Like a million dollars. I know.' I saw him again, sitting there watching over me, staring at the floor. He'd never know I had seen him. Unless, of course, I told him. I looked at him now. He was wearing a pair of stonewashed jeans and a grey cotton sweater I had bought him in the January sales. A lot of women would find him very attractive right now. A lot of women would be right. I was in more trouble than I realized. Help me, I thought. Or just leave me alone.

'I bought a bottle of something. But I didn't know how you'd be feeling. Maybe you'd just prefer to go to bed and have supper.'

'No. No. Let's drink.'

He went into the kitchen and came back with a tray, a bottle of champagne and two new, elegant glasses, thin and fluted. He eased out the cork and poured carefully. I watched the bubbles flow. Then he pushed a glass across the table to me. It was the moment when somebody proposes a toast. We waited, but nobody did.

He took a swig, then put down his glass. 'I have something to say to you, Hannah. Except I don't know if this is the right time.'

'I don't think there'll be a better one,' I said.

He nodded. 'I'm not sorry I walked out on you. You should have told me. But then you know that. I am sorry that I didn't come back. I should never have left you to make that walk on your own. I almost didn't. I drove the car a mile down the road and sat in a lay-by for twenty minutes wondering what to do. I just couldn't see that you'd thank me for trying to look after you.'

I smiled as much as my lip allowed. 'Don't give yourself a hard time, Nick. You were right. I would have been furious. It wasn't your fault. He knew I was after him. If it hadn't been then, it would have been some other time. I'm glad I got it over with, really.'

He carried on looking at me. I knew what he was feeling. I had seen the same thing in Frank that first night. God save me from chivalry. 'When I saw what he'd done to you, I wanted to kill him,' he said quietly. And God save me from other people's emotion when I can only just cope with my own. You'd think a therapist would know better.

'Yeah, well, I had a similar reaction myself,' I said, trying for lightness but missing by a mile. I got up and walked over to the window, pulling back the curtain. I caught a blurred reflection of myself in the glass. Quasimodo. I looked out on to the street. 'The plane tree's starting to leaf,' I heard myself say. 'It really must be spring.'

He came up and stood by me. After a while I turned to him. My heart was beating fit to burst. Slowly he put out a hand to my face. I'd been waiting for him to touch me ever since I walked into the flat. But even though I saw it coming, something short-circuited inside me. I swear I didn't know I was going to flinch away until it had already happened. He pulled his hand back abruptly.

'It's OK, Hannah. It's OK.' I nodded, swallowing hard,

except I couldn't get my saliva down. 'I won't touch you. You're OK. I'm not one of them, all right?'

'I know,' I said. 'I know that. I do.' And to my fury I began to cry.

He stepped away from me. And I could see him covering up the hurt with expertise: becoming Nick the professional with a difficult client, watching, judging the moment, making sure it was the right response. 'Let's just leave it for a bit, eh? Why don't we sit down and have another drink? Then I'll get supper.'

I shook my head. 'Listen Nick. I . . . I have to be on my own for a bit.'

'OK,' he said easily. 'We need some coffee, anyway. I'll take a walk down to the shops.'

'No. No. I mean properly alone.'

He looked at me for a long time. I kept thinking about what he was seeing: Hannah, and not Hannah. But a lover now, no longer a patient. And it may be cruel to say it, but it was a relief to feel confusion in place of his infinite understanding. 'Are you sure about that?'

I nodded. He moved over to the chair and picked up his coat and briefcase. Jesus, I thought. Am I sure? Is this really what I want?

He put on the coat slowly. 'I'll call you tomorrow then,' he said lightly, and walked towards the door. Each action reeked with significance. I could hardly stand it.

He picked up his car key from the hall table. Then turned. 'I just need to know one thing. Is this about you, or about us?'

'I don't know,' I said. 'I don't know.'

And I didn't. But he seemed to. He looked at the floor, then up at me. 'Oh, Hannah,' he said softly. Then, 'Will you be all right?'

I gave a little shrug. 'Yep.' But it came out more as a question than a statement.

'Yes,' he repeated. 'I think you will.' Out of his coat

pocket he had pulled a single key, with a globe key ring on it. He stood running it though his fingers. We both knew which door it opened. And closed. He looked down at it. 'If it's all right with you, I'll hold on to this for a while. You never know. You might need someone to do the shopping.'

And he smiled. I'll repeat myself at the risk of being crude. There must be fifty ways ... Let's hear it for Paul Simon. And for Nick Thompson. Not such a bad therapist after all. I smiled too. This time when he turned he didn't look back. The door closed behind him. I waited till his footsteps had gone down the hall and out the main door. Then I walked over and put the chain on behind him.

I drank another glass of champagne and made myself an omelette. The booze turned me nasty, but by then I was too drunk to care. So I no longer had a lover. All the more room for my toy boy. I wouldn't call it overwhelming, but there was no doubt that since our tryst in a dark country lane the thought of him had crept insidiously closer to my heart. What was it Frank said about their forgetting you quicker than you forgot them? With good reason. Every time I moved, I had a memory of him where my stomach met my bowels. And when that faded, there was always the mirror to refresh my passion. Good fantasy stuff, eh – the detective becoming obsessed with the criminal? And on the way exposing some dark, pathological similarities, making them a true match for each other. To be honest, I've always found it a bit of a cliché. Until now. Now I understood it. Not so much symmetry as tit for tat. He beats me to a pulp, I want to do the same thing to him. That kind of longing can turn you inside out. Just like sex. Problem is he was playing hard to get. Still, when you want someone enough . . .

Until that moment I don't think I had really thought about the future. About whether or not I was still working on the case. As far as Don Peters was concerned, it was over for me. He'd implied as much at my bedside and I'd said nothing to disillusion him. He was hardly likely to check. After all he had six hundred phone calls to keep him occupied. Whereas I had a clear mind and an ache that only one thing would cure. I took my omelette to bed with the rest of the champagne and indulged my madness.

Like all good fantasies he was never far away. Page two of the *Guardian* showed his picture. Mr Nobody. I wondered if he was distressed at how badly he'd been reproduced. The *Independent* had a box entry with a further story on page four. I was on my way to find it when I came across the other little newsworthy tale.

I wouldn't have noticed it but for the words 'animal rights' in the third line. They pulled me like a magnet. The headline read HUNT DOGS IN DEATH MYSTERY. Apparently it had happened just a few days ago. The hounds of the Otley Hunt in Suffolk had been due out last Sunday for their weekly search and destroy mission, but when the huntsman had gone to the kennels he had found three of the beagles dead. Initially there had been fears of animal rights poisoning, but according to the local vet all three animals had died from natural causes. They were still awaiting the post-mortem results, but they seemed to have suffered some kind of heart failure. Strange but true. Three heart attacks? Maybe it wasn't so innocent after all. Maybe the Animal Liberation Front had come in the night and scared them to death with pictures of beagle experiments. Pity the local vet. He must have had his work cut out for him. I remembered the Framlingham man, with the farm dog wrapped tenderly in his blanket. And Greg, the farmer, so solicitous for his animal's well-being. And there was something about the scene that lodged in my mind. Something. But what? I was pouring the last of the champagne into my glass when the phone rang. The bed got its own libation as a result. It was Frank. Just checking.

'So how much did it scare you?'

'What?'

'The phone ringing.'

'Er . . . Four out of ten.'

'You OK?'

'Too many men asking the same questions, Frank. I'm fine. A little drunk.'

'That you are. Does this mean Nick isn't there?'

'No. He's gone home.'

'I see. Is that all right?'

'Yes . . . No,' I said. 'Next question.'

'I rang to see how you were and to give you some news.'

'Yeah?'

'Let's do the welfare bit first, OK? A job has come through that's going to take me out of town till Friday afternoon. I didn't want to leave without checking you'd be OK.'

Who loves ya, baby? 'Thanks. I'm fine. Really. I'm sitting in bed with the newspaper and a half – no, fully empty bottle of champagne. Still in the happy-to-be-alive stage, I think.'

There was a pause. 'You don't sound great, but I'm going to believe you. Right. They got the results of Shepherd's post-mortem back.'

'And?'

'The substance he used to kill himself was Malkarin, a specialized form of animal poison. The kind that they use in laboratories once the experiments are over.'

Ooof. 'What do they think?'

'The money's on poetic suicide.'

'How about poetic murder?'

'Animal rights finishing off what they began, you mean? Nice idea, but too melodramatic for the boys and absolutely nothing to back it up. No forced entry, no sign of a struggle. Also this stuff was traceable. It could only be got from Vandamed laboratories.'

I saw him again, that haggard face, brought down by suffering. So Tom Shepherd had died like an animal, doing to himself what he must have done to a hundred rats and mice. It gave such an awful, blasted symmetry to it all. 'I see.'

'Also the inquest verdict on Mattie Shepherd has come in.'

Ah, I had forgotten. The date had been set for a while. I should have been there, would have been if I could . . . Well, they had my evidence, anyway. My face would only have upset the coroner. 'Don't tell me. Another suicide verdict.'

'Hannah, I strongly advise you to stop drinking. Either that or don't take the sleeping pills. They never worked for me, anyway. What I'm trying to tell you is the remains have been released and there's a funeral service for her tomorrow at a chapel of rest in Finchley. I've got the address. I thought you might like to go.'

I was away from the phone scrabbling for a pen, so I only got back in time for the last bit. '. . . the ignition.'

'Sorry?'

'How long have you been gone?'

'Long enough. Tell me again.'

He sighed. 'I'll tell you, but it doesn't make a lot of sense. Forensics' final report on the car came through last Friday, in time for the inquest. As far as it's possible for them to tell, the bomb was definitely set to be triggered by the ignition.'

'What?'

'You heard. Which means either it went wrong, or –'

Or fourteen-year-old little Mattie had been going somewhere, after all. So how come Daddy hadn't told me that she knew what to do with a car key? No doubt he didn't want to have to think about where she might be going with his precious papers. I saw her standing in front of me, that earnest look on her face. '*Where would I run to? Anyway, I'm fourteen, remember. I don't even know how to drive.*' Well, well. And I had so much wanted her to be telling me

157

the truth. Maybe that had been the problem. I gave it some thought. And I felt a little better. After all, in the end what are lies but the stuff that plots are made of?

CHAPTER SEVENTEEN

Here Come Those Tears Again

It was raining, soft spring drizzle like a mist sticking to your coat and frizzing your hair. It turned out to be a crematorium, which seemed in bad taste to me given the way she died, but then I wasn't her parents. Parent. My God. I'd been so busy with my own pain, I hadn't had a chance to feel anyone else's. Christine Shepherd, a woman who left her family only to find that her family had left her. I thought of Veronica's slim, capable hands. Good for pleasure. Let's hope they were as good for pain.

I was late. I had trouble finding the right clothes. Then I had trouble finding the right road. The service had already begun. Frank had warned me it would be a private affair. But he had slipped the wink to the boys and I got in through the main gate without any trouble. Presumably he hadn't known about the private security firm inside. There were two guards at the chapel door. And I wasn't on either of their lists. Of course my looks didn't help. Well, would you want a face like mine in a chapel of rest? I didn't push it. They would be finished soon enough and whatever I had to say to Mattie could be said out in the rain, without the help of some professional preacher who had only met her through a set of newspaper cuttings.

The service had been arranged at short notice, which presumably accounted for the modest display of flowers outside. There was a simple wreath of chrysanthemums and white gardenias with a card from Christine. I chose not to read it. There were a couple of bouquets from people who sounded like distant relatives and an enormous great cross of flowers from Vandamed. And to the side a small, less ostentatious display of roses. I think it was that that drew me to the card. Well, roses and I would always have a very special relationship. The message read: 'To you both. James H.'

James H? The writing on the card would be that of the florists, of course. But the message? Some cheapskate relative mourning two corpses with one bouquet, or more than that? If I knew Detective Inspector Peters he'd have somebody out here before long just to match up the cards to the people. Simple detective work. First come, first served. I turned my back on the two security guards and slipped the card into my pocket.

It was raining harder by the time the chapel doors opened. The organ Muzak announced the procession. I stood to one side and watched them filter out. Christine was one of the first. She walked slowly, helping a much older woman on her arm. The woman was crying heavily. Mattie's grandmother? But on whose side? Maybe I didn't need to ask. After them came a middle-aged couple and a younger woman pushing a man in a wheelchair. Then Veronica, on her own, in a stunning black suit. And finally a small clutch of smart men. All-purpose executives – apart from one. The boss. Marion Ellroy.

They stood for a moment in the rain, not quite willing to acknowledge that it was all over. I gathered my courage in both hands and approached. The first public outing for me and my new look.

'Mrs Shepherd?' Both Christine and the older woman turned together. The old lady stared at me in pure horror. Christine's reaction wasn't much better. But then her defences were down.

'I – it's Hannah Wolfe. You remember me? I –'

'My God, what happened to you?'

'Er . . . Someone tried to steal my handbag. Listen, I wanted to say how sorry I was. I mean about your husband . . .'

'The car's here. We have to go now, Christine. Your

160

mother needs to get back.' Veronica, polite but insistent, intercepting in the nicest possible way. 'You'll have to excuse us, Miss Wolfe. There are family duties to attend to.' Which was ironic, considering how difficult it was going to be for her to become one of the family. Once again I admired her courage as much as her poise. I also admired the way she didn't stare at me.

The family group passed on towards the doors of an extremely large black limousine. I watched them go.

'It seems you didn't give it up without a fight.'

I turned to see the man no doubt responsible for all the elegant expense and security. Not to mention my hospital bed. He looked good in black. It endowed him with a kind of *gravitas*. 'What?'

'Your handbag.' He was looking me straight in the face and it didn't seem to give him any trouble. I appreciated the lack of pity. 'I was hoping you might come. From what I hear you're a very plucky young woman.'

To be honest I didn't quite hear whether he said plucky or lucky. It warranted the same answer, anyway. 'I had good doctors. Thank you.'

'You already did. Have the police found him yet?'

'Him?'

He smiled slightly. 'I don't know you very well, Miss Wolfe, but I can't imagine you'd have let a woman do that to you.' Very funny. I gave him what passed for a smile these days, knowing full well that my upper lip made it more like a sneer. 'I'm sorry. I didn't mean to offend.'

'You didn't. It's just my face.'

By now a flunkey had spotted him and was running over, carrying a huge black umbrella to shield his master from the acid rain, but before he reached us Ellroy waved him away and we walked on together, getting wet in perfect equality. When we got to the bank of flowers, he stopped for a moment and seemed genuinely moved by the sight of them. Or maybe it was just the cost of the Vandamed display. I stood to one side and waited. He took my arm for the remainder of the walk, steering me ever so gently towards his car. But when we got there he let me go. 'Can I offer you a lift, Hannah? I feel sure we have things to talk about.'

I shook my head.

'Is that no to the lift, or no to the conversation?'

'Both,' I said softly.

He sighed. 'It wasn't a bribe, you know.' And I got the impression that I was proving something of a trial to him, a man used as he was to getting his own way.

'I know that.'

'Tom was a good friend as well as an employee. I'm going to miss him a lot. The police tell me you saw him the day he died.'

I nodded.

'How was he?'

'Depressed.'

'I wondered if he said anything . . . I mean something that took you back to Suffolk for some reason. Maybe something about Malcolm Barringer, although I don't see how they ever would have known each other . . .'

'No,' I said. 'He didn't say anything at all.'

He shook his head. 'Jesus, I'd like to get my hands on those bastards.'

'Yes. So would I.'

He looked at me, then put out his hand. 'The offer still stands, you know.'

'If I was still working, I'd take it,' I said. 'But I'm afraid I've had enough.'

He nodded. 'I know how you feel. Well' – I took his hand and shook it firmly, one professional to another – 'good luck to you, Hannah Wolfe.'

I stood and watched him walk away – the best meal ticket I would ever have.

When I got back to my car, the family entourage had already left. Luckily I was a woman with 'intelligence'. I drove into London slowly. By the time I got to Sutherland Avenue it had stopped raining. I parked across the street from the limos and sat and waited. It wouldn't have been my choice for a wake. But then she could hardly have taken them back to Veronica's flat, and this had been Mattie's home. Presumably it could be hers again now, though I couldn't imagine she'd want it.

They started to leave at around 4.00. The man in the wheelchair took the longest. I gave them ten minutes alone, then went up and knocked. Veronica put the chain on before opening the door. The last time I had been here he had done the same.

'She's had enough for one day. Whatever this is it can wait till another time.'

'Except every time I wait, something worse happens,' I said. 'To me as well as other people. I don't want to talk to her. I just need to see his study.'

It's what's called the foot-in-the-door technique. I'd like to tell you I knew what I was doing, but truth is better than fiction so I'll admit to a certain level of improvisation. Miss Marple would have called it intuition. I'm more a Freud girl myself. Whatever it was, it got me inside the house.

I had a clear memory of that room from ten days before: carpet rumpled, cabinets exploding with files and documents, and Mattie standing by the phone with that sheaf of papers in her hand. Things had changed. The place was very, very tidy now. And the cabinets were locked. There was a selection of keys in the top drawer of the desk. It didn't take long to find the right one. Given how little was revealed, there didn't seem much point in having locked them in the first place. Where were all the files? Someone had done a big clear-out. I went through the little there was. Being an arts and languages graduate put me at a distinct disadvantage, but even I can tell the difference between cancer cells and agricultural feed. And there was nothing about pigs.

I was still looking when I heard her in the doorway. I turned, guilty without cause. Unlike Mattie.

'Find anything?' Veronica had changed into a pair of summer trousers and a white T-shirt. Lovely. I wondered how often men got the wrong idea. I shook my head. 'How is she?'

'Asleep.' She looked around. 'Tidy, isn't it? The police said it's not uncommon. For a man to put his affairs in order. I say he might at least have left her a note.' She ran her hand over the oak desk surface, spotless. After death comes the housekeeper. 'I don't like this room,' she murmured. 'It smells of secrets.'

What had Mattie said about Christine using this phone for her private calls? Like mother, like daughter. I heard again Mattie's voice as I came in on her that night. '*Listen I'm not stupid . . . I know what I'm looking for. And I'm telling you . . .*' Telling me what, Mattie? If I stood here for long enough in the silence, would you tell me again?

'Yes,' I said to Veronica, 'I know what you mean.'

She shot me a glance. 'Were you looking for anything in particular?'

I hesitated. 'No.'

She smiled, as if she understood the lie. 'You know, I didn't expect it to end like this. I only met him twice. But I can't say he seemed like the suicide type. Too angry, too stubborn. Too sure of himself to admit making mistakes. I never thought he'd be this vulnerable.'

Me neither. But I didn't want to talk about it. 'What will you do now?'

'When everything's sorted out, we'll go away. I have friends in Australia. A lot of people would like to see us fail. But for Mattie's sake we're going to try and make a go of it.'

Yeah. A little optimism at last. Just what this story needs. 'What about this place?'

She smiled. 'Oh, this place is taken care of. Vandamed

has agreed to buy it. Above market value. And they're paying his pension in full. With a little golden handshake on the side.' She paused. 'Suicides don't qualify for life insurance, apparently.' Some time soon I must sit down and add up just what all of this had cost them. 'Model employers, eh?' she said in a bitter echo of before.

We went downstairs together. On the landing a door opened. The sleep had left Christine Shepherd looking pale and rather lovely. As if all the grief had finally washed her clean. Behind her I recognized the landscape of Mattie's bedroom. Talking to the dead about the future. Australia, I thought. New country, new life. Who says there's no such thing as rebirth? But no children. I wondered how they felt about that one. Yet another question I didn't feel I had the right to ask.

'Did you find what you were looking for?'

'I think I found what I expected. Mrs Shepherd, did you, Mattie or your husband know anyone by the name of James?

She frowned. 'James? No. I don't think so.'

'What about in Suffolk? Was there anyone at work he was particularly close to? Anyone he might have talked to?'

She thought about it. 'There was a man on the experimental farms. A vet. He got ill before we came to London. I think he took early retirement. But his name wasn't James. At least, I don't think it was.'

And sometimes what you get is better than what you hope for. There was just one more detail. I didn't like to bring it up really, in this atmosphere of healing. But I needed to know and she was the only one who could tell me. The problem with the ignition switch. She told me what I expected to hear.

'Well, the fact was she couldn't. I mean not really. Tom had taught her the basics on the country roads but she'd never really driven in traffic. I don't think she could.'

But being Mattie, of course, she'd give it a go anyway.

Just as loverboy had known she would. It all seemed so obvious now.

Veronica saw me out. I wished her luck. She was going to need it. I wanted to tell her how brave I thought she was. And how capable. But it didn't seem right, being so personal. She did it for me. 'You should try arnica.'

'What?'

'For the bruising.'

'Yeah. You got anything that'll help the pride?'

She smiled. 'Who was it? Do you know?'

'A man.' I paused. 'Bastards, aren't they?'

She gave a little shrug. 'Depends how close to them you get. I hope you get a chance to slug him back.'

'You got any advice?'

She grinned. 'Go for the balls. I've always thought they'd be better without them.'

So now I had a theory. Well, to be honest I'd had it for a while, but it was still so young and weak that it could have expired at any time. Given how much grief there's already been in this story, I hope you'll understand if I keep it to myself for a bit longer.

Back home I made a few phone calls. The florists who'd supplied the roses were as helpful as helpful could be. But then I was a bereaved wife wanting to thank all the donors and too distraught to remember all my husband's friends. They said they'd call me back. It was 5.15. I also needed to contact the local registrar's office for Framlingham to check on a small country death, but I didn't want to clog up the telephone lines, just in case.

The phone rang five minutes later. I jumped on it. Not what I was waiting for, but as good as. Now the story was moving again, everybody but everybody, it seemed, wanted to get in on the act. It was Ben Maringo. The man with the rabbit, the baby and the prison record. And he knew a man who knew a man who had something to tell me.

'They could always call. I mean I don't think my line is being tapped.'

'I'm just passing on a message, all right. If you want to talk to them that's where you have to go.'

'OK. Give it to me again.'

I wrote the address down. It was fifth-lamp-post-on-the-right stuff. Not at all the kind of place where innocent people go to meet. Especially at night.

'What's wrong with the daylight?'

'I told you –'

'Yeah, yeah, I know. You're only the messenger. Tell them I'll be there. But that if anybody tries to beat me up I'm going to be very pissed off indeed.'

'What?'

He didn't understand. But then I didn't think he would. Still, a girl should at least pretend to learn from experience. I dialled Frank's number. The answering machine connected.

'Hi, Frank. Thought you'd like to know. It's Wednesday evening and I've been invited to a dark place to meet some animal rights activists.' And I gave him the address.

CHAPTER EIGHTEEN

With a Little Help from My Friends

I parked my car as near as I could get. In daylight it would have been no problem. In daylight you could almost have seen the Holloway Road from the playground, and if you were in trouble, your voice would be heard in the council flats a hundred yards behind. At night they'd still hear you but choose to believe they hadn't. The place was darker than I had anticipated, mostly because the two street lamps provided by the council had been hit by delinquents. Mind you, how dark does it really get in London? Not like a country lane. Not like that at all.

The gate was locked. I jumped over the fence. On the right my torch lit up a sandpit with a metal climbing frame arching over it and a small, wide slide. On the left was a long rocking horse, the sort that hasn't changed design since the 50s. I looked at my watch. 1.25 a.m.

You think I'm stupid, right? Out at night without even a kung fu lesson between me and my last débâcle. Well, if it's any consolation I did have something nasty in my pocket. But I was banking on not having to use it: since from where I was standing now one animal rights activist was no longer the same as another. Though such was the growing nature of my obsession that deep down I was almost sorry it wasn't going to be him. Dark places, dark thoughts. If you don't let them in, they just scare you more by rattling the window panes. Behind me a swing creaked.

'Hello.'

I turned swiftly. Maringo was sitting on a roundabout holding on to the bar like an overgrown child. I really hadn't seen him. But then he must have had a lot of practice walking softly in the night. 'Hi. How's the baby?'

'Cutting a tooth.' First sign of a carnivore. But no doubt he'd thought through all that. 'What happened to your face?'

I had hoped the night might help. But even shadows can be uneven. 'I ran into a fist. It was moving at the time. Where are they?'

'Here.' It was a voice in the darkness behind me. Not a good idea in my present state. I started to turn round.

'No,' it shouted.

'He doesn't want you to look at him,' said Maringo quickly. 'In case you recognize him later.'

'Tough,' I said angrily. 'The last time I turned my back on someone I ended up in hospital. If he's got something to say, he can say it to my face or not at all.' And I started to walk away.

'All right,' the voice behind me called. 'But remember, you've never seen me, right?'

I turned and walked towards him. From the darkness emerged a small man with a shock of black hair and a bomber jacket. He was right. I had never seen him. Thank God. 'I'm listening.'

I think my face made quite an impression. Certainly when he spoke, his voice was more sulky than belligerent. 'I'm here because Ben Maringo vouched for you. Understood?

'Understood.'

'You don't need to know who I am or where I come from. All you need to know is what I tell you. The ALF had nothing to do with the deaths of Tom or Mattie Shepherd.'

'I know that,' I said, and my little theory gave a cry of joy at being so alive. 'But you did send him threats.'

He let out an angry breath. 'Some, but not all. And only because of what someone sent to us.'

Confessions. The perfect growth hormone for my theory. I couldn't wait. 'So tell me.'

He shot a quick glance at Maringo. My sponsor gave the slightest nod of the head. The bomber jacket took a breath.

'OK. At the end of last November one of our cells started receiving anonymous information through the post. It was about work being done at Vandamed's research centre in London. The cancer unit. It suggested that certain experiments were contravening regulations, and that the head of the unit had authorized them. If it was true, it would have been dynamite. Trouble was we couldn't get into Vandamed to prove it.'

'Tough security, eh?'

'The best. Has been for years.'

Interesting. 'Why didn't you leak it to the press? If it was that juicy?'

'Precisely because we couldn't verify it. The information was hearsay, nothing official. Given our reputation, we can't afford to get it wrong. And we've been taken for a ride before.'

'So you tried a little intimidation instead?'

'Sometimes it works.' He didn't sound too repentant. 'Some of these bastards do have a conscience underneath it all.'

'But not Tom Shepherd.'

'Put it this way. According to our "informant" he didn't exactly have a shining record.'

'You mean AAR? What's illegal about that?'

'We're talking morals here, not law. Unfortunately they're not the same thing in Britain, in case you hadn't noticed.'

Let's hear it for self-righteousness. Good guys, bad guys; I tell you if it wasn't for the deaths I wonder how much there would be to choose between them. 'So tell me about the morals.'

'AAR. Aaargh.' And he rolled it off his tongue like a country yokel. 'It'll probably go down in the science history books as a miracle drug. Except like all "product enhancers", as they like to call them these days, nobody's too keen to talk about what it does to the product. Don't expect you've given a lot of thought to the quality of life of pigs?'

Here we go again. 'You'd be surprised. You're telling me AAR is worse than breeding sows with more teats so they can get shagged out faster producing more and more piglets for the Safeway meat counters? Seems to me whatever happens it's always the women who suffer.'

Behind me I could almost hear Ben Maringo smile. His 'friend' had less of a sense of humour. 'Right. But we're talking a different kind of oppression here. AAR is a drug.'

'So's aspirin,' I said, just because a girl's got to have some fun in her life. 'From what I hear, at least it's better than BST or the stuff the Italians fed to their calves.'

The man snorted. 'So it's a synthetic compound, not a hormone. You try and explain the difference to the pigs. It still goes into their systems. Still makes them bigger faster than they can cope. The only thing that keeps most of them alive until the slaughterhouse is the antibiotics.'

It sounded a little melodramatic, even for a convert. But what did I know? 'What's wrong with them?'

'Infections, weakness, you name it. And stress. Pigs are notoriously nervous animals. Cram 'em together in a dark shed, and apart from starting to eat their own crap, which causes further disease, they can also get violent. So they dope them, too. But since Vandamed not only makes the booster drug but also the antibiotics and tranqs that counteract its effects, they're not complaining. A nice hermetic system, eh? You get the meat, they get the money. And God help the animals.'

'God or you?'

'I told you, we didn't plant any bombs. Even with his record, there are names higher up the list.'

I thought of asking who they were. But it wasn't the moment to push my luck. 'So if it wasn't you, who was it?'

'Someone who wanted us to get the blame. Someone who knew our methods. Knew the kind of people we targeted, and the sort of threats we make. Four of the warnings that Shepherd got were from us. I could tell you exactly what

they said. But according to the police there were six altogether, and I can guarantee you that only the last two were
specific death threats. Those came from someone else. The
same people who strapped the fire bomb under the petrol
tank. Also something we'd never have done.'

'If you're innocent, why didn't you go to the police? Tell
them what you've just told me?'

'Didn't you just hear what I said? These guys knew what
they were doing. We didn't go to the police because they
wouldn't have believed us. And because the people who
didn't kill Mattie Shepherd have done other things. And to
deny one, we might find ourselves having to admit to
others. The best we could do for ourselves is to keep quiet.
Whoever framed us knew that, too.'

He was right, of course. Given the boys' position on
animal rights, the departure from style of the death threats
and the way the car bomb was placed were niceties they
might find it all too easy to overlook. It wouldn't have been
the first time. As stitch-ups go the needlework was very
fine. But then it would have to be.

'So what would it take for someone to know enough to
duplicate your methods that precisely?'

'It's not an insider, if that's what you mean. That boy in
the police photographs. He's not one of ours.'

I snorted. 'I wouldn't go on the photograph. His own
mother wouldn't recognize him.'

'No. But we would. I've told you. He's been checked. He
didn't come from us.'

Very IRA. 'So where did he come from?'

'Over the years we've made a lot of enemies,' he said,
more with resignation than with bitterness. 'Take your
pick.' I already had. Maybe he had too. We kept our
thoughts to ourselves. 'OK,' he said abruptly. 'I've said
what I came to say. We don't owe you anything now,
Maringo, right? I'll see you around.'

And we both watched him disappear into the darkness.

There was a long pause with just the low rumble of late-night traffic on the Holloway Road in the distance. I suppose I was waiting for the sound of a car engine to start up, to prove he had really gone. But then maybe some people are green all over. I wondered if they used unleaded petrol in their fire bombs. Terrorists on bicycles. It just seemed wrong somehow. But then how about killers on motor-bikes?

I turned to Maringo. 'Thanks.'

He nodded. 'Sounded like you were there already.'

'Not really.'

'But you've stopped eating pork?'

I thought about it. He was right, I had. 'Yeah. But I don't know if it's for the right reasons.'

Now it was over I felt altogether a little less sure of myself. As I walked to the roundabout my knees had a definite wobble. I sat down. I pushed my foot along the ground and we started to move, making a slow stately circle in the dark. The world in the round. Quite a different perspective.

'Does that mean you don't know who did it?'

'The who I think I've got. Problem is, it doesn't make a lot of sense without the why.'

'Maybe I can help. I've been doing a little research of my own into Tom Shepherd's career. And his miracle drug.' He smiled. 'Well, academic training dies hard. I thought you might like to know that when it was tested in its original form for the treatment of asthma, there was a tiny but significant side-effect. In the clinical trials the drug was found to have some effect on the heart.'

'What do you mean "some effect"?'

'I mean a certain tiny percentage of people – particularly those with any history of angina – complained of pains, palpitations, that kind of thing.'

Palpitations, eh? Just at that moment I was having a few myself. 'And what would that mean when it was translated into AAR?'

173

'Something or nothing. Hard to tell. Depends on too many things. The dosage, how it was administered, the possible combination with other medications, antibiotics and the like. There're so many permutations. That's why these drugs take so long to test properly. But I suppose it's possible that under certain conditions the pigs would have suffered heart problems too. There's a particular breed of pigs – Peitrains they're called – who are susceptible to heart trouble anyway. They might have seen an increase there. Or it might have been more widespread. I have heard for instance that just over a year ago Vandamed made some adjustments to the consistency of the drug feed. It was pretty late in the day for such changes. I mean they'd taken their time developing it and if they wanted to make a killing they'd have to move fast to get maximum profits before their patent ran out. Anyway, what they did was to reduce the dust intake in the feed. So less of the drug could get in through the respiratory system. It may or may not have been connected. Either way, of course, as long as it was just the pigs, who gives a damn? . . . I mean we're talking dumb animals here, remember?'

Ben Maringo, may your child grow tall and strong like a tree, bringing honour to his father's house and vegetarianism unto the world. I had a few more questions. One was about farm drug trials, and what happened to the pigs after the trials were over. I already knew most of the answers.

I got back at 2.45 a.m. I was too excited to go to bed. But that was OK. I had waited a long time to feel this way and there was a lot to do before morning. Plots can be complicated things when you come at them backwards. I sat at the kitchen table and worked till dawn, then lay down and closed my eyes. I didn't think I'd sleep. But I was mistaken.

The phone woke me at 9.50. It was the Finchley florists. She gave me the name of a shop in Golders Green. They had phoned through the order yesterday morning. It had been quite a rush job, apparently. But that was all she could tell me. Golders Green, eh? Not exactly the most exotic place to wind a story back to. But everyone has to retire somewhere. I made other phone calls to a couple of Suffolk vets and that registrar in Framlingham I hadn't been able to contact earlier. Even more pleased with myself, I then set off, stopping at an instant printer's on the way. How instant, of course, depends on cost and quality. I had to wait. But if a job's worth doing it's worth doing well, that's what Frank always says, and he's a man who knows more than most about fake IDs.

Golders Green was easy. Getting James H's address proved a little trickier. Under usual circumstances I could have depended on my charm to get me through. But now that work depended on it I had had to go back to the mirror. I used the one in the bathroom. It had been the easiest to turn around again. What I had seen was not encouraging. There had been some progress in the lip and the left cheek, but the eye was still sliced up and vicious. In my imagination I had been healing faster. But when it came to facing the rest of the world, looking like something the Kray brothers had just finished with was probably not the best way to encourage strangers to open up to me.

Still, I had the drive to think of something else. As stories go, it was one of my better ones. It was so tragic I was even a little ashamed of it: the surviving widow of a car crash that had sent me through the windscreen and my husband even farther into the blue yonder. Hence the message on the roses. 'To you both.' All our friends had known about it, though not all of them had been able to make it to the funeral. And try as I might, I just couldn't put a face (and therefore an address for my thank-you card) to the name of James H.

Neither could the assistant in the shop. But then for a while she was looking in the wrong column. Because, as it turned out, the man who'd sent the flowers had gone under

175

a different name altogether. I could have told her that, but it seemed better to let her work it out for herself.

She eventually traced him from the Barclaycard details, although when she realized the discrepancy she got just a little flustered. A case of some stories being so tall they're in danger of falling over. But by then she had the order book in front of her. And such is my profession that although I may not have fully mastered the art of self-defence, I have become awfully good at reading upside down. Not to mention a certain talent with pseudonyms.

'Of course. Maurice Clapton.' I smiled. 'Beamish Drive, isn't it?'

She nodded. 'Yes.'

'That explains it. He's a vet, you see. And my husband was a pig farmer. He used to call Maurice James. You know, after Herriot.'

If the penny dropped, I certainly didn't hear it hit the ground. No matter. In the end I think she was glad it took so little to make an injured, bereaved woman happy. I got back to the car and wrote the address down. 'Maurice Clapton, 23 Beamish Drive, NW10. Except when I looked it up in the A–Z, it wasn't in Golders Green at all, but about three pages north-west. All in all it had been a pretty circuitous method of ordering flowers. But then I suppose he had to take some precautions. According to the map I had a drive of about half an hour. Of course I could have saved myself a lot of time and trouble and gone through the Vandamed personnel department. Or even the local Framlingham vet. But you get possessive this near the end of a story, and I needed my visit to be a surprise.

Despite its unpromising name, Beamish Drive turned out to be a smart piece of real estate, although I've never understood why people should want to pay so much money to live somewhere that's neither the city nor the country. There were lots of big detached houses with well-kept front gardens. The Claptons' was more adventurous than most –

176

a riot of colour and fancy brick work, squares of flower beds full of tulips and late daffs and even the odd clump of wild bluebells. Someone had spent a lot of time on it. She was still spending it.

Mrs Clapton was probably in her early fifties, but well preserved. She had black hair, which may or may not have been aided by science, cut in a neat shingle and one of those complexions that doesn't crumble to dust after the menopause. She looked homely and efficient. And quite content watching her garden grow.

I took my briefcase with me and walked smartly in through the garden gate. 'Lovely garden. You've done wonders.' She looked up at me and her face softened with pity, but being British she assumed she hadn't let it show. 'This must be what – only your second spring? You must have really green fingers.'

Her pleasure eclipsed her curiosity just for a moment. 'Yes, well, they had let it go to seed rather. We put new soil in and I feed it regularly. Er ... I'm sorry, do I –'

'Gillian Porter. Vandamed personnel.' I stuck out my hand in that confident manner born of two-hundred-pounds-a-day training courses. 'We haven't met. But I know all about you and your husband. Er ... you must excuse my face. I was in a car accident recently. Lucky I'm here at all.'

'Oh, you poor thing. But you mustn't worry. I hardly noticed it.'

'Thank you. I'm here to see Mr Clapton, really. Is he around?'

'Yes, he's in the house, reading.'

'Good. I tried to call but there's a fault at the exchange, and as I was passing near this way anyway ... Well ... We've started up a new pension leisure scheme, and I thought you'd both like to hear about it. There's an opening offer of a Mediterranean cruise. Special company rates. Limited places. Mr Ellroy was keen that you and Mr Clapton should have first refusal.'

'Oh, I say, that sounds wonderful.'

'How is he, Mrs Clapton?' I said, dropping my voice to the concerned, confidential level.

She shook her head and the halo of efficient optimism shed a little glitter. 'Well, you know. Better than he was. But still not his old self. I think it's affected his confidence as much as his health.'

'I understand. Well, if I could just check a few details with you before we go in, that way I won't have to bother him.' I smiled. So did she. We were getting on famously. But then I was having such a good day I just wanted to share it with everybody.

I pulled out my note pad and jotted everything down. And amid the facts it came so naturally, the odd sizzling little snippet of information. Well, you could see she was a bit lonely really, just her and the garden. They hadn't been here long enough to make friends. Only fifteen months since the heart attack, and although, as she said, he was better physically, in other ways he was a changed man, keeping himself to himself. Still, they couldn't grumble. Vandamed had been more than generous. And continued to be so. The pension was really most extraordinary. Above and beyond . . . and very much appreciated. Of course, it had been as much of a shock to the company as to him. Maurice had been such a healthy man. There had been some heart trouble in the family, but way back and he had always been careful. Liked his food, but watched his diet and had done a fair amount of exercise. Came with the job, really. Being a company vet meant you were always on the move. Especially since the big pig trials started. He'd been involved right from the beginning, overseeing the feed distribution, checking the animals, making sure they were healthy. Tom Shepherd's right hand man, really. An important job. Quite stressful. Maybe that had been part of the problem.

Of course, the terrible news about Mattie Shepherd and now about Tom hadn't done his recovery any good. They had been good friends till Shepherd had been promoted to London, just after Maurice's heart attack. They had worked closely together on the trials and got on well. He used to call him James, after Herriot's vet. They would go fishing at weekends. And she had sometimes had the little girl over for tea. Didn't get on so well with the mother. Seemed a bit of an outsider, really. Sweet child though, if a little lonely. They had both missed her since they'd moved.

'But Dr Shepherd kept in touch, didn't he?'

'Oh, yes, yes. He visited Maurice last autumn – October I think it was. Then . . .' She paused. Well, so would I in her shoes.

'What about since his daughter's death? I know he found it difficult to talk to other people. We were quite concerned about him actually, rather hoped he might get in touch with Mr Clapton, just to get it off his chest a bit. Old friends, that kind of thing . . .'

'Yes, Well, yes, he did ring. Last week, I believe.'

'I see. Do you remember when?'

'No, well, I can't remember the exact day.' Interesting, since she clearly could. 'I mean I answered the phone, but he didn't want to talk to me. Maurice said he was awfully depressed. He was quite worried about him. I believed he –'

'Myra?' The front windows had been open and voices do carry in the spring air. 'Myra? Who are you chattering to out there?'

Women caught gossiping in the sunshine. And why not? We exchanged a small conspiratorial smile. And then she led me inside.

CHAPTER NINETEEN

Positively 4th Street

Given its size the house felt surprisingly poky inside. The back windows of the lounge where Maurice was sitting reading the newspapers looked out on to a rolling garden. More lawn, fewer flowers this time, ringed by fruit trees, but still a lot of work for just one gardener. And inside the room – well, I could waste your time with a lot of description, but if you're anything like me, now we're on the move you'll be impatient for substance rather than scene setting. On the other hand Maurice Clapton may be a late arrival but he sure as hell is an important character and it might help you to know what he looks like.

Not happy to see me, that much was clear immediately. And not as gullible as his wife when it came to the Mediterranean cruise story either. But until she could be prevailed upon to get the tea, we both had to keep up some sort of pretence. Luckily I had come prepared. She padded out to the kitchen clutching a sheaf of brochures with promises of home-made jam and scones. It would only take her ten minutes. I had the time, didn't I? Well, every plot needs at least one traditional woman to keep the home fires burning. I thanked her and watched her go. Then turned my attention to him.

He was a little older than her, stocky but not fat. And he had the kind of face that might have been called upon to play Father Christmas at children's parties. Ironic, really. I tried to imagine him and Tom Shepherd sitting in silent companionship by the river-bank waiting for the fish to bite. A friendship built on the carcasses of animals. And later of humans.

We sat staring at each other. Either he already knew

everything about me, in which case I didn't stand a chance, or Vandamed had only told him what he needed to know. From the few trailing threads of the plot I had hold of, my money was on the latter. If he was who I thought he was, it would be important to them to keep him feeling safe and secure. And as far away from the action as possible. I cleared my throat. Come on, Hannah. On with the moustache and dark glasses. It's just another part of the job, pretending to be people you aren't. And in this case the better you do it the more satisfaction you'll get.

I gave him a wry smile. 'I'm sorry for the pretence, Mr Clapton. But I needed a good excuse. Marion Ellroy sent me.' I fished out my card and flashed it at him. He glanced at it: 'Gillian Porter, Security Supervisor, Vandamed'. Looked good. So it should, it had cost enough. 'I used to work with Marion in Texas. He brought me over just after Mattie Shepherd's death.' So my accent wasn't perfect, but a man with his Suffolk drawl probably only had *Dallas* to go on. He also had his mind on other things. Right from the start he was nervous as a kitten. It was a pleasure to see. 'It's just we've . . . er . . . well, we've run into a little trouble with Tom's estate.'

'What kind of trouble?'

'Apparently the police have found some documents. Nothing serious. But they're obviously on the look-out for any possible animal rights tie-in and . . . well, we gather that one of them makes mention of certain problems with the original pig feed.'

'I thought they said that Tom had cleared everything out of his study before he . . . before he died.'

'Yes, well, that's what we believed. But something seems to have got overlooked. It was dated January last year, I gather. A week or so after you went into hospital. Marion thinks it was probably the draft of some kind of memo that never got sent. We haven't seen it yet, but obviously we'd like to know what it might have said, just to be prepared.'

He snorted. 'Well, if it's the feed it'll be about the dust and the dangers of lung ingestion. But I don't understand why Tom should have written it then. I mean he told me he talked to Ellroy about all this the day after he saw me in hospital.'

'Well, they may have got the date wrong. Do you think it might mention you or just the animals?'

'My Lord, I don't know. I suppose it could do. But why should he write it at all? I mean by then it had been sorted out. He said Ellroy had promised to authorize the changes in the feed production immediately. That was the only reason that Tom agreed to leave the project and take the London job.'

Inside my shoes my toes were positively curling up with pleasure. I shrugged. 'You don't think he might have written it for his own protection, a kind of insurance, in case anything came out later?'

Clapton shook his head. 'He would have told me. Or sent me a copy, as he did with the other one.'

Brain orgasm. Even more exciting when you can't show you're having one. I nodded sagely. 'Yeah, I'm sure you're right. In which case we've got nothing to worry about.'

I gave him a big smile. Corporate security regained. He, however, was still worried. In fact he looked positively distraught, not a good sign for a man with his heart condition. But did I care?

'I don't like it,' he said. 'I mean Marion swore to me I wouldn't be bothered again. That now Tom – well, that that was an end to it.'

'And so it is.' I watched his face close down even further. Time for me to change shape. Not as impressive as a morphing video, but a lot cheaper. I stood up and walked to the back windows. 'You're going to have a fine crop of roses this summer, Maurice,' I said in a voice that had never been anywhere near the Mason–Dixon line. 'Just like the ones you sent to Mattie's funeral.' I turned. 'Did you

182

ask for roses specifically or did the florist choose? Actually I'm not sure that Marion Ellroy would have approved of you sending them. Bit of a give-away, really, with that message. It's the sort of thing the police check, you know, even do routine follow-up interviews. But you'll be all right. I took the card off the bouquet. So now it's just you and me who know.'

'I don't understand . . .' But, of course, when he thought about it he began to. His face went a funny colour. 'Who are you?'

I put a hand into my left pocket and handed it across. 'Sorry. Must have given you the wrong one earlier. Name's Hannah Wolfe. I'm investigating Mattie Shepherd's death and her father's part in the AAR cover-up.'

For just a second I thought I was going to lose my primary witness to an act of nature. Or rather nature helped by a little product enhancer. He stood up and put his hand over his heart. 'Get out of here,' he said hoarsely. I shook my head.

From the kitchen Myra shouted out, 'Did you call, Maurice?' I let the silence grow. 'Maurice?'

'It's up to you,' I said quietly at last. 'I don't care who I tell.'

He stared at me. And it was clear from his eyes that he'd been waiting for me in his nightmares. He just hadn't known what shape I would take. 'No,' he said, raising his voice to meet hers. 'No, Myra. It's fine.'

Then he sat down heavily. 'I don't have anything to say.'

'Sure you do,' I said cheerfully. 'I tell you what. I'll make it easy. I'll start, then you pick up where I leave off. OK?'

How much of this do you need to hear? I suppose that depends how far you got without me.

Like all good stories you need the background to understand the action. After I had talked to Maringo, I had dug a little deeper into the patent system of drug manufacture.

183

He'd been right. In Vandamed's case time was running out. The development of AAR had already taken a while, even before Shepherd was brought in on it. He'd got things moving, but then there had been clinical trials and the extended farming ones. Even if it got its expected government approval – which technically could happen any time – it would still only leave them six years as the sole marketers. That was enough, of course. In that time they could get back their costs and start the profits rolling in; profits which, in Marion Ellroy's multinational Utopia, would no doubt help find a cure for cancer and all other major diseases not yet bought up by the drug companies. On the other hand Vandamed wouldn't want to leave it any later. No sir.

So you'll appreciate the importance of the timing when fifteen months ago Maurice Clapton collapsed in his humble cottage and was rushed to hospital with a major heart attack. On its own, of course, a heart attack is just Nature's way of telling a man he's eating too many chips. But in this case there was more to it. For anyone bright and willing enough to look. And, as everyone in this story agrees, Tom Shepherd was that kind of scientist. After his friend's heart attack he started doing a little digging around. And as soon as Clapton came out of intensive care, Shepherd talked to him about what he'd found.

What they discussed was the possibility that the drug in the pigs' feed might somehow be ingested into the lungs of those administering it. By his wife's admission Clapton had been very involved in the practical side of the trials. And according to Maringo's sources the consistency of the feed as it was then produced did give off considerable dust. Easy to breathe in. One of the farmers, a man called Peter Blake, had suffered heart palpitations earlier the year before. Nothing serious, but Shepherd had heard about it, and well, Shepherd was an honourable scientist . . .

So he went to the bosses. Whatever he said obviously put

the fear of failure into them, which was to prove worse than the fear of God. Most likely he would have recommended the cessation of the trials and a return to the drawing board. But, of course, that was something they didn't want to hear. So they reached a compromise. Ellroy agreed to an immediate overhaul of the feed to reduce its dust percentage. And Shepherd ... well, Shepherd allowed himself to be satisfied. In more ways than one. He came out of the meeting with the promise of promotion to head of research, and a little gift for the vet who had helped him along the way – an early retirement package the like of which would make your mouth water (if, that is, you knew about it, which one suspects the rest of the employees did not.) Not exactly being bought off. Just rewards for services given, and silence assured.

So Shepherd went off to London, and Clapton to Beamish Drive. But despite, or maybe because of, the rewards Shepherd was not a happy man. According to his wife this was the time when Dr Jekyll became Mr Hyde, a man obsessed, not able to talk to anyone about anything. Guilt at the small print of his pact with the devil? Or just the exhaustion of trying to do two jobs at the same time, the one he now had and the one he was too worried about to give up completely?

Meanwhile back in the country the dust level had been reduced and the trials were progressing very nicely, thank you. Well, except for the odd little vagary of country living. Over the next eight months Tom Sheperd kept his ear to the ground and by autumn, what with the odd dog keeling over, his scientist's nose was twitching again. Which meant it was time for another chat with his friend and confidant, the vet.

Not bad for someone who isn't even a pretty face, eh? Except from here on out it was all a little bit sketchier . . .

'So what exactly did Shepherd say when he came to see you last October, Mr Clapton?'

The trouble was I had done so much of the talking that he had grown used to his own silence. He shook his head. 'I don't know what you're talking about. I haven't seen Tom Shepherd since he visited me in hospital over a year ago.'

'Oh, come on, Maurice. Don't insult me. I already know he was here.'

'Says who?'

From the kitchen doorway Myra chose this minute to call out with requests for milk and sugar. I let her voice waft between us before gracefully declining either. I smiled at him sweetly. 'It was just a short chat. Gossip, really.'

He scowled. From the bosom of the family. 'He just came for a visit, that's all. A friendly call.'

'So he didn't say anything about Malcolm Jones's farm dog?'

'I don't know what you're talking about.'

'Of course, on paper there was nothing immediately suspicious about that death, was there? I mean I gather she was almost twelve years old and well past her prime. But the same couldn't be said for Edward Brayton's house dog, could it? I mean according to your colleague in Framlingham she was just playing in the yard one moment, dead the next. He was very puzzled about it. Told me that himself. Still, he's only a local vet, isn't he? Doesn't have your depth of knowledge and experience. Yours and Tom Shepherd's.'

I waited. Eventually he looked up at me. And we both knew it was over. I didn't even need to mention the hounds in the Otley Hunt stables. 'It was the dogs that gave it away, wasn't it, Maurice?' He stared at me, then nodded abruptly.

'Except, of course, this time it had nothing to do with the feed.'

'No,' he said almost too quietly for me to hear.

'Because the dogs hadn't eaten the feed. They'd eaten the trial pig meat, hadn't they?'

'Yes.'

'And they weren't the only ones. So had some of the farmers. And so had you.' I saw it in his eyes, but I also needed to hear it from his mouth. 'Hadn't you?'

'Yes,' he said softly.

'I'm interested why you didn't tell Tom Shepherd that back in January.'

He was flustered. But then it wasn't an easy one to answer. 'I . . . I didn't think it was relevant. I mean I wasn't the only one. Lots of us were doing it.'

'Absolutely. You and Peter Blake, to name but two. Of course, officially you shouldn't have touched it. Officially it should either have gone to the dogs or the knacker's yard. But if you had told him then, you might not have qualified for that handsome medical handshake of yours. Not to mention the even more handsome pension.'

'I deserve that money. I've been twenty-five years with the company. And the doctors said I'd been under great stress.'

'Yes, I'm sure you had. And I bet it hasn't let up, either. Must have been a great strain trying to decide whether or not to mention it to the other farmers.'

'As far as I was concerned, the problem was with the feed. The meat was perfectly safe. They'd done the tests.'

'Oh yes, they'd done the tests, but not enough. Or rather not enough to be sure that in some cases, where the drug was used in conjunction with certain antibiotics, the hormones wouldn't pass over into the food chain. Because that's what happened, isn't it? And that was what Tom Shepherd had found out last October when he came to talk to you.'

He sighed. 'More or less, yes.'

'And what did you say?'

'I told him to let it be. Not to rock the boat. I mean all he had was questions. There was no proof, no proof at all. The incidents with the dogs could have been pure coincidence. And even if by some remote chance they weren't, it was because the dogs ate the offal, where the residue build-up would have been much worse. Humans would never be affected to that degree. That was, and still is, my professional opinion as a veterinary surgeon.' Well, he had to try it, really, but it wasn't with much conviction.

I waited. He closed his eyes. 'Do you know how much Vandamed had spent developing AAR to that stage? Upwards of four million pounds. They weren't going to throw it all away because of a couple of freak results. It wasn't as if Tom's own hands were that clean, anyway. If he had gone to them, they would have just reminded him how he got his new job in the first place.'

'You're saying he took your advice and didn't go back to Ellroy?'

'That's right. He didn't.'

Well, it wasn't his first lie and it wouldn't be his last. 'So he kept his suspicions to himself. But just in case, just for his own protection he wrote it all down, didn't he? The whole deal. Wrote it down and sent a copy to you for safe-keeping?' He opened his mouth. 'Don't bother to try and pretend. You've already told me he did.'

He scowled. 'What of it? By that time it was too late anyway. The police said he was already starting to receive those death threats.' He snorted. 'Animal rights. Poor old Tom. Who would have thought it?'

'You know, you're a really bad liar, Maurice.'

'Listen. I know nothing about what happened, you understand. Nothing. I've worked hard all my life. Done the best I can for the animals in my care. I nearly died because of their wonder drug. But in the end I've made it work for me. I'm sorry for Tom and I'm sorry for Mattie, but my grief is my own affair. And I'm not going to let it take away from what's rightfully mine. Mine and Myra's.'

'Even though Shepherd and his daughter are dead?'

'Animal rights, not me.'

Interesting, the power of auto-suggestion. 'And what about

the others? The ones in two or three years' time who buy a leg of pork and end up deader than the pig it came from?'

He shook his head. 'Even if it were possible, which I dispute, thousands of people have heart attacks every year. Most of them are prime candidates. Tom said himself it's almost certainly random. It'll affect less than one pig in a thousand, if that. It probably wouldn't make any difference anyway. They'd need to stuff themselves silly and then some.'

'And what happens when someone finds out?'

'How they're going to do that? Some chap with heart trouble snuffs it. Who's going to think to ask him how many pig's kidneys he's been eating recently? No doctor would make the leap. Unless they already knew.'

'Or unless someone told them.'

'I told you. I nearly died once. I want to stay alive a bit longer.'

'Well, you're going the right way about it. I mean, seeing as you've already outlived the only people who could have prejudiced your happy retirement, I'd say their deaths put you home and dry.'

'Mattie Shepherd's killing had nothing to do with this. It was animal rights. And Tom committed suicide. Injected himself with his own rat poison. Everybody knows that.'

'Yes. But nobody but you knows what he said that afternoon when he called you.' I waited, then pushed. 'However, let me give it a guess. He'd worked it out, hadn't he? Worked out who was really behind his daughter's death. How far did he blame you, I wonder. Not enough, obviously.'

'I don't know what you're talking about,' he said in a voice of a man sleepwalking through lies. 'Tom committed suicide. It was nothing to do with me.'

'Yes. Well, let's just hope the anxiety of continuing to believe that doesn't give you another heart attack.' I stood up. There comes a point when you just don't want to be around someone with so little courage. Especially when you're going to be so much in need of your own.

'It's been an education, Mr Clapton. I can see now why Tom Shepherd kept coming back to you. I mean everybody needs a good friend when they're in trouble. I'm sure you'll do the same for me too, though you should know that according to his secretary Marion Ellroy is at meetings all day in London and not contactable until this evening's reception. I wonder what they can be celebrating? Maybe you'll know when you get your next cheque in the post.'

I picked up my bag and walked to the door. In the kitchen I saw Myra putting the finishing touches to the laden tray. 'Oh, one more thing. Your farmer friend Peter Blake was buried last weekend. A simple ceremony at the local church; nicely done from what I could see. One pig's kidney too many, eh? Don't expect the Vandamed retirement newsletter mentioned that? But then you did say you didn't want to be bothered. No need to worry, though. According to the local registrar's office the death certificate read "natural causes". Well, he'd already had palpitations. And everyone knows how much he liked his food. Tell your wife I'm sorry I don't have time for her scones. Too much cholesterol.'

CHAPTER TWENTY

This Little Piggy Went to Market

I had to get away from the house with its front garden of spring wonder. I drove down the street and parked by a hole in the road left by British Gas. Farther down the pavement a girl was taking a dog for a walk, or possibly the other way round. It was a young labrador full of puppy energy and the smells of life, entranced by every tree and lamppost. She must have been twelve or thirteen, another would-be Mattie. I felt sick. From what I had heard and for what I had done.

I understood now that I could never have saved her. The papers in her hand, the phone call, the car keys, it was all part of a complex, orchestrated dance of death, and I had never even got near the dance floor. But Shepherd's death had been more mine than I had realized. By telling him what I knew about Mattie's animal rights affair and her fingers in his filing cabinet I had lit a fuse which could lead only back to him.

I could see him now in his study, knowing exactly where to look and knowing exactly what it was he wouldn't find. Who else to call but the man with the copy? The only man he felt he could trust. For so long I had thought he must have been calling Vandamed, to warn them that the proof of his secret – whatever it was – had gone. It never occurred to me that they might be the ones who had taken it.

The question is, did it occur to him too? Vandamed's own brand of rat poison. Murder or suicide? Maybe it didn't even matter that much. Poor old Shepherd. If only he'd been able to tell me. Or someone else. They might not have loved each other till death did them part, but she was his wife. She would at least have listened.

Come on, Hannah. No time for pity now. I looked at my watch. It was just before 2.00 p.m. Frank had said he'd be back after lunch. I needed to talk to him so badly, but I didn't have a lot of time to spare. Knowing Maurice's itchy finger with the dial he would already be on the phone now, calling his minders. If he made it sound urgent enough they just might find the boss after all. As for the reception that Ellroy was due to attend that evening, well, it was apparently rather hush-hush. If it was to celebrate what I thought, then it was interesting that Clapton hadn't been invited. Maybe I wasn't the only one to have doubts about his reliability.

I drove back into town and went straight to the office. No one was there. There were four messages on the answering machine. I rolled them back. Two inquiries from bona fide members of the public, one from Frank's wife and one from Hannah. I listened to my own voice telling of an after-dark appointment with animal rights. What a lot had happened since then. It was impossible to tell whether or not Frank had called in and heard it. But if he had, he'd left no message in reply. I sat down at the computer and wrote him a little essay.

It took longer than I expected, but then there was a lot to say. Insurance, really. Just like poor old Tom Shepherd. Making sure those who ought to know, do. Of course, it wasn't without its loose ends, but with luck Frank and I would have those stitched up by the end of the day. I printed it out and saved the file. I called it 'PORKIES'. Because that was basically what it had all been. I put it in an envelope on his desk. On the top I wrote 'FRANK' in big bold letters, and then, 'Read this before you do anything else.' Then I used the fax line as a phone to dial into our answering machine and left a fifth message. It read: 'There's a letter on your desk. But if you get this message later than 3.30 p.m. Thursday, meet me first. From 6.00 on I'll be at the Hortley Hotel outside Framlingham.'

I reckoned it would take me the best part of two hours to

get there. After that I had no real plan at all. I knew enough to know that I shouldn't move without Frank. But I also knew I couldn't leave it too long. Besides, if Vandamed had something to celebrate, it was most definitely the time for us to join in.

The Hortley Hotel was just as I remembered it. But the weather wasn't as good. Already the blossom was ragged, soaked and blown away by wild coast winds. It was just six days since Nick and I had been here, petting under the apple boughs with a future together still a possibility.

Nick. I hadn't given him much thought these last two days. I let him walk into my imagination and take off a few clothes. But the signal was weak, cluttered with the aftermath of another man's violence and my need to pay back my debts. And it went deeper than that. In the end despite all the pig meat I think Nick and I had probably died of natural causes. His post-mortem would no doubt favour a different pathology – one that included my lack of commitment and an unbalanced, obsessional attitude to work. And, of course, he'd be partially right. All I would say in my own defence is that as male problems go it is always more evident in the female. And that I am not unaware of it. As he – and others before him – had said, maybe it was just a question of meeting the right man. Of course I find the idea insulting (when did anyone ever suggest it to Philip Marlowe?), but I don't rule it out altogether. I'll keep you informed on that one. For now the only man I really needed to meet was my boss.

I had alighted on the Hortley Hotel more out of chance than design. Near and yet so far. But it felt like a good choice, a place public enough not to stand out, and private enough to be alone, where the clientele – it was Thursday night so there was little passing trade – was more small-town business then average pig farmer.

Even so, as local memories go, last weekend was recent enough for me still to be something of a celebrity. I went to work on my physiognomy. The hospital nurse had equipped me with some clever make-up (Nick had obviously triggered in her illusions of a romantic recovery), which I hadn't bothered with up until now as it looked too crude, but when applied thickly enough it did something to obscure the bruising. The eye it couldn't touch, but a pair of tinted glasses helped. Of course it didn't exactly render me invisible, but then what woman wants that . . .?

I got there just before 6.00 p.m. I sat nursing a large orange juice and looked out over the gardens down to the pond, waiting for my favourite ex-policeman to arrive.

I was so busy thinking, winding the Ariadne thread of the story back towards the centre of the labyrinth, that I didn't notice him come in. So the first I knew was an unexpectedly soft, lilting voice, really quite attractive, not at all like the carrion call across the dark stream behind the pub.

'Hello, Hannah. Sorry I'm late.' Loverboy at last.

At least he was better-looking than Frank. To have found me he must have been looking hard. That made me happy. How much he would have destroyed following in my footsteps was a little more worrying, but I would no doubt find out soon enough. For now I was too excited by the meeting. He had great physical presence, I grant you that. But then, of course, I had more reason than most to remember it. He was older than the Vandamed mug shot, more mature even than Mattie's furtive snap, which made him not that much younger than me. Full frontal, the face was a little too broad to be really stunning, and the hair was different, dark now and cropped right back, more James Woods than James Dean. But the same man, and one that most women would be tempted to get into bed with. Unless, of course, you knew where he'd been.

He watched me for a second and there was a kind of pride in the look. A man surveying his handiwork. I wanted to ask him if it was better than sex, but didn't want to hear the answer. For Mattie's sake I hope he was equally adroit at both. He put out a hand on the table in front of me. I glanced down. In the fleshy curve between thumb and first finger there was a small but perfectly formed bite-sized welt. I looked up at him. Put your fingers in my mouth next time, buddy, and I'll chew them off. Only now did the fear return. I felt a sick surge of panic in my gut. And something worse near by.

'Are you pleased to see me or is that just a knife in your pocket?' I said, and my voice was OK, a little throaty but firm. Humour. Refreshing the bits that other emotions can't reach.

'Well, you know how it is, Hannah? Some women you just can't leave alone. We're going now, all right. Arm in arm. Just like we can't get enough of each other. If you make any move or say anything at all, I'll stick you with six inches of steel.' And I knew that he meant it.

We got up and walked out, his arm around my waist, the edge of the blade lying like a shard of ice against my side. A man reading a copy of the *Financial Times* glanced up as we passed, then back down at the state of the economy.

The driveway was deserted. His van was parked off the road, an ordinary tradesman's Transit, nothing fancy, a hundred of them to be seen every day pootling down country lanes. The back door was already open. Just as we got there he wrenched me round to face him; lovers' rough stuff, an embrace too tight for breath, let alone a knee up into the groin. For a second I almost thought he was going to kiss me, but once again it was all for show. Where his lips should have been there was a nasty-smelling rag. Over the nose and into oblivion. Chloroform; you'd think a drugs company could manage a little more sophistication . . .

It was dark, but the smells were not Ford Transit kinds. Welcome back to the sweet stench of the piggies. I could hear them near by, a raucous screeching sound, panic and fear in equal measures. I moved and felt rustling straw beneath me. Away in a manger. Nobody ever mentions the pig shit. And the noise. Not just animal but mechanical: somewhere in the background the clanking and turning of machinery. I moved some saliva around and spat it out on the ground. I wiped my lips on the back of my hand, then pulled myself up on the edge of the pen.

At the far end of the shed the pens had been dismantled to be replaced by one big enclosure. Inside pigs huge with hormone flesh were packed so closely together that they could hardly move. They were jostling against some big wooden doors at the end of the pen. I thought about the geography of the building. Outside those doors would be that crude little concrete corridor connecting one shed to the other. At last I understood its function. I also understood the function of the machinery. I wasn't the only one. No wonder the animals were squealing. These big piggies go to market. Vandamed had no doubt stopped giving them the tranquillizers. What had Maringo told me about having to withhold drugs for a certain number of days before slaughter to avoid cross-over? Bit of a joke really, considering what some of them would be carrying around in their kidneys. The sight of them made me feel sick. Or maybe it was the smell. Or the remains of the chloroform. I turned and slid down on to the floor again, propping myself up against the side of the pen. Better this way round. Apart from the view.

There, leaning over the opposite rail, watching his captive wild life was the managing director of Vandamed International, British Division. He looked surprisingly at ease in his suit amid all the shit and filth. I've had enough of this, I thought, being put to sleep by thugs and waking up in strange places with suave men watching over me.

'How you feeling?' he said raising his voice over the screeching.

'Better than the pigs.'

He glanced at them, then back at me. 'I suppose it doesn't help. Knowing they're part of history.'

Time for the civilized conversation. Thank God for a man who'd read the books. 'You got the go-ahead, then?'

'Two days ago. Successful final trials. Now full-scale production.'

'Shame the architect didn't live to see his house built.'

'It is indeed. We could have made it a grander celebration. As it is, without Tom – well, it's just a token effort. A couple of managers from the meat industry, some journalists –'

'And a few suckling pigs,' I said, as the sound of their terror welled up all around us.

He shrugged. 'All humanely dispatched according to the rule book, I assure you. You know, this is a big moment for us, Hannah. By the end of next year we should be in a position to start feeding some of the profits back into the community. We're planning on creating a Shepherd research fund. It'll be a lot of money.'

'What will it research? Unexplained heart attacks among the nation's pig-eaters?'

He shook his head. 'Shame. I thought you might pretend you didn't know.'

'How could I do that when Maurice Clapton's already been on the phone to you. I assume he got through?' He didn't say anything for a bit. In fact he looked quite troubled. Or as troubled as a man can look when facing a future of promotion and profit. 'Such a corporate-spirited chap, eh? Sending you the only copy of Shepherd's report. Which just left the problem of the original. I must say it was a great plan, Ellroy. You target Shepherd by sending incriminating evidence to animal rights, then have Mattie keep up the flow. And using your "student/infilitrator" to recruit her was a masterstroke. Sex and politics. Irresistible to a young girl. Shame she couldn't find the one thing you were looking for. Not that it mattered that much. I mean when Shepherd threatened to cause trouble, all you had to do was to send a few death threats of your own, find the right time and place, and boom, Tom becomes a martyr to science, Mattie confesses, and the police go on a wild goose chase around school gardens and student campuses, with all roads leading back to animal rights. Nobody's bothering much about secret reports. What were you going to do? Offer to help the police go through his papers to check for industrially sensitive material? Why not? After all, you were the good guys, weren't you?

'As I say, great plan. You weren't to know that Shepherd would screw it up by spending the night in the lab and sending someone else to bring Mattie to London. And of course, she didn't know anything about it. For her it was business as usual. Back in the house and up to Daddy's study again, on the look-out for something tasty to take back to loverboy. Only this time she looked in the right place. For the record it was under the carpet. Well, where else would you put your dirty work? Trouble is, she was bright enough to realize what it was she'd found. To know that this time she had dynamite of a different kind – enough to blow Vandamed International clear out of the water and make her young gardener love her for ever.'

He opened his mouth to say something, but decided against it. Across the shed the outside door had opened, a long rasping noise of iron. Standing there, under the light of a single bulb, was the man of my dreams. Come back for more fun. I swallowed hard. What had Frank said about the face he wouldn't see in hell? I wish I could have been so sure. I gave him a big, sassy smile. There are certain times in one's life when you need to make an impression.

'Well, hello there. I thought you'd left me for someone else. Come on down. I'm sure the price is right. It usually is with Vandamed. We were just talking about you. About how you called Mattie the night she died. Remember?'

He was walking towards me. My words were my weapons, sharp little knives slicing through the air, whistling ever closer to that smooth skin. 'I'd like to think that it began as a humanitarian call. To make sure she didn't get into the car by mistake. But I'm afraid when push comes to shove you're not that interested in humanity, are you? So when she told you what she'd found, you had to do some fast thinking. Not something I suspect you have much experience of.' I gave him a quick shy smile. 'I mean now she'd seen it, you could hardly risk her confronting her father, could you? Or anyone else for that matter. So what did you do? Told her what a clever girl she was, and how she'd be even cleverer if she could get the car keys and drive herself to an arranged meeting place so you could share in the find? I have to hand it to you. It was a nice strategy. Appealed to both the rebel and the romantic in her. So she acted her socks off to get herself out of the house with the report tucked away in her back pocket. Very clever. So clever in fact that it's hard to believe it was all your own work. That someone more senior wasn't standing next to you, prompting you on.'

They were near enough to each other even to look a little like father and son. Who knows? Maybe that's how they felt. Not quite.

'I didn't —' Loverboy began.

'Shut up.'

He did as he was told. My, when it came to imposing corporate solidarity, Marion Ellroy was the tops. Even if he didn't look as good. I turned my attention from the pleasures of the flesh to the challenge of the brain.

'Still, you took one hell of a risk, both of you. Killing her and leaving him. I mean if Shepherd had realized . . .'

Ellroy shook his head. 'But he didn't, did he? Or rather not until you told him. You see, Hannah, it doesn't pay to go into these things too deeply. You saw him. He was smashed apart by her death. Too lost to cause us any trouble, for a while at least. Until you told him about Mattie and her animal rights boyfriend who used to work at Vandamed, that is. Then he went looking and found his report had gone.'

I picked up the baton. The trouble with this relay race would be what happened at the finishing line. 'And so Shepherd called the one person he trusted. Clapton, who listened, told him he'd come over right away and then called you. And the rest is animal poison. How did you do it?'

'You don't get it, do you, Hannah? I'm telling you we didn't have to do anything. What you told him made him realize that he was the one really responsible for his daughter's death. After that there was only one way out. It would make you feel better if it had been murder, wouldn't it? But the chain was on the door and there was no sign of a struggle.'

I shook my head stubbornly. 'The Notting Hill rapist used to get in through the back windows. You talked yourself in through the front and just got out that way. And it takes very little to stick a needle in someone's arm. Especially someone who thinks they deserve to die.'

He said nothing, only smiled ever so slightly, as if accepting the compliment. He was right, of course, wanting to believe was not the same as wanting it to be true. But that didn't help me now.

He nodded. 'Well, I think this is the moment when I tell you what a smart girl you are.'

'Woman, please,' I said. 'It's deeply patronizing to be called a girl.'

'Woman, then. You know, Hannah. I'd dearly love to invite you to join us. The offer I'd make you would be embarrassingly generous. But then I know you're not interested in money.'

I stood up. 'On the contrary, I've just been playing hard to get. Waiting for the offer I couldn't refuse.' I smiled and put out my hand. 'I accept.'

We looked at each other. And there was just a hint of hesitation. On his part. 'And what about Frank?' he said softly.

'Frank need never know.'

'How about what he knows already?'

Trick questions. The best preparation for being a private eye is the entrance exams for the Civil Service. A letter on a desk and a message on an answering machine. To have followed me to the Hortley Hotel they must have found one of them. And finding one presumably also meant finding the other. But not necessarily the root as well as the branch. 'Thanks to you, nothing,' I replied. 'A tape message can mean whatever I choose it to mean, assuming, that is, you haven't wiped it already. And you obviously have the letter, which means that Frank doesn't. So I tell him I made a mistake. Thought I'd solved the plot when I hadn't. It's happened enough times before.'

Ellroy looked at me for a while and there was a kind of sadness in the gaze. Then he shook his head. 'Porkies, Hannah,' he said very softly. Ah well, even the villains understand technology now. 'Nice try, though.'

And it was now that I started to feel something which I knew must be fear, but strangely felt more like sleepiness. A desire to stop, just curl up in a corner and let it all go away. I pulled myself back into the land of the living. 'You can't kill me,' I said. 'There's such a thing as too many bodies. Shepherd you might get away with. Me, no one would believe.'

He pursed his lips. 'Hannah, you're obsessed with this case. Everyone knows that. Your boss, your boyfriend, the police, everybody. It's driven you to extremes.

'It drove you to make contacts in the animal rights movement. Through them you managed to track down the man who worked undercover at Vandamed and deceived Mattie into betraying her father. You were so determined to solve it alone that you didn't even give him to the police until you were forced to. So when he contacted you and asked you to go a playground in Holloway at 1 o'clock in the morning, you agreed, although you didn't tell the police. You did tell Frank, though. The message is on his answering machine to prove it. And, believe me, no animals rights activist is going to come forward to contradict him. So the next evening you meet that same activist in the bar of the Hortley Hotel near Vandamed headquarters. Only this time you don't tell Frank – you're right, of course, that last message has gone from the machine. And this time people see you together. Recognize you both. You're very friendly. You leave together arm in arm.

'It's a dangerous strategy, yours. Infiltrating the enemy camp. And in this case you have to sing for your supper. Agree to go on a little underground mission to prove your good faith. Simple enough to do. Break into Vandamed while they're busy celebrating the news of AAR's government bill of health, and put a fire bomb in the abattoir. A fine, poetic comment about the cost of making a profit.

'Unfortunately, as happens with such things, something goes wrong. This time one of you doesn't get out. I'll leave you to work out which one it is.'

Of course, he who can make one plot work, can usually make another. In lieu of a fatal flaw I clutched at straws. Good in the myths, small beer in reality. 'Why just me? I mean why not get rid of us both? Kill the killer and no one ever penetrates the conspiracy. His dead body would tie it all up in a big red bow. Or maybe that's what you had in mind already.' And there was perhaps a touch of unease between them. 'See,' I almost shouted at loverboy, 'you didn't read the small print on the contract.'

He turned to Ellroy and there was, I suppose, just a second when their attention was elsewhere. Not enough for the classic getaway but what else could I do? I was out of the pig pen and on my way to the door. He had to jump over two fences to get to me. I nearly made it. If I hadn't been shaking off the last of the chloroform ... Well, it's academic now. I still think it was better than not trying at all. But I paid a price.

The first instalment was the feel of his hands upon me.

No messing, this time. He held me by the hair, very close. We definitely had something going between us. You could feel it in the air. Even the boss recognized it.

I had moved from the man with the words to the man with the action. It would be a different kind of fun from now on. Ellroy stood and watched us in each other's arms. Just like him, I thought. Better to do things from a distance. And I had a sudden picture of Shepherd's living room, with Ellroy sitting watching as a man with nothing left to lose stuck a needle into his own flesh. Part of his job, really, persuading people to carry out his decisions. 'You all right, Joe?' A name now, although it was much too late. Joe nodded, holding me hard against him. 'I'll see you later, then.'

'Don't do it,' I shouted out at the top of my voice, and I would like to tell you that it was just another part of the act. I would like to tell you that, but I can't. 'Don't let him do it. Please.'

Ellroy stopped and seemed to think about it for a second, but in the scale opposite my life sat a six-year patent and two people's deaths. He shook his head. 'You've got three-quarters of an hour, Joe. Just make sure you get out of the building before then.' And he turned and walked past us without giving me another look.

The door clanged shut behind him. Joe started to drag me towards the pig corral. And as we moved closer, I heard my own voice rising up to join theirs.

CHAPTER TWENTY-ONE

It's the Famous Final Scene

We crossed to the death shed under cover of darkness, the sudden fresh air slapping me around the face. He had no hand free to clamp my mouth, but there was little point in screaming since there was no one to hear.

The next door led to another world as we both knew it would. Inside the machinery was silent now, though the pigs weren't fooled. Behind me I could still hear them squealing out the injustice of it all. He held me close as he propelled me through a forest of hanging carcasses towards the killing floor. Travelling from their deaths towards my own. To keep my brain alert I decided to be interested in what I saw.

It was a large, bare room, the floor criss-crossed by a dozen drains, the ceiling decorated with a long, dancing line of steel hooks suspended like giant *S*'s from a conveyor belt that snaked its way round and out through heavy plastic doors towards ... well, I would find out soon enough. I went back to the hooks, the stuff of a thousand movie images of death. At least they were honest. Show a pig a packet of bacon and it might think it stood a chance. Here, at least, it would know.

It hadn't been long since they had been in motion. This, after all, was a champagne break, not an end of shift. I could see where water hoses had been used but not enough; there was still blood on the floor and the walls, and steam rising from a huge galvanized steel bath at one end with what looked like a large chip fryer resting above it. What it actually was I didn't know and didn't want to know. Bloody chambers. Except by the time the pigs got here they would already be dead. You had to remember that. The business was meat, not deliberate cruelty. The only cruelty was our appetites.

Either way it made the pigs luckier than me. Our waltz across the room had made me grow restless in his arms. He had even slipped once on the messy floor. It made him nervous. Or impatient. He pushed me heavily through the plastic doors. They slapped against my face and the smell of pig closed in about us.

Inside he let me go. Why not? There was nowhere to run to. Or nowhere that you'd want to go. We were standing in a small concrete box, no bigger than a bathroom. The floor was littered with pig shit, the stench like a blanket over your head. The only way out, apart from the hooks and the plastic doors, was a heavy iron grille gate leading to the concrete corridor and at the end those sliding double doors which could be opened to a smaller or wider degree. Beyond there was only the desperate smashing of pigs' feet. I'd cry for them later. For now I had my own death to fight against. I looked around for any help I could get, but he was nearer to it than I: on a large hook on the wall, like a monstrous pair of headphones, was a set of stunner tongs, its ends plunged in a bucket of dirty water. Electrocution in stereo.

What a nasty little place to have to die. I moved as far away from him as I could get, my back against the wall, and we stood watching each other. The power of concentration. The walls of the chamber fell away and I lifted myself out of the stench until I could almost taste the sweet night air around us: a lovely country lane with the grass and the ditch and the sheen of sweat on my skin.

At least this time I could see him. And he me. My dark glasses were long gone, and the cut above my eye throbbed gently from the memory of his attentions. So here we were, together alone at last. I had been waiting so long for this moment: the final intimacy, the shared psychopathology.

But the truth was, when it came down to it, he wasn't

that fascinating after all – simply one more man intent on violence. Maybe all that dark symmetry had just been a premonition of death. But if I was no longer attracted, he was. He stood poised on the balls of his feet, watching me with a still, intense interest. Spring and a young man's fancy.

So all those tired old film directors were right. Men and women. Violence and sex. It comes with the territory, an inevitable function of power. Or maybe just a way to take your mind off the job. I tried to do the same. I thought of a car ride through a glistening Wiltshire morning and Mattie's question asked so many aeons ago. *'How many men?'* One-night stands. I used to be so good at them. But one night meant there would be a possibility of another. Eighteen men. Please, God, don't make it nineteen. Even if it would give her and me something in common other than death. On the other hand when it came to gaining time I didn't have a whole lot else going for me. And as any woman can tell you, a man thinking with his cock is not a man thinking with his head. He took a step towards me. I flinched. He liked that. I sort of knew he would. I took a breath. 'Are you sure we've got the time, Joe?' I said loudly. 'You wouldn't want to be caught in a fire with your trousers down.'

It took him a while to work it out, but when he did, it appeared to cause him enormous mirth. He laughed out loud. 'My. You do have a high opinion of yourself. Don't worry, I'm not going to fuck you. You're not my type.'

Not just death but sexual rejection. As days go this was proving one of the toughest. So it wasn't sex. In which case what kind of desire had I been reading in his greedy looks? Come on, Hannah. Your only chance is to know him better than he knows you. And you don't have a lot of time. Not his type. Too old, perhaps?

Then it dawned on me. 'But *she* was, wasn't she? Your type, I mean,' I said softly.

He frowned. 'Mattie?' And something in the way he said it made me realize I had touched a chord. 'Yes, Mattie was lovely,' he said. It took my breath away. Not just because it was true, but because it was clear that whatever his pact with the devil, there had been a bit of him that had not wanted to kill her. I had been right, but for the wrong reasons. That one had been Ellroy's decision. And that was what Joe had been trying to tell me in the pig shed when Ellroy stopped him. Another time it would have been the stuff to drive a wedge between them. But it was severely too late for that kind of subtlety.

'You're killing the wrong person, Joe. I liked her, too.' But there was the tiniest crack in my voice and I knew I had lost. 'For her sake let me go.'

He looked at me, and I watched something spark in his eyes. Mattie slid away, rubbed out by a stronger, wilder emotion. I didn't totally understand it at first, so clung on to what we'd had. 'Do you want me to plead?' I whispered so that my self-respect wouldn't have to hear it this time. And then came the smile. Big and with an inner light. Its craziness scared me. He knew it immediately, and he liked that even more. He took a step towards me.

'You're frightened,' he said quietly, almost tenderly, and it was not a question.

This time I didn't speak, just nodded. I watched his tongue touch the edge of his lips, then withdraw inwards: a preparation for a different kind of eroticism. What was Frank's phrase? 'Different strokes . . .' Gotcha, loverboy. What he wanted from me wasn't sex but something else. Something I wanted to give him even less. The pleasure of my terror. Except some of it had leaked out already. A part of me was already lying in that road again, paralysed by the prospect of pain and the knowledge that it was in his power to inflict it on me. My fear, his desire. So our conjunction of souls did have some purpose, after all. I tell you, I've always wondered about masochism. Hasn't everyone? Show me a woman who hasn't had even a brief private flirtation with the story of O, or a secret yearning for some dark corners of porn. The defeat of political correctness by the power of fantasy. But we're talking consenting adults there. Control being something that you choose to give up in expectation of the pleasure it will bring you. Not like now. Now the deal was different. But maybe not. Maybe this could still be my choice. I went inside and touched the fear. My body hurt from the effort of trying to keep it suppressed. I looked into the vortex and stopped resisting.

As intellectual decisions go it was a pretty visceral one. I started to cry, not normal tears, but great solid wedges of sobs that choked and made breathing difficult. I heard myself clutching for air, my arms and legs shaking uncontrollably. Like sex. A woman moving towards the outer orbit of control.

He saw it and thought it good. Through a veil of tears and mucus I watched him move towards me, starting to relax, getting into his own rhythm. Sex and death. Everything you wanted to know but never quite got in a Woody Allen movie.

'Please,' I said, and my voice shook like a woman on the edge of orgasm. I was fast against the wall now. The stun gun was about three or four feet away, idling on its hook, looking for work. I saw him glance at it and I knew what he was going to do. 'Don't hurt me.' He moved to the wall and threw a large switch. The place hummed into life. The chain of hooks juddered and creaked as the conveyor belt started its dance. Then he picked the tongs out of the water and switched them on. The cacophony of sound was extraordinary. Dentists' chairs and Baron de Retz torture chambers. The noise of death whooshed down the corridor that connected slaughterhouse to pig shed and through the doors. The animals bellowed and smashed against the wood in a collective frenzy of fear.

He was a few feet away from me. I fell to the floor,

curling my body in on itself. I knew what I was doing now. Knew it from the country road when he had lifted me up from the ground before hitting me again, and from the moment in the hotel when he had been itching to put a hand out to touch the scar. A final part of the ritual of violence, the moment of intimacy before he hurt me.

He was standing over me watching me cry. I got to my knees and gave a long, low moan. Faking it. Who says it's an unacceptable female strategy? He started to bend down towards me, laying the tongs on the floor near by. They gyrated crazily, the noise made worse by the clang of the concrete underneath. But he was too absorbed in the object of his desire to notice. As his hand came out to me I let him take hold of my face and gently move it up towards his, while I in turn slid my hand across the floor towards him.

And I knew, more than I have ever known anything before, that right at that moment I had as much power as he did. All I had to do was connect with it and turn it into violence. His touch made me shiver. I let the thrill of the moment wash through me. And in doing so I took him somewhere he wanted to go so badly that just for that second he dropped his guard. Behind us the noise of the pigs was deafening, punctuated by the crash of their bodies against the wood.

I formed the word 'Joe' on my lips like a kiss in the dark. He leant down towards me to hear it better and when he was close enough I closed my fingers around the stun gun handle and flung myself up and into his arms. I kept the tongs low and open, and as our bodies fused I rammed them into his groin, crushing the handles between my fingers with all the strength I could muster.

His roar of pain was more animal than human. Now it was his turn to hit the floor, doubled up with the voltage of love. I saw myself in a dark country lane with my stomach coming up through my throat. And I felt this river rush of energy. I lifted my foot to kick him, to keep him down, but as fast as the rush came it went and the compulsion turned to revulsion. I turned.

He was between me and the plastic doors so I had only one way to run. I wrenched open the grille gate and started to stumble down the corridor. But as I did so he shot out a hand and grabbed my foot. I think I must have screamed. I know someone did. This time I completed the kick. It caught him on the side of his chin. Not hard, but enough for him to let go. He was still having trouble moving. But I couldn't be sure it would last. It wasn't over between us yet. I knew that. I also knew whatever happened next it would never be over. Not really. All I could do was put an end to the now.

In front of me the doors to the shed were starting to splinter open under the frenzied weight of the animals behind. I walked towards them. Right at that moment I have no memory of what I thought. And maybe even if I had I wouldn't tell you. All I know is what I did. I bent down and unbolted the bottom of the sliding doors, two massive steel bolts. Then I reached up and did the same at the top. Immediately the doors started to rip open under my grip. There was a catch in the ceiling a few yards away, where you could secure the doors to form a smaller opening, controlling the flow. Given the force of their bodies, I would never have been able to secure it anyway. The fact is I didn't try. I flung myself up on to the top of one of the concrete walls of the corridor as the doors smashed apart and the pigs stampeded in, a solid bulwark of meat on sharp hooves, mad with the sounds and smells of death and the size of their own bodies.

He was right in the middle of their path. I had no option but to watch, as he tried to pull himself up on the shit-stained floor and then as he went under, the pigs smashing forward, crushing the tongs underfoot and stampeding through the plastic doors into the open hall of death. I don't remember feeling anything. Except perhaps a sense of release that something held in was now set free. But whether or not that was me or the pigs I couldn't tell you.

After, when they had passed (or maybe when I had seen enough), I jumped down from the wall and walked out through the doors into the shed. The corral was empty. I stood for a while looking back into the mouth of hell. But time was at my heels. A firework display had been planned for tonight, and if I was not to be part of it, I needed to reach spectator distance. Poor pigs. From the fat of the land into the fire.

I walked towards the main door of the shed, stopping to unlock the pens where there were any remaining animals. They rushed out into the darkness after me. Then I walked across the grass and along the tarmac road towards the lights of the main office block.

I was maybe fifty yards away from the shed when the explosion hit. I had not expected it to come so soon. Time, of course, suspends itself at moments of crisis, but even so there was no way our dance towards death had lasted a full three-quarters of an hour. Clever old Ellroy. Thinking of everything. So Joe had been a dead man from the start. In time to come that may give me some comfort in the confessional. But then I just kept on walking. I felt the heat of the flames at my back but didn't turn. I had seen it all before, marvelled at the fireball of light and noise, felt its power, been left with the fragments of life that haunted my nightmares.

The sirens joined the roar of the flames, and security guards poured out from the cracks in the darkness. I had reached the office block. I could see the lights in the penthouse where the movers and shakers of the food industry had been tasting pigs. Some were already on their way out, wine glasses and canapés still clutched in anxious fingers. But in front of them all came Ellroy, a man used to making the running.

It took time for him to recognize me. Maybe I looked

different. I don't know. But when he did, his face went blank and lost. Fear. Even from this distance I felt it seeping out from him. And I too liked the smell of it.

He quickened his pace. By the time he reached me he was way ahead of the others. Just him and me at the centre of the plot. The place every private eye longs to be. I grinned at him. And I must have looked mad, because that was what I saw in his eyes.

'You got a lot of problems, Ellroy,' I heard myself say.

'Where is he?' he muttered in a harsh whisper.

'Where you always intended him to be,' I said gaily, a smile still on my face.

He grabbed hold of my upper arm. 'Listen to me,' he said in a snarl. 'If he's gone, then you just wiped out your only evidence. Shepherd's dead, which means his report was never written. And we've got a library full of positive tests and government approval.'

'You've also got Clapton. And believe me, he's not the heroic type,' I said quietly.

And this time it was his turn to smile. 'Stress,' he said. 'It's a killer.' He shook his head, slowly. 'Think about it, Hannah. All you have is the body of a known infiltrator and animal rights terrorist. Everything else is just your word, a hysterical detective who got too caught up in her own grief. And who's still going to have to explain what the hell she was doing in there with him in the first place.'

Thinking on his feet. What he was good at. And, of course, I knew he was right. In the end it's rather reassuring that the best bad guys have the kind of minds that make you wish they were on your side, fast, complex and sure. We had run out of time. The security guards were upon us. So were the guests. And the pigs. Most of all the pigs – poor sad, mad animals careering like lost souls around the compound. I took my cue from them. Tell the truth, but not the whole truth. Get what you can and let the devil take the consequences.

I turned to the crowd. 'There was someone in the abattoir,' I said. My voice was loud and steady and not without righteousness. 'I think he was animal rights. But the pigs killed him. I saw it happen. They just went crazy. There's something wrong with them. They've got some disease.'

The words echoed up into the night and a terrible ripple went through the assembled company. I looked straight at Ellroy. I didn't need to tell him what the deal was. He already knew. I'd cover up his cover-up, if he revealed the truth about the pigs. My silence for his words. 'It's only money,' I said quietly. 'You can always make more.'

He lifted his head and closed his eyes for a second. And I knew we had a deal. He turned to the public relations man at his shoulder. 'Hannah says something's wrong with the pigs,' he said slowly. 'You better get everybody out. And call the Ministry.' I shook his hand off my arm. Then I turned and started to walk towards the main gate. And I tell you, it was the best exit I have ever made.

Epilogue

You wanted one anyway, go on, admit it. I mean stories need pay-offs, especially ones that end in such an orgy of action. Too much emotion, too little thought. It leaves you churned up. Like electricity looking to earth itself, everyone benefits from a way of winding down.

What more do you need to know? Well, you would have found the day spent in Ipswich Coroner's Court interesting. The case of Joseph Petrie, twenty-seven, of no fixed abode, whose body was found burnt and crushed to death in the ruins of the Vandamed abattoir.

A gift of a case, really. And one that tied up all the loose ends. Because as baddies go Petrie turned out to be something special. A real salmonella egg. Maringo's bomber jacket pal had been wrong (or maybe he just lied better than I thought). Petrie *had* once been involved with animal rights. But it had been a while ago and he was always more keen to disrupt the peace than save the animals. He had specialized in arson, and violence but quickly got chucked out of the movement because he was so careless about where he chose to start his fires. From then on he was out for revenge ... and fun. He got into Vandamed's good books by pulling the plug on a certain laboratory break-in eighteen months before. And from there – well, with his talents his uses to the company proved inexhaustible. Ellroy got him some new names, even something of a new face to judge from the police pictures, and the rest is history. History but not common knowledge, if you understand the difference.

On the other hand as compromises go it wasn't bad. Petrie may have been seen as a maverick nutter expelled from animal rights, but the health risk exposed by his death turned an estimated 4 per cent of the population to vegetarianism, or so said the *Sunday Times*, and who are we to argue with their statistics? In fact AAR is all over the papers these days, not to mention Vandamed and the Ministry which gave them the go-ahead. And of course where there's talk there's money. The out-of-court settlement to farmers who might have eaten the meat, but only needed to pretend they breathed in the feed dust, cost Vandamed a small but satisfying portion of next year's profits. Not to mention the large research fellowship in Tom Shepherd's name.

Ellroy, of course, is back in Texas under something of a career rain cloud. One of the first deliveries to him there was a full version of my rewritten – and revised – report, a copy of which is lodged in the Holloway Road branch of Barclays Bank. That way I feel safer every time I get into my car and switch on the ignition.

And that, broadly speaking, is that. So good did not completely triumph over evil. Well, when did it ever? Frank says I did as well as could be expected under the circumstances, which is not as well as he would have done, but then he has to say that, doesn't he? I mean he's the boss.

Mind you, when we go to the pub now more often than not it's him that does the buying. And he's switched from pork scratchings to low-cholesterol chips. Well, from little acorns . . .

Oh, and Nick brought back the key. One evening when I was home with no pressing cases to solve. I was thinking of cooking some supper. He was thinking of doing the same. Save water – wash up with a friend. It seemed a better way of saying goodbye.